Alexa is a teller at the Bank of ———, and the bills that she carefully extracts from her drawer have that dangerous, tangy odor—or aroma, I should say—of sex. *Alexa's sex*.

I know that smell as I know my own body; the curves and the dips, the hard places of bone and soft places of flesh. I've had my nose against enough women's cunts to recognize even a fraction of a scent from far off. But Alexa's fragrant bills aren't far off. They're close, in my hand, and they are steeped in the nectar of sex.

I always stand in Alexa's line, whether there are other tellers open or not, whether there are ten people ahead of me…or more. I stand in her line with my head down, as if in thought, while actually I am taking deep breaths, trying to pull her smell from the air.

In my dreams, I am bathed in her scent, am saturated from the ends of my blue-black hair to the tips of my glossy sapphire-polished toes. In my humble opinion, heaven would be an existence drenched in Alexa's heady perfume, in her swoon-scent. Draped in it, drenched in it, dream-filled, wondrous.

Alexa, I want to make you mine.

Also by ALISON TYLER:
The Blue Rose
The Virgin
Blue Sky Sideways and Other Stories
Dark Room: An Online Adventure
Dial "L" for Loveless

VENUS ONLINE

ALISON TYLER

ROSEBUD

Venus Online
Copyright © 1997 by Alison Tyler
All Rights Reserved

No part of this book may be reproduced, stored in a retrieval system, or transmitted in any form, by any means, including mechanical, electronic, photocopying, recording or otherwise, without prior written permission of the publishers.

First Rosebud Edition 1997

First Printing March 1997

ISBN 1-56333-521-2

Manufactured in the United States of America
Published by Masquerade Books, Inc.
801 Second Avenue
New York, N.Y. 10017

Dedicated to SAM,
with love from your Vampire Mau

VENUS ONLINE

***Book One:* Alexa**   *9*

***Book Two:* Omen's World**   *153*

***Book Three:* Simultaneous Stories**   *219*

Book One
ALEXA

You have entered The Dangerous Café. There are 24 people present.
Gemini: Omen, welcome.
Harley: ::on bended knee:: Mistress, O.
Angel: <winking> You're late.
Omen: Yeah, Angel. But the night is long…plenty of time to deal with you.
Angel: Oh, please…
Elijah: Careful what you ask for, Angel…
Vanilla Girl: O, didn't you get the invitation? I E-mailed it last week.
Omen: I had some unfinished business to attend to, 'Nilla. Would you like to hear about it?
Vanilla Girl: Yes, please, Mistress.
Omen: It involves pain, 'Nilla. Can you visualize being

11

stretched out on my drawing table, arms fastened above your head, legs spread, ankles tied securely with thick leather straps?

Vanilla Girl: Oh, yes, O.

Omen: You wouldn't be able to move at all, would you, 'Nilla?

Vanilla Girl: I wouldn't try to move, O. I'd stay still for you…like a good girl.

Omen: But you're not a good girl, are you, 'Nilla?

Vanilla Girl: No, Mistress.

Omen: <smiling> Would you cry out for me?

Vanilla Girl: <swallowing hard> Yes, O…

Omen: Would you beg me to take you, beg me to hurt you?

Vanilla Girl: Yessss….

Omen: Because you know that's the way I get off, don't you, 'Nilla? I need pain to get off. I need to give pain to get off. It's the only thing that takes me. The only thing that really sends me.

Vanilla Girl: I know, O.

Omen: Do you need to take it?

Vanilla Girl: Yes, O. You know me.

Omen: I do, lovely one. I do know you.

Vanilla Girl: Tonight, Mistress? Will you take care of me tonight?

Omen: Another time, 'Nilla. I don't want to interrupt the scene in progress.

Vanilla Girl: Please?

Omen: No, 'Nilla. Don't make me angry.

Vanilla Girl: <eyes lowered> I'm sorry, O.

Omen: <deep breath> What are the rest of you up to?

Justine: <sighing contentedly> Punishing the fire-haired Venus.

Omen: <interested> And who, may I ask, is Venus?

Justine: A sweet young thing with a glorious mane of red-gold hair, aren't you, Venus?

Venus: <head bowed> Pleased to meet you, Mistress Omen.

Omen: She's well-mannered.

Justine: Yes. We just got through a training session about that, didn't we, Venus?

Elijah: The tears are still wet on her cheeks.

Harley: The skin is still hot on her ass.

Dameron: The hair is still damp on her pussy.

Justine: She struggled, but we overcame her fears.

Omen: Ahhh, then I did miss something....

Gemini: A show, Omen.

Dameron: A good fuckin' show...

Justine: Venus, on your knees. Pay your respects to Omen.

Venus: ::crawling:: Yes, Mistress.

Omen: I thought you weren't into girls, Justine. Have things changed since I last came to play? Has the world turned upside down? Has the sky fallen?

Justine: I'm going through a phase, I guess. I have Marcus tied firmly to the bed right now—in real time, you know—I'm letting him stew while I get my kicks.

Omen: Good to hear. I wanted to make sure I hadn't missed out on your "girl phase." I'd kick myself if that happened.

Justine: You'll be the first one to know if I switch to girls off-line. And if I have a need to bottom for you...

Omen: Glad to hear it. Now tell me more about Venus.

Justine: We only met her tonight, but based on her innocent looks and devilish needs, I'd say she was a perfect match for you, Omen.

Omen: And tell me more about her hair. You know I love to wrap my fist in thick, long hair, like to use it as a set of reins.

Harley: When you make your fillies whinny?
Omen: <winking> You got it, Harley.
Venus: ::bowing before Mistress Omen::
Justine: It's radiant hair, O. Lush. Perfect for you.
Omen: Why haven't we met you before, Venus?
Venus: <softly> I'm new, I suppose, Mistress.
Omen: New? Just stepped free of your ocean shell, Venus?
Harley: Covering her secret treasures with her flowing tresses and a few well-placed flowers.
Omen: <grinning> You like that image, too, don't you?
Harley: <winking> Of course.
Omen: I do, too.
Gemini: She's dreamy, Omen. Young and impressionable.
Dameron: Just the way you like them, O. You should have seen how she squirmed.
Omen: And who mastered her tonight?
Gemini: Justine…it was Justine's turn.
Vanilla Girl: She was pretty when she cried. She knew just how to do it. Begging us to stop, but not really wanting it. She didn't use her safe word. She wasn't even close.
Omen: And her safe word was…?
Vanilla Girl: Sin.
Omen: Hmmm…I like it.
Vanilla Girl: I thought you would.
Dameron: But she wasn't acting, 'Nilla. Those tears were real.
Vanilla Girl: <wistfully> Yeah, I know…
Gemini: <sighing> Real and beautiful.
Dameron: You missed everything, O. There was an examination, first.
Omen: And who performed that?

Harley: I did, O. I got her fastened down on the table, spread her legs, poked and prodded.

Omen: A true evil scientist in the making, huh?

Harley: No, just routine procedures. Turned her over to take her temperature. Spread those porcelain globes of her ass and slicked her hole with some K-Y.

Omen: Now, that's a pretty image.

Gemini: Oh, it was. She was so exposed, blushing, crying... begging us to take pity on her. To leave her a little dignity.

Dameron: But she didn't want dignity. She needed to be stripped of it.

Omen: You're quiet through all this, Venus. How did it feel? How did you like all the attention?

Venus: I—I was embarrassed, Mistress O.

Omen: But you liked it, didn't you?

Venus: Yes.

Omen: What did it feel like?

Venus: Which part?

Omen: The exposure, being stripped down to your soul. Having people watch...being on display.

Venus: <stammering> I don't know, Mistress....

Dameron: Don't listen to her. She knows. She knows plenty. She spread her legs willingly and let Harley probe her asshole and her cunt. She sighed with pleasure when he slid on a pair of rubber gloves and went to work.

Omen: Do you play in real time, Venus?

Venus: Mistress?

Omen: Are you a cyber-whore, in this for a bit of cyber-fucking? Or have you had these experiences in your day-to-day off-line life?

Venus: I—

Omen: Don't lie to me.
Angel: No, Venus, don't do that.
Dameron: Tell her what she wants to know.
Venus: I'm sorry, Mistress O. I am a novice at this. I haven't experienced an examination like that in my real life, if that's what you're asking me.
Omen: That's just what I'm asking you...but do you want to?
Venus: Yessss....
Omen: Good girl. That's the answer I was looking for.
Venus: <relieved> Thank you, Mistress.
Harley: See how easy it is? Reveal yourself and you will be rewarded.
Justine: And punished.
Vanilla Girl: But that's what she wants.
Gemini: And therein lies the reward.
Omen: <grinning> It's as if you all practice in your off-time.
Justine: Oh, we do, Omen. We do.
Dameron: Don't you practice, Omen?
Omen: I don't need to.
Justine: Cocky thing, isn't she?
Venus: Practice what, Mistress?
Omen: Don't worry about them, Venus. They're just playing. Talking. Fucking around. Understand?
Venus: I guess so.
Omen: I think I might be able to satisfy some of your needs, Venus. But I'd like to talk with you more.
Venus: Yes, Mistress O. Anything you want.
Omen: I want to meet you alone, young one. Tonight.
Venus: I can't tonight, Mistress O. I'm sorry.
Omen: Then tomorrow night. Late. Very late. I have an appointment, but I could meet you after.

Venus: Tomorrow…I promise.
Omen: In the private room…Ether.
Venus: <whispering> Yes, Mistress. Yes. I won't let you down.
Omen: Good girl. Don't ever let me down.

PREFACE:
Midnight, San Francisco Time

It's late or it's early. Depends on how you look at things. On how you look at time. On how many hours you spend sleeping. I'm an insomniac, and midnight is my personal favorite time to be awake. I can sit on my fire escape and stare out at the city, at the twinkling carpet of lights spread out before me. At the golden, unseeing eyes of cars speeding along the freeway. I can sip from my steaming mug of java, stare into the night, and think.

Coffee at midnight. I'm not asking for a good night's sleep. But as an insomniac, I rarely, if ever, have one. It's to the point where I don't even know what I'm missing. So I sit on my fire escape, watching the last light click off in the apartment building across the way, and I daydream...or night-dream...or fantasize...about paradise.

I took a writing class in college in which we wrote papers about our personal concepts of paradise, and since then, it has been my favorite thing to think about. My favorite place to create.

What's my idea of paradise?

Tonight, it's me in a room with more than twenty other people. A dark room, or a dimly lit room. Doesn't matter. Candles burning in wrought-iron sconces on the wall? Maybe. A glittering silver ball spinning over head, a remnant of the 70s disco craze? Perhaps. A neon-lit sign flashing OPEN in glowing blue letters. Yes. That's it. Open. Open. Open.

I'm naked on a table, strapped down, my hands over my head, my legs spread wide. There are others, standing close, staring down at me, but though I hear their voices, I can't discern their features.

One comes forward and introduces himself as Harley. He says, "Be still and close your eyes," and then he begins to examine me. Slowly, carefully, exposing me. Spreading my legs wider apart. Probing my insides. Embarrassing me. My skin is hot to his touch; my heart beats rapid-fire in my breast. I try to breathe in deeply to calm myself, but it doesn't work. Instead, I gasp as I feel his exploring hands continue their endless search.

Nearby, the voices grow in pitch and excitement. Another figure pushes through the crowd and takes Harley's place. She says to call her Justine; and at the sound of her husky voice, I open my eyes and stare at her. She's intensely beautiful, I know this somehow, but all I can see are her lips as they form each command. She has red-slicked lips, dark with a crimson sheen, and they part as she says, "Behave."

I want to please her. It's all I want. She tells me things and I obey. I've never known myself to act this way, but it feels right. It feels more than right, it feels like my destiny.

She undoes my wrists and ankles and has me roll over. She reties my limbs, then moves forward and strikes me. I squirm and ask for more. I say, "Please, Justine, please…" She hurts me and I cry, but feel myself growing wet from the pain. My thighs are glistening with my juices. My pussy throbs as the waves build inside me.

Justine continues to beat me, firmly, impersonally, callously, and I come. Viciously. Thrashing against my bindings, begging for mercy but wanting none of it. Climaxing harder than I ever have.

When it's over, there are tears streaming down my cheeks. I can't meet anyone's gaze. Justine unties me and pulls me into a standing position. I look down at the floor, and I contemplate my disgrace. Until Omen comes. And rescues me.

Paradise.

On my fire escape, the dark night surrounds me. There are people everywhere—in my building, in the building across the way. Every light in every speeding car represents a human being. But it doesn't matter. On my fire escape, I am alone.

I turn to catch my reflection in the window. My hair is scraped back from my face. My eyes look haunted, hungry. My lips are parted, as if I want to speak, but can't. (Who would I be talking to?) I'm holding my white porcelain coffee cup, and the steam escapes around me in thin gray swirls. As I stare at myself, a light comes on in the apartment building behind me. A light on the top floor. I turn my head, and catch a figure in the window, looking down on me.

No longer alone, no longer in need, I duck my head in a mock bow, open my window, and climb inside.

Midnight has come and gone.

But my night has just begun.

You have entered The Dangerous Café. There are 13 people present.
Harley: Venus, you're back.
Angel: She couldn't stay away.
Dameron: She wanted more.
Venus: <shrugging> I guess....
Vanilla Girl: You're new to the scene on all levels, aren't you?
Venus: Just got a computer. <grinning> A little late on the scene, I'd say.
Elijah: Better late than never.
Venus: Yeah, well...
Dameron: You missed Justine. She had to deal with her real-time lover.
Venus: Do you meet here every night?
Angel: No...there's usually one or two chosen nights every week.
Dameron: How did you find out about the café?
Venus: Stumbled into it.
Harley: <impressed> Most people don't. You have to search us out.
Venus: Well, like I said, I just got online. I went exploring.
Elijah: Boy, did you ever. First night out and we were right on you.
Venus: It's not exactly my first night online. But my first night "talking."
Dameron: You've been a wallflower, then? Listening in but not participating?
Elijah: That would make sense. I think I've seen you around.
Harley: But why did you talk tonight?
Venus: <blushing> I knew what I was looking for. I thought I could make it happen with Justine.
Vanilla Girl: You must have done a lot of listening, though. I mean, I've never seen a performance like that from a novice.

All Night: I missed it…what happened?

Dameron: Venus had her little self explored, probed, beaten, hurt…

All Night: Damn…

Master X: Tell us more….

Venus: Actually, I wanted to know more about Omen…or, Mistress O.

Vanilla Girl: She wants to know more about you, as well.

Venus: Yeah…

Vanilla Girl: I mean, once you left, she asked us all for information.

Harley: Probed us, is more like it.

Dameron: You just like to say the word "probe," Harley.

Harley: <grinning> You got me there.

Vanilla Girl: Do you play in real life, Venus?

Venus: I want to…I mean, I think I want to.

Vanilla Girl: A novice on all counts.

Dameron: Everyone has to start sometime, 'Nilla.

Vanilla Girl: I know. I know. Maybe I'm jealous of her naïveté.

Dameron: Thinking back to the good old days before you became such a slut, 'Nilla?

Vanilla Girl: You're one to talk!

Venus: Can you help me out? Give me pointers?

Dameron: I think you're doing just fine, Venus.

Harley: Amazing, is more like it. The way you contracted on me. The way you blushed when I embarrassed you. When I poked and prodded…

Venus: But I don't know how to do anything. How to act. How to speak.

Elijah: You were wonderful tonight. Your innocence is overwhelming.

Angel: You were beautiful. Crying. Begging.

Venus: Does everyone act like that?

Dameron: Some act tough and take longer to be stripped down. Some crack quicker than you did. It doesn't matter. The important thing is to paint a picture. See it in your mind. Describe it for everyone else.

Angel: If your cunt is wet, you have to say it.

Dameron: If you're bleeding, describe it.

Angel: If you want more, beg LOUD! SCREAM!

Vanilla Girl: Go out and taste it in real life, Venus. Then you'll understand this all better. Then it will make more sense to you. And it will come easier for you.

Venus: Have you all experienced it? Do you all "play" in real life?

Angel: Most of us have tried different things, haven't we?

Dameron: Of course.

Angel: By the time you reach a certain age, Venus, you know what you want.

Vanilla Girl: What you need.

Master X: What you deserve.

Venus: <head lowered> I know.

Vanilla Girl: Do you, love? Then find it.

Master X: And if you need any assistance...

Venus: Oh, no. Thanks...I've got all the help I need.

Good-bye to Venus. There are 12 people present.

CHAPTER ONE:
The Chameleon

I work in a bank in the downtown section of San Francisco. I took this job when I was twenty-two, straight out of college. In the past four-and-a-half years, I haven't ever stopped to consider whether I like it or not.

As the world of banking has become increasingly dependent upon computers, many financial institutions have faded out their teller systems, encouraging patrons to use the electronic models instead. Penalizing customers who choose to do their business with humans. However, the bank I work for believes in old-fashioned service. This means knowing customers' names and faces and interacting with them at a personal level. I agree with this philosophy and enjoy the opportunity to speak with a variety of people throughout the workday.

Although it does cut into my daydreaming time....

"Good morning, Alexa. I'd like to withdraw fifty dollars," Mrs. McNamara says to me. She's an attractive gray-haired woman who comes in at least once a week.

I smile easily, and count the bills for her. "Forty and ten makes fifty."

She lifts the crisp bills from the counter and fingers them before placing the sheath of money into her wallet. As she does, she shows me an old picture of her grandchildren and a new picture of her toy poodle.

"Lovely," I say absentmindedly. "Just lovely."

She pauses before leaving, leaning a little closer to me. "What perfume do you wear, Alexa?" she asks. "It's so...interesting."

"Hmmm." I pause. "I'm not sure what I put on today."

"I like it." She pats my hand the way someone might pat the head of a small child. She breathes in deeply. "It's light. Elegant."

I thank her, then scan the room for another customer. There are none in my line, but a few are filling out slips at the table in the center of the bank. I return to my private musings until another of my regulars approaches. He's wearing a bright yellow Mackintosh raincoat—I haven't seen one since I was in elementary school.

"Good morning, Mr. Jurgens. A deposit today?"

He nods and slides the checks forward with a sigh. "I hate this weather," he tells me while I enter the figures.

"Typical for the season," I say, as if that's some sort of consolation. My fingers fly on the computer keyboard, adding amounts, printing his receipt. I hand it over with a smile and a wish for sunnier days, then settle back into my thoughts.

I've always been brilliant with money and quick with numbers. Throughout elementary school, I was in gifted math classes, sometimes even outsmarting the teacher, correcting her when she made mistakes. My know-how with numbers blended seamlessly into an affinity for finance, which is why I'm working here. But actually, it's more than that. I'm not much good with anything else.

During college, I was known as "the quiet one" in my dorm hall, "the pretty one" in my sorority, and "the smart one" in my math seminars. I got straight As in the most difficult mathematical courses, got As in everything except English comp. That didn't make much sense to me—I mean, if fairness were to come into play, were to count for anything at all. Numbers have always been second nature, almost a second language, and I hardly had to stretch myself for sterling grades in high school or college trig, calculus, statistics…. But I struggled in English, with nothing—or very little—to show for it.

Professor Anastasia Longstreth's English composition was a difficult class to get into. She had her own way of teaching and was a favorite among students and faculty, alike. She was constantly lauded for her unique methods, for her way of transforming even the most mediocre essayists into capable, clever writers.

I'd been advised to take Longstreth's English composition by my freshman counselor, who said, "Students who don't naturally excel in writing tend to improve dramatically after taking Anastasia's class." That sounded almost like a TV ad, and I called him on it.

"I've never done well in English," I told him. "I can spell, and I know my parts of speech, but I can't string together a unique or interesting sentence. Don't promise me magic."

But I wanted it. I wanted to be creative.

My counselor said, "Anastasia's a brilliant teacher. She breaks concepts into easily understandable nuggets. She works with her students on a one-to-one basis, offering the most in-office hours of any of our other professors. Try hard to get into her class."

With that recommendation, I stood in the long sign-up line at the registration center and penned my name in the second-to-last opening slot. Then I went back to the dorm to spin self-satisfying mental movies in which I starred as a famous writer.

Colette, watch out, I thought.

In Professor Longstreth's class, we wrote descriptive essays, personal stories, memoirs. We turned in diary entries, developed imaginary travel journals, created advertisements for products that didn't exist. We described ourselves on paper as if to explain our images to someone who had never met us before but was going to need to find us in a crowd. For that assignment, I stared in the mirror in my dorm room, seeing—and at the same time somehow *not* seeing—my familiar, sharp-featured face staring back at me.

"I have long marmalade-colored hair," I wrote, sort of stealing from a Tom Waits' lyric, but making it my own. "I have green eyes that change hue with what I wear or how I'm feeling. I have a slightly pointed chin—my mother calls it 'elfin'—and a long neck. I have pale skin that never tans or burns. I have—" too many sentences that start with "I have." I crumpled up the paper and tried again, and again, never getting it right—because "it," in this case, was me.

"I am five feet ten and weigh 130 pounds…." That sounded too much like a personal advertisement. "I look like someone who doesn't know how to write a descriptive essay…."

On our first day in class, Professor Longstreth held up a black-and-white photograph of a couple and asked us how it made us feel. She said, "Look at this picture for as long as you like. Throw yourself into it. Are you the man or are you the woman? Are you the photographer, or someone seated just outside the frame of the shot?"

Instead of staring at the picture, I stared at the professor. She was in her mid-thirties, tall, slender. She had on a black silk cape-collared jacket and a long skirt of the same fabric. She wore amazing leather boots—shiny, with square heels and laces up the front. I had instant visions of licking her boots, polishing them for her with the warm heat of my tongue. I wanted to go on my hands and knees and unlace the ties, then refasten them tighter. I needed to kiss the insteps of her soles, hold her heels in my mouth to clean them—and then I shuddered. I had never thought of anything like that before.

Never.

I tilted my head and stared at her some more. Her skin was as pale as mine, and her eyes were a type of blue that made me instantly think of a box of Crayola crayons—Cornflower Blue. She looked around the room, meeting my fixed gaze for only a fleeting moment, and then said, "Take out a sheet of paper and write down your feelings about this picture. Later, we'll put these notes together into five-paragraph essays. I'm sure many of you have worked with that style before, but I'll go over the format for those who need a refresher. For now, however, I'd like you to be loose. Be free. Write down anything that comes to mind. Words. Phrases. Images."

Instead of getting in touch with my feelings about the picture, I got in touch with my feelings about the professor. I continued to stare at her. There was a wall of windows in the classroom, and the fading afternoon light poured through and brightened the dull college room. Brightening everything, but positively illuminating Anastasia.

Professor Longstreth's hair was brushed so hard that it shone with a blue halo in that glimmering light. Her dark tresses hung loosely down her back; a few wayward ringlets curled over her forehead and fell in perfect spirals past her shoulders. I imagined sitting behind her on her bed and drawing a wood-backed, boar's hair brush through her shining mane. I visualized our dual reflections in a mirror over her dressing table, the way we'd look entwined.

Professor Longstreth continued, "When you view this picture, where do your eyes focus first?"

My eyes focused on the silver rings she wore on three fingers of her right hand and then on the matching silver hoops in her ears. The earrings were hardly noticeable, except when she turned suddenly and her hair waved gently back on her shoulders, away from her delicate earlobes, revealing the thin silver glinting against that ebony backdrop.

Around me, pens clattered on the pads of college-ruled paper. I realized that I'd been left behind by my daydreams. I felt a warm flush of embarrassment creep along my jawline while I wondered what the others were writing about. Suddenly fueled with a need to succeed, I stared at the picture that the professor had set in front of us on a wooden easel, trying to catch up. I recognized the image from one my friend Carolyn had in her dorm room. It was a photograph called "The Kiss," taken in the 1950s in front of a hotel in Paris. My classmates continued to write while I stared at the poster, remembering the recent news stories surrounding it.

One version stated that the lovers kissing were models hired by the well-known photographer Robert Doisneau. When the photograph became famous in recent years, an elderly French couple tried to sue for a percentage of the royalties, because they had been the couple in the picture. But somehow the photographer (or the agency that supplied the models) had kept the receipts from forty years before and was able to prove that the man and the woman—so in love in the picture—were other people entirely, and that they had each signed release forms for their time.

Knowing the story sort of spoiled the image for me. How worked up can you get over a lawsuit kiss, a phony embrace? Finally, I wrote on my blank sheet of paper, *Love is a Facade*, but I didn't know where to go beyond that. If love is a facade, then what is reality? If there are no illusions of romance left to us, then why do we even bother with the pretense of it?

Still, I tried. For that first assignment, I envisioned myself the woman in the picture, even mimicked her slightly swaybacked posture once I'd retreated to the solitary confinement of my dorm room. But I couldn't get into it. I didn't want the man's hands on me, his lips on mine—I wanted to be in Anastasia's embrace. I wanted to please her.

When pretending to be the female model didn't break my writer's block, I imagined that I was the man, touching the woman's shoulder gently, lost in his love for her.

But that didn't work either.

I ended up typing something that I didn't believe in, and the professor could tell. She scribbled the words "Let yourself go" on the top of my paper and gave me a C. My first grade under an A– in ages. I was horrified—not that I'd crash my grade-point average, but that the professor didn't like me, didn't find me a fulfilling student.

For each assignment, I kicked out my roommate and locked myself in our dorm room. Alone, I stared at the directions Professor Longstreth had given us, willing the elusive muse of creativity to alight on my shoulder.

She never did.

I paced the minuscule dormitory room, to my closet and back to the bed, over to my roommate's closet and then back to the antiquated desk that had been built into the wall generations before. I walked in circles, surely driving the students in the room below me mad. But I couldn't give Professor Longstreth what she was asking for, what she wanted.

Numbers have always come easily to me. When a correct numerical answer is lurking nearby, I can find it. If there's a theorem to be proved, I can prove it. But words are my enemies. They fail me every time.

I sneaked down to the cafeteria after hours, slinking through the back entrance, parting the huge, padded doors stealthily and finding my way into our glorious dining hall.

Others knew the secret as well. There were encampments of students, spread out on blankets under tables, some making out, others studying by battery-powered light while eating stolen leftovers from dinner. I usually went in for the coffee, making monster batches in the huge silvery vats. Fellow dorm-mates would crowd around, helping me drink my caldrons of evil brew. I was already an insomniac by my senior year in high school, but I'd only discovered coffee in my freshman year at the university.

I'm certain our college knew about our after-hours high jinks, but we cleaned up after ourselves, and nothing was ever said. (Our parents paid exorbitantly for our admission to the school—which probably helped smooth out any troubles.)

In the dimly lit dining hall, I'd turn on my own flashlight and stare again at the assignment of the week written neatly in my notebook, already knowing the words by heart. But I could never concentrate for long. Images of Anastasia would race through my mind, replacing any concept I'd hatched for writing the paper. After hours of nothingness, I'd return to my room and sprawl on the bed, drifting in a fantasy world of ungraded bliss.

I've heard people talk of out-of-body experiences, mostly occurring in the face of death, or on an operating table, or under heavy drugs. But I'd have nightly out-of-body experiences in which I followed my professor on her daily route: through her teaching load, her office hours, her trip home to an apartment off-campus. I visualized the inside of her studio; the way it was decorated, the objects d'art she must have scattered throughout the undoubtedly classy space. I lost many X-rated hours dreaming of her—hours that should have been spent honing and polishing my "C-rated" papers.

Professor Longstreth pulled me aside one day, about halfway through the quarter, and told me that she felt I was having trouble expressing myself clearly on paper. A kind way to put it.

"Spend some time alone, Alexa," she advised.

"I'm always alone," I told her honestly. "Even when I'm with friends."

"Talk to yourself, then," she suggested.

I hesitated, hoping I wasn't going to sound like too much of a smart ass. Finally I blurted out, "But isn't that the first sign of insanity?"

She gave me a long look, then took a step closer. I was aware of her perfume—some kind of sandalwood, musky but light—aware of the way a lock of her hair fell over one eye; she had to brush it back with her fingertips. Aware of the matte brick-colored lipstick she wore, and envisioning it smeared along the flat of my belly as she kissed me there, as she took me.

"What are you afraid of?" she asked, coming closer still, invading my space. "What happened to you to make you so distrustful?" Her voice dropped. "What happened, Alexa?"

I shook my head, stammered some words that had no meaning, and fled to my next class, wondering, *Am I that transparent? Am I made of glass?*

But I tried even harder for her. I lit tall, twisting ivory candles on my desk when I prepared to write an assignment for her, thinking that the shimmering, incandescent light might help get me in the mood. I closed my eyes and contemplated the so-called reality in which I lived.

I ended up writing the title of the assignment over and over again in my loopy girlish handwriting. Then writing my professor's name—Anastasia Longstreth, Anastasia Longstreth—in fancy cursive, then in block letters. Huge and towering. Then minuscule. I was like a junior high school kid, writing the name of my beloved on my binder. I was like a Renaissance painter, wanting to capture my love on canvas for eternity, wanting to drench her sublime features in gilded paints and late-afternoon sunlight.

But I was only a college freshman with an unbearable crush, wanting to please my teacher, wanting to make her like me. Having nothing to say.

Professor Longstreth gave us topics that were broad, enabling us to choose our own themes. My fellow students apparently relished the assignments, writing tomes when only a page or two was required. However, these topics left *me* helpless. I tended to excel when pointed in a specific direction and told to do research, or add numbers, or check facts. Instead, I would be forced to look into myself to answer her confounding questions: Your Favorite Memory—*How could I pinpoint one? How could I find even one?* Something You Collect and Why—*I collected nothing.* Your Concept of Paradise.... Ah, this would have been easy if only I'd had the nerve to be honest.

Paradise?

Swinging in a hammock—hammocks always feature prevalently in paradise, don't they? Watching a sunset, wrapped in the pacifying embrace of my teacher. Her hand strokes my hair, smoothes my bangs from my face, twists my tangerine-colored curls in thick, gossamer-soft corkscrew coils around her fingers.

A compare/contrast essay?

The warmth of her flesh contrasts with her cool silver rings against my cheek as she glides her hand along my face.

A topic sentence?

Anastasia Longstreth equals English Professor to some, but to me her name has always represented the embodiment of my dream lover.

Paradise?

Being tied to the hammock, rocking in the swing and sway of the ocean breezes as they stir both the string-woven frame and my own slender frame along with it. Watching my teacher as she stands above me, looking down, her face a mixture of seriousness and desire, of solemnity and lust. Her mouth, usually firmly set, is relaxed and easy. Her dark blue eyes, are filled with the promise of all that I need. Filled with the promise of truth.

Paradise.

Locked in a slick and sweaty sixty-nine with that same staid professor in that same swinging hammock. Her strong legs, usually hidden beneath slacks or skirts, are naked and scissored around my back. My arms are around her thighs, my tongue busy, circling and darting. Tasting her. Drinking from the split of her body, reeling in the waves that build inside her and cascade over to me. Lapping at the glistening drops of her come as it pools in my mouth and makes me weak with hunger for more.

Her knowing tongue, searches out all of my secret places. She increases the speed, the intensity, and I feel the rush of her honeyed breath against my clit, the probing insistence of her tongue, the delving of her curious, yet experienced fingers.

She says my name, "Alexa." Says it differently from when we're in class. She doesn't sound stern, doesn't sound concerned, she simply says, "Alexa," and I shudder, wanting her more.

Words don't come easy for me. Numbers are my friends. I count the circles I make with my tongue around her clit. One, mmm, two, mmmm, three, mmmmm. I count the sound of my heartbeat pounding in my ears. There's a roaring in my head louder than the ocean's steady, forward drive.

"Alexa…."

I want to tell her how she makes me feel, but I don't have the words to sound real and not phony. Passion? Yes, but it's not strong enough. Ardor? A ten-cent thesaurus word. Desire? Desire pales against what I feel for her. Longing, yearning, needing...I long, I yearn, I need for her to make me come.

One, two, three circles. Deep breath.

"Alexa…"

And then no more thoughts of words or numbers. No more thoughts at all. Just, sweet, sweet paradise. The things that dreams are made of.

But those visions weren't going to happen, and I wasn't going to expose myself. Instead, I ended up turning in the most pat, precise papers, with no true feeling, no revelations. "Paradise, to me, is discovering something new, learning a skill, finding an interest…." Blah, blah, blah, blah, blah.

Ms. Longstreth wrote in bold red ink on my final composition: "You seem to be hiding."

She stated it tentatively; "You seem…" But she was right. That's what I do. I hide from my friends, from my lovers, from myself. I've found it's the easiest way to get through life. Blend into what people want you to be. Chameleon yourself. Reveal nothing.

You can't get hurt that way. You can only continue, in the same manner that you always have, moving neither forward nor backward nor side to side. Stagnant, perhaps, but unable to be damaged, unable to be marred, unable to be ruined.

Being hurt can be so bad. Being hurt can mean the end of every careless gesture, every unplanned action. Every kiss momentarily purposeless, but filled with meaning for the future.

Professor Longstreth had asked me, "What happened to you?" which could easily be translated to read: "Who hurt you?" "Who did it?" "Why are you the way that you are?"

Is it fair to lay blame on one person or one instant? I can remember the night, basking in the safety of my first lover's embrace, cuddled together in the worn backseat of his father's car. I know the way Matt's skin smelled, the way his short hair felt when I rubbed my palms against it. He had a marine-style crewcut, which was the fashion in our high school ever-so-briefly, clipped to the point where his skull showed through and tanned. It was a look that some surfers at my school liked. They could hit the waves in the morning before first period and show up relatively clean and dry at 8:30. Matt wore his hair this way, and he used butch wax to make it stand up.

I loved the feel of his bristly hair, almost like animal fur; the way he sort of purred when I stroked it. I remember how his strong chest felt when I ran my fingertips over it, delighting in his built-up muscles, his pumped-up pecs. And, most importantly, I remember the look of intense horror he gave me when I opened myself to him and told him what I wanted.

"You want me to do what?" he asked, incredulous. Stricken.

"...nothing...never mind." Ruined.

"Lexi, you're kidding, right? Tell me you're kidding, that this is your idea of a sick joke."

"Uh-huh. Yeah, Matt..." Moving away from him in the back of the car. Wrapping my arms around my own trembling body as if I could protect myself from his utter disgust. "Yeah, I was just kidding." *Just kidding, that's all. No one could want what I asked for. No one could need that. No one deserves that.*

I've never tried again. I'm sure that sounds like a cop-out; a denial at seventeen shouldn't scar someone for life. But it did me, and now ...*now*, I simply go with the tide of those around me. Offering none of myself that can't be seen on the surface.

Asking for nothing in return.

You have entered Ether. There are 2 people present.

Omen: Thank you for meeting me.

Venus: I've heard about you from the others. I wanted to see what you were like in person...so to speak. Though this method of exchange is fairly new to me. I only recently bought my first computer.

Omen: What did you hear? What did they say?

Venus: They talked about your power. They talked reverently about you. Even the dominant ones are cowed by you.

Omen: Really?

Venus: Yes. Especially Justine.

Omen: <smiling> Justine is a special case. She switches.

Venus: What does that mean?

Omen: Sometimes she's a dom, sometimes she's a sub. She ought to be cowed by me—I've whipped her often enough.

Venus: <trembling> In real life or online?

Omen: <smiling broader> Does it matter, young one?

Venus: I just wondered....

Omen: And I just wondered...What did they do to you last night? I know a little bit...but I want to hear you describe the experience.

Venus: <quietly> They punished me.

Omen: Do you like to be punished?

Venus: Like?

Omen: Don't be flippant with me, subservient one. Do you NEED to be punished?

Venus: Need...that's such a strange word, isn't it? I prefer DESERVE.

Omen: It sounds as if you've got this all worked out in your mind. And yet you still haven't played in real life. Why is that?

Venus: Fear.

Omen: What made it easier to expose yourself online?

Venus: It's not real.

Omen: It is and it isn't. Did you really cry while it was going on?

Venus: No.

Omen: And after...

Venus: After, I came.

Omen: Ahhh...What did you do to let them know that you wanted to be a sub, that you wanted them to take you?

Venus: I arrived. They were on me instantly. So fast that it was startling.

Omen: A new face in the crowd. A new plaything, new toy.

Venus: I guess...

Omen: Tell me what you want. What you were looking for when you signed up for your online server and began trolling the chat rooms?

Venus: <hesitantly> To be cleansed.

Omen: Nice choice of words...how will you be cleansed?

Venus: <eyes lowered> By being punished...purified...

Omen: How long have you wanted that?

Venus: Forever.

Omen: Have you ever told anyone?

Venus: Once—my high-school boyfriend. But just that once.

Omen: What did you do?

Venus: It's not what I did, but what I asked him to do to me.

Omen: And what did you ask him?

Venus: I asked him to overpower me. To punish me.

Omen: Specifically, Venus, what did you say?

Venus: I told him that I wanted him to take off his belt...to use it.

Omen: Use it how?

Venus: Use it on me.

Omen: <insistent> How?

Venus: I told him I'd been bad, teasing him, like a little girl, and he said, "Oh, really?" Playing along for a minute, not seeing where I was going. Not understanding.

Omen: And where were you going, slave? What did you want from him?

Venus: <stammering> I wanted him to bend me over his lap, to stripe my skin with it. To mark me. To hurt me. To cleanse me. I closed my eyes when I asked him, not wanting to watch his face change, his reaction to my request.

Omen: And he wouldn't?

Venus: Couldn't.

Omen: What did he do?

Venus: He balked. He turned a sickly white and then red. He thought I was kidding, hoped I was kidding. I tried to pretend I had been. But I didn't fool either of us.

Omen: And then what?

Venus: We never went out again. I think he told some of his buddies, because they looked at me different when I ran into them at school. A few avoided me; a few sought me out.

Omen: Did you tell anyone else?

Venus: Of course not.

Omen: Never?

Venus: Never, not until now. Not until I got online and began to see how many other people there are like me.

Omen: Why didn't you ask anyone else? You tried with a high-school boy, a young, inexperienced pup, and then gave up?

Venus: He denied me.

Omen: He didn't understand you.

Venus: I couldn't find the nerve again.

Omen: That's too bad, isn't it?

Venus: Is it? I've functioned well.

Omen: But you've been at a loss. You've never experienced what you most want. What you most desire…what you most deserve.

Venus: Worse things have happened.

Omen: Of course, around the world, in the news, in the bigger picture of things. But we're talking about you. You, Venus. And you have never experienced the thing you most want, have you?

Venus: No, Mistress. But it's not important. Not necessary.

Omen: <sadly> You've got it all buried deep, haven't you? You've got it all figured out.

Venus: <nodding> I guess so.

Omen: Tell me what you want. What you want from me.

Venus: I can't.

Omen: If you tell me, I can give it to you. I can make it happen. Think about that for a second, Venus. Think about having it happen in real life, not online, not in your fantasy world. But in real life. In real time.

Venus: I can't.

Omen: I know what you want. But I need you to tell me.

Venus: I can't….

Omen: I won't deny you. I understand that he hurt you, and I won't hurt you like that. Not like that. I promise.

Venus: It was too hard to bear. I can't do it again….

Omen: Tell me, slave. It's not a request. It's an order.

Venus: <deep breath> Pain. I want pain. Cleansing pain.

Omen: Spell it.

Venus: P–A–I–N.

Omen: You don't know the meaning of the word.

CHAPTER TWO:
Paradise

From my position behind the cool black-veined marble counter at the bank, I stand and wait for customers. We're busiest early in the morning, right after we open; again at the lunch hour; and then just before closing. The rest of the day is much more mellow. There are things I can do to fill the long moments; computer programs to be mastered, receipts to be organized, transcripts of accounts to be filed. But on those clear days when the fog burns off, I can see out the windows into the street, and I lose myself, watching.

The bank is situated near the turnaround, where the cable car lines begin and end. Shiny, red cable cars pass at a rolling pace, one after another. At slow periods on unreal, pseudo-summer warm days, I fantasize as I watch them go.

It's raining today, but still I fantasize.

"A penny…?" one of my regular customers asks. Nina works at The Cave, a café down the street. She's sort of punk, I suppose, and the rest of the prim tellers stare at her oddly when she enters the bank. Each time she comes in, she seems to have a new color of hair. I compliment her on it—which is why she chooses my line.

"A penny…?" she repeats, and I stare at her neon-violet ringlets, dumbfounded. Her normally straight hair is wet from the rain, and it's got a life to its own, curling maniacally around her face.

"You're depositing a penny?" I know this can't be the case, but I'm unsure of what she's talking about.

She sets down a request for a withdrawal on the counter and grins at me. "No, silly, a penny for your thoughts. You were daydreaming, weren't you? Wishing it were summer? Wishing the rain would stop? Or wishing you were somewhere it wasn't raining at all?" She sighs. "Like Jamaica…"

I shrug, counting out her bills. "Guess so, but I'm not sure where I was. Maybe riding one of the cable cars."

She nods, then breathes in deeply. "What perfume do you wear, Alexa?" Many people ask me that question. I'm always vague with my answer. To Nina, I say, "I didn't remember to put on any this morning. Maybe you're smelling my conditioner. I bought a new one at the salon last weekend."

She leans toward me and inhales even more deeply. Then she shrugs and says, "That must be it," but she doesn't sound convinced. "Whatever it is, it's pretty.

Sensual." She slides me a coupon printed on electric pink paper that's good for a free coffee. "Come by later? I'm working all day."

I thank her for it, promise to stop in on my break, and then watch the shimmy of her hips beneath her tight blue jeans as she leaves. When the glass doors swing open, I can hear a riff from one of the street musicians who's set up a music stand under an overhang near the bank to hide out from the rain. He's playing a familiar melody, but I can't name it. Something sweet and light.

I listen to the fragments of song and am transported for a long beat or two. For a fantasy passage.

Was I riding the cable cars like I told Nina? No. I was far off, in my personal paradise, rocking in a hammock, bathed gently in a warm tropical rain. My skin—which never tans, never burns—was as dark as one of the copper pennies Nina was offering me for my thoughts. My hair, vibrant in shades of red, orange, and gold, hung free over my breasts, covering me in the fairy-tale style that mermaids prefer.

When I return from my mental wanderings, I wonder whether my eyes have the faraway look in them you see in movie stars' eyes when they're filled with longing—or regret. Like the look in Ingrid Bergman's eyes when she stared at Humphrey Bogart in *Casablanca*.

My next customer steps forward in line. I wonder whether she can see the haunted look in my gray-green eyes. The desire for something I've never had. An unfulfilled yearning swirling deep within that pale green glow.

"Depositing one thousand, Alexa," the woman says,

glancing at the bronze nameplate on the counter. "Alexa Van Horne. That's a nice name."

I smile at her as I print a receipt.

"Thanks..." I look for her name on the deposit slip. Unfortunately, it's just an initial and a last name. K. Jones. "Thanks, Ms. Jones," I say dumbly. "My grandfather said we're descended from Vikings."

She says, "That would explain your red hair," which is what most people say when I tell them that—something I've totally made up—and then she takes her receipt and says, again, "Thank you, Alexa."

I hear my teacher saying my name, the way her tongue hit the roof of her mouth when she said the "l." ALex-a...a sigh at the end. "AL-ex-ahhhh...."

Paradise?

Being caught in a rainstorm and soaked thoroughly. My hair, a darker red when it's wet, is pasted in glassy spiraling curls to my forehead and cheeks. My eyelashes are decorated with tear-shaped beads of water. I peel off my black suit jacket, and my no-longer-crisp white shirt becomes instantly transparent, revealing my lack of a bra, the pert stance of my breasts. The cold water makes my nipples erect and they poke forward, pleasingly, sharp under the pounding torrents.

I stand before a store window and observe my reflection, calmly removing my shirt, my shoes, my slacks and hose, and standing, naked and exposed, in the middle of Market Street.

A crowd gathers, closing around me, watching me. I close my eyes and begin to touch myself, stroking my breasts, pinching my nipples, dragging my nails along the flat of my belly to leave long red welts on my skin. Thrusting two fingers into my dripping cunt and feeling that different kind of wetness that I create within myself. Working myself solo until *she* approaches and takes me in her arms and says...

"I'm withdrawing fifty today, Alexa."

Deep breath, and then I'm back again, wondering, as I always do, if my eyes give me away. But I catch a glimpse of my reflection in the windows and see only emptiness. There's nothing to my straitlaced facade that shows anything but boredom with my job, my life, myself.

"Small bills?" I hope she can't sense my fluttering, uncontrollable heartbeat.

She nods, then turns her head to watch the cable cars.

Olivia's one of my favorite customers. She comes in regularly to withdraw money or deposit checks, and she always waits in my line. She possesses what my friend Raina once referred to as a "San Francisco style," though I believe Raina was describing herself at the time. Still, I like the phrase, took it to mean a description of someone who has her own sense of fashion and dresses like an artist. And if that's the case, Olivia definitely does have a San Francisco style. She has that and the blackest hair I've ever seen. She wears it loose, usually, and it hangs down her back in Medusa-esque, snakelike ringlets.

Paradise?

Having her touch me...

Did I just think that? Did it come into my mind unbidden, an image of her fingertips roaming over my naked body, her dark hair cascading forward as her mouth comes into play. Having her direct me, choreograph our lovemaking, guiding me, then letting me free.

What do you want, Alexa? What do you want?

I press my nose against the back of her neck and inhale deeply to get a firm grasp of the heady, rich animal smell that is trapped in her thick hair. I align my body with hers, spoon against her, aware of the sensation as her body heat warms me, as I cool her down.

What do I want? What do I want…?

Paradise.

"Do they come by very often?" she asks me, still turned away. I can stare at her outfit because she's not watching me. She has on a pure white turtleneck under a black V-neck cashmere sweater, and she isn't wearing any jewelry. There's a closed black umbrella at her side for protection from the melodramatic weather.

She's stunning in her simplicity—always. Watching her is like watching an Italian fashion magazine come to life. Beyond-chic. I wish I had taste like that.

"Every few minutes," I tell her as I pull the bills from my drawer. "The turnaround is right outside." She doesn't even face me I count the cash out for her.

"Do you ride them to work?" she asks.

"Yeah…every day. Rain or shine."

"You're lucky," she says, without offering any further explanation.

Finally, when the bills are laid out neatly on the counter, she turns and scoops them up, sliding them into her eelskin wallet without checking my math, and murmuring under her breath, "I adore cable cars…."

I do, as well. From the fire escape at my apartment I

can watch tourists' reactions as they hit the top of the hill and look down. I watch little kids, gripping their mothers' hands, their eyes wide with fright and excitement, and I am envious of them. I do not show that emotion. Fear. I keep everything inside. My eyes don't open wide when I crest a big hill.

My heart doesn't beat faster when a lover embraces me. My teeth don't chatter when I'm cold.

I have trained myself over time to keep it all inside, visualizing my emotions in a deep freeze, like the flowers they sell now that are flash-frozen. Perfect, but dead. Or, if not as pretty as those flawless flowers, then embalmed and preserved like an Egyptian mummy.

I know that inner-denial gave my grandfather an ulcer in his early thirties when young bucks with college educations were promoted over him. I know that by refusing myself the luxury of revelation, I am forgoing pleasure. But I have never learned how to be open. Now, at twenty-six, it's much easier to be closed.

In my line at the bank, people smile at me. There are certain customers, like Olivia and Nina, who search me out, wanting to deal only with me regarding their accounts. The other tellers call me "friendly", but I've heard the gossip, too. Women talking in the bathroom behind closed doors, saying in their calmly catty ways as they squat to take a piss, "Alexa seems nice, doesn't she?"

"Uh-huh…"

"But under that, I'm sure she's a coldhearted …" Fill in the blank.

I don't care. I couldn't work up the emotion to care even if I tried. The only thing that hurts sometimes is this: I have no talent, other than with handling money. I walk along the streets in North Beach, passing the musicians with their velvet-lined cases open for tips, their shining horns or worn guitars or lilting violins weaving the glorious music that can come only from the soul.

I pass painters, with their wooden easels facing the bay, capturing the beauty of our city on their canvases. I linger at art fairs in the park near the Haight, touching the glossy exteriors of hand-thrown pots; staring wistfully at the photographs of children playing, of lovers kissing; running my fingers over colorfully woven rugs and blankets. And wishing, endlessly wishing, that I could express myself artistically, as well.

Maybe then I could expose the raw heat that fills my core. Maybe then I could reveal who I truly am. Because inside me—deep inside me—there is another, much louder entity. One who wouldn't smile so pleasantly all the time. One who has needs that I cannot even bear to consider.

One who frightens me.

("What are you afraid of?" my professor asked me, "Tell me," her body language screamed. "You can tell me, Alexa…you can tell me anything.")

So I continue, waiting for I don't know what. Pleasing those around me. Keeping myself tightly under wraps, like the mummies at the British Museum. I'm as tightly wrapped as they are.

You have entered Ether. There are 2 people present.

Omen: Do you make yourself come at night?

Venus: Are you asking me if I masturbate, Mistress?

Omen: Yes, slave. That's exactly what I'm asking you.

Venus: Yes...but why did you ask if I do it at night?

Omen: I'm not sure....I suppose I had a vision of you in your bed with your hand between your legs...stroking, teasing, caressing...bringing yourself to climax in the center of a soft feather bed.

Venus: Yes, I do, Mistress. It relaxes me. But I don't have a feather bed.

Omen: Now, you've got my interest piqued, young one. Do you come during the day, too?

Venus: Sometimes...

Omen: When? Before work?

Venus: Sometimes...

Omen: Coy thing, you're hiding something.... Tell me.

Venus: <eyes lowered> Nothing, Mistress. Nothing.

Omen: What do you use? Your fingers...a vibrator...?

Venus: My fingers.

Omen: Have you ever used a vibrator?

Venus: No...I'd never have the nerve to buy one. Can you imagine? Walking into a store...<grimacing>

Omen: The idea doesn't turn you on?

Venus: It embarrasses me. Everyone knowing what I was going to use it for.

Omen: How about the idea of me taking you into a store, dragging you to the display of the largest, battery-operated monsters, making you hold it while I turned it on.... Do you like that image?

Venus: <eyes lowered> Yes, Mistress.

Omen: Of course you do. You just need to visualize the big picture.

Venus: I've never even been into a store that sells them.

Omen: Sheltered one...have you used anything aside from your fingers?

Venus: What do you mean?

Omen: Some women have their own special toys. Not necessarily "sex toys," more like household objects they use to get themselves off....

Venus: I don't know....

Omen: You must have heard stories of women fucking coke bottles, squatting on door handles....

Venus: Well, sometimes, in the tub, I use the spray from the faucet to come.

Omen: Describe the sensation.

Venus: <blushing> I lie on my back with my feet up against the tiled wall. I position myself directly below the spray of the water. I can adjust the temperature with my toes, swiveling the faucet one way or another.

Omen: <liking the image> Lovely, lovely. Do you prefer warm or cool water to make you come?

Venus: Usually, I start with warm and slowly go colder and colder. It makes it last longer, somehow.

Omen: When did you first use water pressure to masturbate?

Venus: That was how I learned to do it...with the faucet in our tub at home. We had this great claw-foot tub, and I could sprawl completely in it, with my legs draped over the side.

Omen: How old were you the first time?

Venus: Nine or ten. I'm not sure. It seemed like I hated baths up to that point, didn't see the need to be really clean—I was sort of a tomboy. Then, when I learned the magic of water pressure, suddenly I was the cleanest kid in the family.

Omen: Did anyone ever find you …I mean, in that compromising position?

Venus: One of my sisters…

Omen: Really?

Venus: Yeah, but I think she just learned to do the same thing.

Omen: Do you come every night?

Venus: When I want to sleep.

Omen: It helps you?

Venus: It's the only way I can.

Omen: Otherwise…?

Venus: I stay up, pacing, wandering around my apartment. I used to smoke until a few years ago. When I did, I would stay up half the night, killing a pack of Marlboros.

Omen: What do you think about when you come?

Venus: What I told you before…

Omen: Pain?

Venus: And pleasure…. They're intermingled now in my head.

Omen: Where are you when you come?

Venus: In my bed.

Omen: No, I mean, where in your mind are you?

Venus: Different places: a dressing room, a rooftop, a bridge….

Omen: Real places?

Venus: Yeah. But not always the real scenarios. I transform reality.

Omen: Don't we all?

Venus: I suppose.

Omen: Tell me what you think about. Specifically.

Venus: Men. Women. Nameless, faceless. Actors in plays that I write in my head.

Omen: Tell me a scenario. Paint me a picture.

Venus: I'm not good with words.

Omen: You must be good with words to play online. You have to describe what you see, what you want, what you offer. You have to spell it all out. I don't know what you're thinking, and I can't look into your eyes to make an educated guess.

Venus: I'm not good, though, Mistress. I've never been able to…to reveal myself.

Omen: Then listen to this as a command—I'm sure it will be easier for you if you are obeying a direct order. I can sense that about you. You crave direction, don't you?

Venus: Yes, Mistress.

Omen: Now that we've got all that cleared away, I want you to describe a scenario. What do you see when you close your eyes and your fingers start to play?

Venus: I envision myself being exposed, sometimes. Being taken. Not having a choice in the matter. Not having to fake it.

Omen: Fake what?

Venus: Not having to wear a false face, a calm facade. Not having to pretend.

Omen: Do you pretend a lot, slave?

Venus: Yes, Mistress…all the time.

Omen: What if you didn't have to pretend anymore?

Venus: What do you mean?

Omen: What if you could tell me a scenario and I could make it happen?

VENUS ONLINE | 59

Venus: online.

Omen: In real life…at my apartment…or yours.

Venus: I'm not ready.

Omen: I think you are. I think you simply need to explore a little…

Venus: No, Mistress. Not yet.

Omen: Meet me somewhere, slave. Meet me somewhere, soon.

Venus: I'm sorry. I'm just not ready yet. It's too fast.

Good-bye to Venus. There is one person present.

CHAPTER THREE:
Under Wraps

I visited the British Museum as a college freshman, on a summer vacation with two college friends. While they sought the Elgin marbles, I stared long and hard at the mummified bodies, thinking vaguely that I could relate to them. The ancient mummies were exposed under glass in their tattered linen wraps, but at the same time they were carefully hidden from prying eyes like my own.

My girlfriends, Elaine and Carolyn, were far more concerned with the handsome, raven-haired docent who hung about nearby. He grinned at the three of us, asking, in his attractive accent, "May I answer any questions? May I help you, ladies?" (And you could read the *want* beneath it: Can I take you? Can I touch you? Can I fuck you?)

Elaine tittered and asked him question after imbecilic question, leading him from room to room, quizzing him, "How old is that marble?" when the sign on the wall told everything they could want to know, and more. Carolyn followed, a few steps behind, asking, "Where is the Rosetta stone?" when they were five feet away from that piece of history.

My girlfriends were both cute, both flirtatious, tossing their long hair, almost in unison, as if they'd practiced the move like psychotic, sexually ravenous cheerleaders. Pulling on the hems of their summer dresses as if nervous, but knowing exactly what they were doing. Revealing their long limbs, the slim lines of their bodies, their California tans. But the boy sought me out, whispering facts to me about the mummies. Telling me that he'd seen one unwrapped once and asking if I wanted him to describe it. Taunting me the way a little boy would ask a neighbor girl, "Do you wanna down to the cellar? Do you wanna play doctor? I'll show you mine if you show me yours.... I dare you."

"Some mummies are five thousand years old," he told me.

I nodded, knowing that much already.

"Right there," he continued, pointing. "That was a king. The Egyptians usually preserved their royalty, embalming them so that their bodies would join their souls in the afterlife. The poor people couldn't afford the expense of the process. I don't know if poor people even made it into the afterlife." A long beat. Then; "Do you believe in one?"

"Do I believe in heaven?" I asked him, paraphrasing from a John Lennon song, and he grinned at me and brushed his hair out of his eyes to meet my questioning expression.

"*Do* you?" he asked, moving closer, almost touching me. I bit my lip and stared at him, wanting to answer, but unsure of what to say. Finally, taking a deep breath, I responded, "I'm not sure...but I believe in paradise."

Paradise?

In his arms, pressed against the glass case, thrust against it. Letting him lower my white jeans and cotton underpants. Letting him observe me, scientifically, parting the outer lips of my ginger-furred pussy, feeling the wetness on the tips of his fingers. Only a controlled experiment, of course, only submitting myself in the name of science.

His tongue flicking out to taste the warm, dark flavor of my sex. Licking at me rapidly, taking me to the edge of heaven in a heartbeat.

Paradise.

Elaine frowned when the boy stuck so closely to my side. She didn't like losing out—especially to me, someone who was so obviously not in the game. She came over, putting one arm suggestively around the boy's shoulders, saying, "What's your favorite exhibit? Take us to see it. Do you like the Elgin marbles? Do you think that they should be returned to Athens?"

But, like Cinderella and her wicked stepsisters, I won out.

"It took seventy days to mummify a body," he told me softly, reverently. "There's a quote from the Eighteenth Dynasty that says, 'When you have completed seventy days in the embalming place, you shall have a good burial in peace.'"

I stared at him in admiration. "Do you like the mummies as much as I do?" My eyes focused on him. "You know more than it says on the little posted squares by the cases."

He shrugged. "It's interesting, I think. More interesting than stolen marble." Said loud enough for Elaine to hear.

I grinned and offered my hand. "I'm Alexa."

He shook it, held on slightly too long for a polite handshake, then said, "Nice name. I'm Alex…" A broad smile before continuing in his odd form of Egyptian foreplay. "Did you know that nothing which had touched the dead person's flesh could be thrown away?"

I shook my head, shuddering at the thought.

"Everything was preserved—all the linen, all the wadding, everything. The embalming chamber was swept out and the garbage—or so-called garbage—was stored in sacks. They made sure that not even the tiniest particle of the deceased's body would be lost. All of the refuse was buried separate from the sacred tomb, but close to it."

Elaine, still nearby, grimaced and said loudly, "Oh, ick!" making a face. The boy simply turned his back on her and slipped me his number, saying, "I work here only for rent money, just part-time." Puffing his chest out, proudly, "I'm really a writer, typing away on my first novel in the evenings. I have a scooter. I could show you London."

Those looks of hot, wet envy that Elaine shot me sealed the deal. "We're staying at the Dorset Square," I told him. "You can pick me up at nine, if you'd like." And then I went back to the mummies. Squinting at them through the glass. Ignoring Elaine entirely.

The three of us girls returned to our hotel after the museum, riding on the top of an open double-decker bus and letting the unexpected—and rare—London sunshine beat down on us. I slid on my sunglasses, crossed my legs, and kicked back. Flaunting my success. Elaine didn't speak to me, but Carolyn sat at my side, telling me that she thought the boy was cute. Asking if I really was going to meet him.

"Sure," I told her, shrugging. "Why not?" I looked at her over the top of my sunglasses.

"You don't know anything about him," she said, sounding concerned. "What if he's a murderer?"

"That'll be something for those trashy London tabloids, won't it?" I asked her. "American tourist killed by British Museum docent. Body found among the mummies. No part of the deceased was thrown away..." Already quoting from the boy.

Carolyn shot me a look. "I'm not kidding. I don't think you should go by yourself. At least, take one of us with you."

"As a chaperon?" I asked, trying not to sound as nonplused as I felt.

She shrugged. "I don't know. Safety in numbers..."

We arrived at the stop closest to the hotel and walked down the steps to the street. Elaine strode quickly ahead of us. Carolyn hung back with me.

"I'll be fine," I told her. "Don't worry."

She looked me over. I do know how to take care of myself, and Carolyn knew it. Finally she said, "Check in with us when you get back, okay? Knock on the door or ring us up."

I promised I would and then retreated to my own room. Elaine and Carolyn were sharing a suite, but I'd opted to spend a bit more money and stay in my own private haven. I rarely have had the luxury of my own room. I grew up in a family of girls and never lived in a room without at least one bunk bed. Dorm life was easy to adapt to—two girls crammed in a tight little space—simply more of the same.

The hotel was more expensive than many of the others in the area, and maybe it was a little bit more than we should have spent, but we were on vacation, and the three of us had worked during the year to save up. The luxury was divine—the privacy even better.

My room had its own bathroom done in marble, and I took two showers a day, letting the hot spray wash away tension from the journey, from the year of school and work, from hanging out with Elaine.

I set my alarm, then spread out on the bed and took a nap. I got up at eight and showered, then went through my suitcase, looking for something suitably slutty. I didn't own much trashy clothes.. but Carolyn and Elaine did.

I buzzed their room and got Elaine. She didn't say a word, simply passed the phone over to Carolyn.

"Can I borrow your yellow sundress?" I asked. "The one with the straps that cross in back?"

There was a long pause, and then she said. "I wore it last night, Lexi. It's not fresh."

"But it's not dirty, either," I told her. "And I can get it dry-cleaned tomorrow. I'm only going to be in it for a few hours."

Another equally long pause. Then "All right. I'll bring it over."

She was just across the hall, but it took her fifteen minutes to make it to my room. By that time I had my hair up, with loose curls falling free in a romantic look. My makeup was perfect, startling Caroline, who said, "I didn't even think you owned any. You never wear it."

She perched herself on the edge of the bed while I slipped into her butter-hued sundress. "I know how," I said. "I just rarely bother."

"But you look so much…." she wanted to say better, but was slightly too tactful to go through with it.

"I look so much *different*, right?"

She nodded.

"I don't care," I told her. "This is just a facade, only a farce for a one-night stand."

Her mouth dropped open. "You mean, you're going to sleep with him?"

"Wouldn't you?" I asked.

"Well…Jason…"

"Wouldn't Elaine?" I said then, knowing the answer and knowing she did. "Of course she would." I answered for her. "And you wouldn't think twice about it. This conversation is occurring only because we are talking about *me*."

Carolyn lay back on the bed with her hands beneath her head. The bedspread was a lush down comforter covered with a quilted throw, and when she moved, she sank down in it a few inches into feathered softness. "I guess—" she started. "But you usually are more…picky. You don't fool around as easily as Elaine."

"I'm not a slut," I said, translating for her. "But everyone needs a bit of …relief occasionally. Plus, I'm tired of Elaine's self-satisfied smirk. 'Everyone loves me best.' 'Everyone thinks I'm the most beautiful.' It's annoying."

Elaine was Carolyn's best-best-friend, while I was only at the best-ranking. Still, she took a deep breath and went for honesty.

"She's insecure."

"She's annoying," I repeated more forcefully. "If she can't have someone, or if someone doesn't choose her, she gets into a snit. Like tonight. It's a fucking boring show. You can tell her I said so. And you can tell her, if you want to, that I'm going to screw that boy's brains out."

Carolyn rolled over to look at me. Her eyes were wide, but her look held something of respect and amazement. "Are you really?"

I nodded, sliding into a pair of white hose and then slipping on my boots. They were the only shoes I had besides sneakers.

"Will you …tell me about it?"

I shrugged. "Sure, if you can make certain that Elaine gets over this by tomorrow. I'm not going to continue this vacation with her if she behaves like a child every time something happens that doesn't suit her. I'll re-book my reservations and go to Paris on my own."

There was a knock then and Carolyn looked around frantically, ready to hide, thinking it was the boy. I motioned for her to stay where she was and opened the door. Elaine stood in the hallway, holding a pair of her white satin heels. She'd traveled with four suitcases and had shoes for every occasion—I'd managed with one bag, plus a carry-on.

"Sorry," she said, shrugging, and then thrust the shoes into my hands. "We're the same size, right?"

I nodded, unsure of whether to accept the obvious peace offering.

"He's cute," she said next. "Wake us up when you get back and tell us how it went."

I grinned at her, unable to stay mad. This is how our relationship has always been. A whirlwind of emotions. A roller-coaster ride. She sat on the edge of the bed, next to Carolyn, while I undid my boots and slid into her dainty white satin shoes.

There was another knock. This time it *was* Alex, standing in the hallway, waiting, his scooter helmet in his hands. I waved to my friends, told them to close the door behind them, and left.

"My bike's downstairs," he said. "But we can walk to the first pub."

"How'd you get up to my room?" I asked. "They're pretty strict at the desk, aren't they?"

He gave me a sidelong glance, as if unsure whether I was worthy enough to hear his secret. "One of my schoolmates works the desk. He told me your room number. But don't rat on him, okay? He'll get fired."

"No problem," I said. "I'm sure you would've seen the interior of my room sooner or later."

"...really?"

I nodded, and then we were outside, walking down the street, past a wrought-iron-enclosed garden, past a flower seller's stand, to The Rose and Crown. He was polite, steering me through the pub crowd with his hand on my waist, behaving like a gentleman—although we both knew how the night would end.

He ordered drinks for me, choosing things he thought I'd like when I told him I didn't recognize the names. People were smoking nearby. We bummed two cigarettes and went outside to a private courtyard to smoke.

"Tell me about your book," I said. "I'd like to know what you're writing."

He looked into his glass, then back up at me. "I'll send you a copy if you like, but I don't talk about what I write until it's finished."

"Have you had anything published?"

"Articles in local magazines..."

"On mummies? You know a lot about them."

He shook his head. "No. I pick up bits of information at the museum and I have a good memory. I hold onto things. But no, I don't write about mummies. I write about...darkness, the underground, you."

"Me? How do I fit into that?"

He put his hand under my chin and looked into my eyes. "You're sexy—you know it? Much sexier than your friends. Even though they'd never believe it." He plucked at the strap of my sundress. "This isn't yours, is it? It's one of theirs. You'd never buy something this revealing."

"It's Carolyn's," I told him. "I borrowed it for the evening."

He leered, "I'm not saying I don't like it, but I knew when I picked you up that you hadn't shopped for it yourself."

"How'd you know?"

"I write about people. I'm pretty good at knowing what people are thinking."

I tilted my head, regarding him, daring him. "What am I thinking?"

"That you want to kiss me."

I blushed. "Is that a line?"

He shook his head. "I'm good with people, but I don't date a lot. I don't flirt. I chose you. Does that make sense?"

I shrugged, unsure, then moved forward and kissed him, sliding my lips on his, making it sweet and soft. He smiled when we parted and took my hand, leading me back through the pub, up the street, and to his scooter. He gave me his extra helmet and we climbed on and went roving through downtown London. We stopped in pub after pub, meeting people he knew, drinking Southern Comforts and Long Island Iced Teas—because I was American and this is what they swore Americans were supposed to drink.

"Do I want to kiss you now?" I teased him at the last pub we stopped at. "Do I want your hands on my body?"

I said it a little too loud, and he quieted me with his lips on mine, whispering into my mouth, "Yessss…"

"Do I want you?" I hissed back at him, moving millimeters away from his smile, "Do I want you? You tell me."

I was plastered, not used to being served at eighteen. Up to that point, I'd had only beer at college parties— no hard liquor beyond the occasional punch laced with 151.

"Yes," he said, again leading me away from the pub, taking me upstairs to a private room. There were mirrors on all the walls and I turned around and around, staring at my reflection. Alex opened a window shade and turned off the light, and the room was instantly transformed. Mystical, magical, his body against mine.

I said, "Where are we? Whose place is this?"

"A friend's. Don't worry."

He held onto me tightly, kissing along the line of my throat, wrapping his hand in my hair and pulling my neck back, exposing me.

"Do I want you?" I whispered. "Tell me how you know."

He placed his hand flat over my cunt, through my dress, through my panties. "I know…."

"I don't want to do it in here," I told him. "I want to be outside." The room was spinning, and with the mirrors all around I felt as if I were falling.

"Sure," he said. "No problem," He took me around the waist and carried me down the stairs and out of the building, then set me down. We walked slowly to the bridge and looked into the water. The stroll was his idea, but it was a smart one. He was too drunk to drive, and the fresh air on my flushed cheeks helped bring me back to reality.

Alex held my hand and said, "I liked you from the start. Even before I knew we had the same name."

"Mine's *Alexa*," I said. "They call me Alex when they want to make fun of me. My tomboy attitude."

He shrugged that off. "But Alexa's close to Alex. Real close."

I nodded, and while I was making sense of the statement, he kissed me again, put his hands on my shoulders, and licked both of my lips before parting them with his tongue. It was a long kiss, golden-hued, redolent of the alcohol we'd consumed and the dizzy drunken feeling that goes with it. In the middle of the kiss, the power shifted. I was the one doing the kissing, rather than the one being kissed.

There is something undeniably sexy about being in control; and when it's never happened to you before, when you've never even fantasized about it, the surprise of it makes it that much more erotic.

Feeling Alex's hands on the back of my neck, pulling me forward, toward him, and then my hands on him, matching strength for strength, reminded me of crunching numbers in school. Of making things even, those numbers below the straight line. Of taking everything down to zero.

A win-win situation, I suppose. A tie. And then, ever so slightly, that nudge to my side of the seesaw, my edge of the rope in the tug-of-war, and I was pulling him forward, my fingers at the nape of his neck, caressing that smooth, warm skin. My ravenous mouth taking charge. Probing, violating, sinful, and divine.

His breathing became more rapid, and he tried to pull away. I let him, looking at him, directly in his eyes. He said, "I knew. I saw you and I knew."

"You didn't want the others?" I asked, testing him.

"No…from that first glance, that first image of you over by the glass cases. You were so intent. I knew."

"Knew?" I asked.

He blinked, sucked in his breath, and said, "That you'd be the way you are. That this would be the way it is."

"How is it?" I was drunk enough to fuck *with* him

before actually fucking him. "How is it?" My mouth so close to his, my breath stirring his hair. "You tell me how it is."

And he blushed, looked down, stammered, "Just perfect, Alexa, perfect and good."

And then my arms were around him again, my mouth sealed to his, our bodies pressed together. Unifying. Undeniably simple, and undeniably right.

I leaned in, bringing my lips to his ear, whispering, "You knew...did you know how it would feel? Did you know we'd be here? On this bridge? Doing this?"

He didn't respond verbally; but, with a moan, pulled my panties down my thighs, unbuckled his jeans and slid them down, got ready to enter me. I couldn't get enough of his mouth. I kissed him ravenously. Kissed him endlessly, letting his cock press against my naked thighs. Letting him rub it and grope forward with it, trying to push it in me. Trying to feel the wetness that had coated my outer lips and slicked my thighs.

There was an iron railing on the edge of the bridge He leaned me up against it. Then, as I'd done with our kiss, I switched the power on him, moved suddenly and turned in his arms, so that he was against the railing and I was against him.

"I knew..." he said, and then shut his eyes and let me work. "I knew."

You have entered Ether. There are 2 people present.

Omen: Tell me your darkest secret.

Venus: I don't keep secrets from you, Mistress. I tell you everything you ask. I am totally honest with you.

Omen: I mean, I want you to tell me something from before, before I knew you. Reveal yourself to me. I demand it.

Venus: Yes, Mistress. Let me think…. I'll tell you a secret.

Omen: Your biggest one.

Venus: Sexually speaking?

Omen: Of course, Venus. I'm not asking whether you cheat on your taxes.

Venus: I don't.

Omen: Or whether you devour whole packages of Oreos late at night when no one's around, eating only the stuffing from each one. Licking them clean.

Venus: I don't.

Omen: I want to know something you haven't told anyone else. Ever.

Venus: Okay, let me get my thoughts together.

Omen: I'm waiting. I don't like to wait, slave. Tell me a secret. Now.

Venus: I did a boy once.

Omen: Yes? Is that supposed to shock me?

Venus: A one-night stand. I let him touch me, let him take me, let him do whatever he wanted to me.

Omen: And?

Venus: And then, on a bridge, in the middle of the night, I controlled him.

Omen: You mean, you fucked him?

Venus: Not really. Not exactly. I did, I guess, but there was more to it. That's my secret. That was the only time I ever took charge.

Omen: Describe it.

Venus: He was my size, almost exactly. I'm tall for a girl, he was normal for a guy—about 5'10". He was heavier, stronger, but he didn't abuse the situation. He started lifting my dress, pulling down my panties.

Omen: And?

Venus: And then I turned, grabbed his wrists, held them down at his side. I'm sure he could have stopped me if he'd tried, could have lifted his arms up and broken my hold, but he didn't.

Omen: Why not, slave? Why do you think he didn't?

Venus: It turned him on.

Omen: Continue.

Venus: His cock was out. His jeans were down. I slid on him, working myself on his shaft. Controlling the ride.

Omen: Did you like it?

Venus: I guess...

Omen: Did he?

Venus: Yeah...he moaned. His head was back, his eyelids closed, his mouth tight. He swallowed hard and said my name, then screamed my name as he came.

Omen: What did you like the most.

Venus: Being outside. Letting people watch.

Omen: There were people nearby?

Venus: Driving by in their cars. No one stopped, but a few people honked at us.

Omen: Anything else? Did you like anything else?

Venus: When he was coming, I moved off him, letting him shoot onto my belly, my thighs....I liked watching it. It made me feel in power. Empowered.

Omen: Do you like to be in power...slave? Tell me the truth.

Venus: No, Mistress. Not really. But I'd never experienced it from either side before—not submissive, not dominant. It gave me ideas. It fueled my fantasies.
Omen: Tell me a fantasy, now.
Venus: Mistress, it's late. Too late. I have to go…
Omen: Then next time. Be prepared.
Venus: Yes, Mistress. I promise.

CHAPTER FOUR:
Two Men Fucking

Every evening, when I get off work, I ride a cable car to my apartment building at the top of California Street. The drivers know me on this route and they tend to banter with me during the ride.

"Got a boyfriend yet?" they tease, always asking the same question. "Pretty thing like you ought to have all the boys calling." They eye me when they say that, sometimes offering themselves to fill the role. Sometimes adding, "I've got a son just your age." Or "I've got a nephew who'd be perfect for you." When they know nothing about me. Not what I want, or what I need.

I shrug and blush. I say, "I'm not ready yet." Or "My work's too important to waste time on men, you know." Long pause. "Men," as if I don't know what to do with them, and they laugh and grin and tease me some more.

Along the way, in between fielding their personal questions and staring out at the blur of the buildings we pass, I unwind from the day, replaying any positive or negative moments that occurred. By the time we reach my stop, the banking day is over, wiped clean from my head, and I'm ready for my nighttime routine to begin.

At home, I change into black silk Calvin Klein long johns—a true luxury—and brew a pot of strong coffee. I buy my coffee beans at The Cave, the local café where Nina works. I've done my research over my four years living in San Francisco. Along with being an ultracool coffee bar, The Cave sells the best coffee beans in the city. The workers there expect me at least once a week, when I come in to buy my latest fix. Sometimes I choose French roast, sometimes espresso, sometimes Hawaiian Kona: the greasiest, darkest beans and the most expensive. That's a splurge I save up for. With my coffee habit, I'd go broke if I bought only Kona.

When the java's ready, I pour a steaming cup—I drink it black, I'm one of the few coffee puritans left among all the hazelnut cream, vanilla-flavored fanciers—and I climb out my window to sit on my fire escape. This is my favorite place. From my perch, I watch the people walking on the street below. I watch the sun set over the hill. I watch the lights go on in the building across the way and the streetlights flicker to life along the block.

Usually I stay in, catch an old movie on TV or rent one for the VCR, often something I've seen many times before. My favorites are the *Thin Man* movies, starring Myrna Loy and William Powell. I also like films of

Raymond Chandler books: *The Big Sleep*. *The Long Good-bye*.

I'm fairly low-key about my downtime. Insomniacs tend to have a lot of extra hours. I don't really do too much with them, though. Before I quit, I'd sit in bed and smoke the night away, lighting one cigarette from the butt of the last. Practicing blowing silver-gray smoke rings to impress my easily impressible friends. I usually smoked French Gauloises because I liked the box. Occasionally I smoked Marlboros, for the taste.

I had to quit after college because smoking at the bank—running outside during breaks and puffing away, often in miserable weather—was more hassle than it was worth. But even now, four years later, I miss it.

Occasionally, depending on my mood, I go out for a late dinner with friends. None of us are married yet, and only one of our fivesome ever seems to have a steady boyfriend at any given time. So we stick together, choosing funky restaurants like The Stinking Rose in North Beach, Stars Café near the opera house, or Zuni, my favorite. We meet for an adventure, but rarely find it. Though on our latest outing, at Zuni, I got a little drunk and walked into one of the large unisex bathrooms off the kitchen. The couple inside had apparently forgotten to lock the door—either that, or they wanted an audience. I was mildly startled, but drunk enough not to immediately back out apologetically.

I mean, I'd never seen two men fucking before, and the image captivated me. Of course, I knew that some men fucked each other—10 percent of the population, and probably more of the immediate S.F. populace, are homosexual. And I knew that videos are available at Tower. I could easily rent one to watch on the subject, in case I ever cared to check it out. But I never had seen one of those movies—never even had visualized the action—and I was mesmerized.

After what seemed like an eternity, but was probably only two or three seconds, I said, "Excuse me," lowered my head, my hair falling over my flaming cheeks, and exited. From behind the closed door, I heard, "No problem, honey...any time."

It was the one in back who'd spoken, the one who was doing the fucking—I knew this somehow. He seemed more capable of finding the words than the one in front. I closed my eyes, memorizing the image, the lighting in the bathroom. The way the walls were painted in gold and reflected in two mirrors—one over the sink, one on the wall across the room. The gold paint made the partners look gilded, their bodies in prime shape, beautiful enough for a sculptor to cast.

Without relieving myself, though my bladder had been near-bursting, I stumbled back upstairs to the white-sheathed table where my four girlfriends sat. The remnants of our sumptuous meal lay before them. Two wine bottles stood on the table, both empty. On the wall was a painting of a café in Paris, with colorful umbrellas over the round tables and the rippling silver water of the Seine in the background.

I stared at the picture trying to calm myself, but I wanted to tell my friends what I'd seen. My cheeks were sweetly flushed with red wine and excitement. Julia noticed and said, "Hey, what happened to you?" She turned her attention entirely on me, propping her fox-sharp chin in her hand and regarding me with her deep, drunken brown eyes.

"I saw...." Then I looked around the table at my friends. Elaine has become somewhat more refined over the years, though she *was* wild when were in college. She cut her leonine mane into a chic bob and stopped bleaching it to the platinum blonde she preferred when we were in our late teens. After college, she got a master's degree in education, and now she's a nursery-school teacher. Still, she thinks she's avant-garde because she dresses all in black and dates musicians when she can. I knew she'd be horrified if I revealed my story.

Raina actually *is* avant-garde, a performance artist who supplements her income by reviewing porn for a few local positive-sex magazines. I met her in my senior year at college in a dance class off campus, and I introduced her to the rest of the gang. She adds spark to our groupings—that's just the way she is. Raina came out to me about three years ago about her bisexuality, but hasn't told the others. But if any of our friends took the time to pay attention, they would be able to figure it out—simply by the way she flirts with women. Our waitress, for one, had given Raina the eye when we'd first been seated, and Raina had replied with a look that would have flambéed anyone paying attention.

I knew that Raina wouldn't really care about the men downstairs. And it definitely wouldn't shock her.

Carolyn, who had become a banker at a different branch from mine, wouldn't know how to process the information. She's been in the same volatile on-again, off-again relationship ever since high school. I don't think she's ever experimented with anything outside her definition of "normal" sex. (I don't believe in the word "normal" anymore. Why should one definition be considered acceptable, while others are deemed bizarre?)

The only one who might understand my piqued interest was Julia, my very best friend since childhood. She's a painter and is extremely creative. She'd accept my odd yearning to know more about the men in the lavatory. She might even share it. And, knowing that I could call her later in the evening and reveal all, instead I said, "Nothing...I'm a little buzzed, you know? I almost walked into the kitchen instead of the bathroom. Can you imagine the chef's surprise?"

And they laughed and returned to their conversation, while my eyes glazed over and I replayed the image.

The half-clothed men were standing in front of the mirror in the cavernous rectangular bathroom. The more handsome of the two, a dark-eyed brunette, was bent over the stainless-steel sink, holding onto the rim with both hands, his knuckles gone white with effort. That was the strongest image I had—the tightness in his body revealed in his hands. His redheaded partner was doing the fucking, and it looked harder and more powerful than anything I'd ever seen. I wanted to go back down and watch. I wanted to stand against the interior wall and listen to them, listen to the noises they'd made.

I'd never made noises like that while fucking. Moans, sighs, animal-like grunts. I'd never actually been fucked, I realized, thinking back. I'd had men make love to me, sweetly, softly, touching my hair and whispering my name as the moment took them. I'd been in control only once. But if what I'd just seen was fucking—and I decided it was the perfect image to accompany the word; that *Webster's* should show a photograph of the two of them next to the definition in the dictionary: To Fuck (v)—then all I'd had to that point was lovemaking.

I struggled with my emotions. Making love should be a positive thing. It should show that I had chosen my beaus with careful consideration. But all I felt now was that my experiences were wimpy in comparison to the way those bathroom lovers had behaved.

I'd rarely sweated during a passionate clinch, but the two men downstairs were both covered in a glistening sheen like a light brushing of olive oil. I'd never panted hard, never gritted my teeth; the man bent over the sink was positively grunting with effort. His beautiful white teeth were clenched; his finely carved jaw was tight; the wires of muscles and sinews in his neck stood out in bold relief. I wanted to touch him, wanted to lick the sweat off his forehead, wanted to run my fingers down the lines of his jaw and his cheekbones and his throat.

My dress, though of summer-weight material because a heat wave had hit the city, suddenly seemed too heavy on my body. I yearned to be naked, to join them—though I was certain they wouldn't have a use for me or my female holes. For the first time in my life I wanted to be a guy, able to enter in the rough-and-tumble world they lived in. I wanted to shed my good-girl exterior and learn how to play hard. Or, not to play at all, but to *live* hard.

Paradise?

Locked in position, head down, arms frozen with the effort of keeping still. My reflection thrown back at me from the mirror over the sink. My eyes wild and hungry and untamed. He stands behind me, shaking his head slightly, whispering under his breath, "This is gonna hurt, sweetheart. Oh, yeah, this is gonna hurt. Can you take it? Huh, baby? Huh, sweetheart? Can you take it?"

"Yeah…please…" Not my voice at all. Some stranger's voice, some stranger's body, some stranger's muted green eyes fixed on mine in the mirror.

He spits on his palm and then greases me up, lubes my asshole, the split between my thighs, then lubes his cock. And then he rises on his tiptoes, the muscles tight in his calves, and he plunges inside me.

"Say it again," his voice urgent, his cock so deep, so hard in my ass that I can't think of anything but the feeling of being filled. "Say you want it."

A struggle for air. Then: "I want it…."

His breathing is as ragged as mine. His need is as consuming. "Say 'please.'"

Oh, God, I can't do it, can't do it. Eyes shut tightly until I feel his mouth on the nape of my neck, his body sealed against mine. "Please…."

And then he pumps me hard, out and in again, thrusting, filling, completing.

Paradise.

My friends tried to include me in the conversation. Of the five of us, Raina is the only one with a real life, in my opinion. She does what she wants, when she wants to. She shocks us for fun, upsetting Elaine every so often, confounding Carolyn with her dirty words and exuberant chitchat about sex and orgasms. Of the four of us, I am the only one who goes to Raina's shows, who supports her art.

Finally Raina said, "What's eating you, Lexi? What's on your mind? You've hardly said a word since you came back from the bathroom. And Carolyn's been talking about money—your favorite topic."

I said, "Just too much wine, I suppose."

She shot me a look, which I recognized as disbelief, and I hurried to say, "I guess I'm thinking about work. We've been really busy lately."

Carolyn, my banking friend, caught me in the lie. "No, we haven't. That's just what I was saying. Things have been really slow."

"Well, *I* have," I said, trying not to sound as snotty as I heard myself in my head. "I mean, with school and everything."

There was silence at the table. I hadn't told them of my night classes at SFSU, my attempts to grow a talent from nothing. I hadn't told them because I hadn't wanted to, and the looks on their faces were a mix of anger at being left out, confusion and, on Raina's, respect.

"What's this?" Julia asked nicely.

"Nothing," I said again, feeling a different kind of heat rising to my cheeks. Not the wine. Embarrassment. "I didn't want to tell you until I finished it…it's nothing. Just a writing class."

Elaine, also drunk, said, "You can't write. Remember your college class? What'd you get? A C–? And she was being kind."

I nodded, brought back rudely from my fantasy. "Yeah, a C-, Elaine. How'd you remember it so well?" A harsh sputter of anger. "I guess you were the one with straight A's, is that right?" Knowing that wasn't the case at all, that she'd had to have me tutor her in math every quarter, but seething at her callous response. Raina rescued us from an impending blowup.

"I'm glad to hear it, Lexi," she said. "If you ever want me to read anything…. I'm a pretty good copy editor, and I'd love to help you if you're ever stuck for an idea."

I nodded again, thanked her, and downed the last of my merlot in a single gulp. Then I pulled my worn leather wallet from my pale blue Coach handbag—a one-time splurge. "How much do I owe?" I asked. "I've got homework…."

Realizing that I was angry at her, Elaine looked down at her plate. There have been few times that we haven't had the sting of competition between us, which is odd, since I refuse to compete for anything. I work at my own pace, toward my own goals. Elaine is the one with the need for a war. Otherwise, she can't be happy.

Raina's warm brown eyes flashed at me. "My treat, as congratulations for going back to school."

"Thanks," I said again.

"Will you come to my birthday party? We can talk more about your class then…."

I promised her that I would and then fled, down the stairs to the freeing air of the street. I took a cab, something I rarely do in our town which is filled with public transportation, and got home as soon as I could. Home to my brand-new computer, to write a story about Two

Men Fucking. The only thing on my mind for that night, the next night, and weeks after.

The sweat on them, the hard glare of their bodies under the light. Why hadn't I realized that I found men together attractive, when men who scampered after me did virtually nothing to stir my blood? I remembered images in films like *My Beautiful Launderette* and the French farce, *Going Places*, that I had shrugged away as simply "Art representations—" not real life, not considering my reaction to them or interpreting it in any way. It's easy to say, "I like Daniel Day-Lewis, that's all," allowing yourself to slide away from the true issue: "I liked Daniel Day-Lewis kissing another man...."

I'd never confronted this feeling, even though it wasn't as if I'd never been exposed to homosexual men. My mother, a travel agent, worked almost exclusively with gay men. As a teenager, I'd hung out in her office, paging through dog-eared copies of *GQ* with her assistant, Roger.

"Do you like him?" Roger would ask me, pushing a lock of platinum hair away from his forehead. He always was returning from one trip or another—travel agent's discount—and he had a perpetual tan and the kind of sun-bleached hair one can get only from lying on the beach of one tropical island or another.

I stared at the glossy page of the magazine, in which an even-glossier young stud, with pale skin and dark hair, stared gloomily back at us. Pouting. Soulful. "Yeah—" a beat—"do you?"

"Not my type..."

And then we'd turn the page and Roger would sigh

and point and say, "But him…oh, Lexi-darlin', look at him…."

"It's just the leather, Rog," I'd assure him, stroking the page. "Look, the guy's got no personality."

And we'd argue together as the fashion spreads blurred.

But I'd never considered the positions. I knew only that some men dig each other, the way some men dig women, and some women dig each other the way some women dig men, and that's the way the world goes.

I retreated to my apartment after my Zuni adventure, turned on my coffee pot, and opened my fire-escape window. I did these everyday rituals without thought, lost in the realization that I'd never really decided what I liked. Or why.

You have entered Ether. There are 2 people present.
Omen: A fantasy.
Venus: Yes...
Omen: I'm waiting.
Venus: Yes...I have one, Mistress. I'm just trying to think of a way to start.
Omen: Just one?
Venus: I mean, one to share.
Omen: Begin.
Venus: I would like to be a guy.
Omen: Gender-play—is that what you mean? Role-play? You wanna be Mommy's bad boy? Do you need Mommy to spank you? To pull down your pants and spank your bare bottom? Is that it?
Venus: No, not play a guy. BE a guy.
Omen: Why?
Venus: I think I'd be less shy, less fearful if I were a male.
Omen: You aren't shy, young one. You're subservient. It's your nature.
Venus: What if I wanted to switch my nature for awhile? What if I'm tired of being subdued?
Omen: Okay. It's your fantasy. Describe it for me.
Venus: I'd be strong, handsome, wanted.
Omen: What would you do, then?
Venus: I'd be fucked—
Omen: By a woman? With a strap-on?
Venus: No, by another guy....
Omen: Are you saying that you're a gay man trapped inside a woman's body?
Venus: I'm not saying anything like that. I'm saying that my fantasy is to be a guy, and to be fucked, hard, up the ass....
Omen: You could fulfill that act as a woman, you know.

Venus: <long pause> I know.
Omen: Have you?
Venus: No.
Omen: Why? Because it's dirty...messy...wrong?
Venus: No.
Omen: Because you're afraid to ask?
Venus: No...
Omen: Then why?
Venus: 'Cause none of the guys I've been with have ever tried.
Omen: You've been with the wrong guys, then. As far as I can tell from our conversations, just being with guys at all is wrong. When are you going to get over it? When will you admit what you want?
Venus: Maybe I am.
Omen: I have an assignment for you, slave.
Venus: Yes, Mistress.
Omen: I want you to fulfill your fantasy...as well as you can, I mean. I'm not talking a sex-change operation.
Venus: Find a guy?
Omen: Or a girl with a strap-on, a huge, powerful dildo....
Venus: My assignment?
Omen: To get fucked up the ass.
Venus: When?
Omen: I'll give you a time limit. How about...within two weeks. Then write to me about it.
Venus: You're serious?
Omen: Deadly.
Venus: You want me to get fucked...
Omen: How can you ask that question? Haven't you been listening?

Venus: I mean, you won't be jealous?

Omen: I'm ordering you to do it.

Venus: Do you mean online?

Omen: Real time. Do you understand? No fantasy finger-work on a keyboard with an imaginary fuck-partner. But strapped to a bed with a red-blooded human who wants to ream what I'm sure is that cute little asshole of yours.

Venus: <hesitantly> Yes, Mistress.

Omen: I want you to practice safe sex, of course.

Venus: Yes, Mistress.

Omen: And write to me as soon as it happens. A full report.

Venus: I promise, Mistress.

Omen: If you fail me, slave, I will have to come and punish you…. Though that's not much of a threat, I guess…since you'd like it. Still, I want you to obey me. I don't handle disobedience very well.

Venus: <head bowed> I understand, Mistress.

Omen: You think you do….

CHAPTER FIVE:
Jack, or John, or Marc, or Bill

As I changed into my long johns after what I've come to think of as my "amazing Zuni adventure," I took a brief trip down memory lane. In my mind, I called up my various lovers and partners: the boy Alex, in London; then many boys at the sorority/fraternity parties, but only because Elaine was there, and Carolyn, pushing me forward.

"Don't you think he's hot?" Elaine would say, pointing out some young buck who was nearly indistinguishable from the rest of his pack. College boys hang out together as if they're joined at the jock strap.

"Which one?" I'd ask, trying hard not to appear as bored as I felt.

"Jack, [or John, or Marc, or Bill] the blond one [or

brunette, or redhead], with the muscles." [They *all* had muscles.]

I'd turn and stare and, more often than not, the boy would stare back in a look that said, "Are you game? Do you wanna play? Do you know the rules?"

Did I? Of course. Just matching his look would give him the permission he needed to approach us. That and the rush of adrenaline in his veins, the beer, the smell of impending victory in the air. He'd look us over, the three of us easily the most attractive of the sorority sisters at any function. Elaine, the coy blonde with the sylphlike body; Carolyn, a naturally auburn-haired stunner with a cameo-perfect face; and me, with my shifting green eyes and calico hair and my model's height. The boy would look the three of us over, and then he'd make his choice.

If Carolyn was in the running, it meant she'd broken up with Jason, her high-school steady, yet again, and was after a revenge fuck. One that she'd call me up and cry about the next day, self-pityingly; "Oh, God, Lexi, what will I do if Jason finds out?"—a sob—"I'll have to kill myself. I will!"

I'd murmur all the appropriate lies to her and ask myself, "And what if Carolyn ever finds out about Jason and Elaine and their summer fling? What then?"

If Elaine was picked, she'd give me a superior look on her way up the stairs to do it. A look that said, "See? I'm prettier than you are. I'm better than you are. They like me more. They want to touch me, suck me, taste, me, fuck me."

I'd just nod and think to myself, "So? Is it really all that great up there in bed with a hunk who thinks he's God's gift? Is this something I need to compete for?"

But if it were me—if the boy set his sights on me—then I felt myself fall into the scripted pattern of guy-meets-girl. I knew the steps; I did the dance. For whatever reason you want to name: acceptance, loneliness, I offered myself up as a willing sacrifice, closed my eyes, and went through the motions.

I don't think I'll ever get the smell of a frat-house bedroom completely out of my sensory memory, though I'd love more than anything to be able to bring in a mental Dustbuster and erase it, vacuum it all away. There was always a musky, he-man odor of unwashed clothes and rotting food, covered—barely—by the overpowering scents of Polo cologne ...and come, if you weren't the first lucky one to be bedded that night.

Jack, the football stud I remember best, chose me over Elaine, sparking her intense competitive spirit immediately.

"You're looking good tonight, Lexi," Jack said, his light blue eyes caressing me, drinking me in.

"Thanks."

"I haven't seen you much since the ice-cream social."

"I've been studying a lot. Finals, you know?"

"Wanna see my room? I just got a new trophy."

Elaine swallowed hard over her anger, gave me a look of hatred, and said, "Hey, Jack, why not make it a threesome?" And the stud's eyes bugged out as if he'd just been goosed. I could tell Elaine was baiting me, and I wasn't going to play her game.

"You guys can go up," I told them, making my way toward the door. "I'm sort of tired."

"No, Lexi...Join us...." A dare. A taunt.

Old Jack looked stunned. Barely able to stand upright after chugging so many brews, he still couldn't comprehend his luck. There was Elaine, blonde and lanky, with a ravenous look in her eyes that guys took to be sexual hunger but was, in reality, an endless need to be filled—something she never succeeded in achieving. It's probably why she binged and purged for so many years, trying to fill an emptiness inside her that nothing—not food or sex or guys—ever could.

Elaine dressed in a collegiate slutty look, tight-fitting dresses and cute slacks-and-vest sets that showed off her round butt and rounder cleavage. I almost always wore jeans and white T-shirt, refusing to buy into the college-whore fashion so popular among my sorority sisters. But that night was hot, and I had on a pastel summer dress that revealed my long legs and tied in back to accentuate my slender waist. Elaine had talked me into buying it, trying to bring me "out of my shell," as she said.

Jack looked at us, from Elaine to me, then back again. "You serious? Or are you fucking with me?"

I shook my head one way, Elaine shook hers the other.

"C'mon," Elaine hissed at me. "He's totally gorgeous. And he's a football player. How can you say no?"

"How can you say yes?" I whispered back. "You don't even know him."

"What's to know?"

Jack remained silent during this hissing interchange, in somewhat of a stupor at his amazing good fortune. Would he have a story for the guys. Shit, he'd have a story for *Penthouse*'s "Forum." (I could hear the letter in my head: "I was at a mixer on Friday night, sorta bumming 'cause my girlfriend had dumped me. Then I saw them: two beautiful sorority sisters standing across the room and looking my way….")

Finally, with Elaine shooting me daggers, I said, "Sure, why not," and ended up leading the way up the stairs.

In each of the four frat bedrooms, we found other couples already in sweaty clinches. I backed into the hallway after peeking my head into the last room, and I shrugged at the other two. "Oh, well," I said. "No room at the inn." But Elaine, unwilling to give it up, pulled my hand and said, "Let's go on the roof."

Up to that point, I'd never come from sex, and I hadn't even thought that was odd. A huge percentage of women have a difficult time coming, I'd read it often enough in the women's magazines like *Cosmopolitan* and *Mademoiselle*. Why should I be any different?

But with the night sky filled with stars, with the lights in the frat houses on around us, I discovered my penchant for exhibitionism. I stripped first, standing in the center of the roof, tossing my dress to the ground. I met Elaine's eyes and waited, offering her the kind of "fuck-you" expression I knew would get her. She slid out of her own skintight number and then, together, we turned to face the handsome, able Jack.

"I—" he stammered, at a loss.

"Well?" I asked, my hands on my hips, thrusting forward, offering myself to him. He had his back against a concrete wall and he slid to a sitting position, watching us.

"I don't know if I can," he said. "I've had so much fuckin' beer, and you both are so fine…."

I smiled, realizing that in some small way, we'd won.

We had cowed the famous football hero, who would no doubt still brag to his buddies that he'd done two sisters from our infamous sorority. I turned back to Elaine, who had her arms over her head, as if in a communion with the night sky and the silver crescent moon above.

"Well…?" I asked again, this time directing my question to Elaine. She cocked her head, as if she hadn't heard me quite clearly, or as if she didn't know what I was getting at. But she knew.

"Yeah, Lexi?" she asked, hands still over her head, stretching her body out in one long, lovely line. She's a swimmer, and her muscles were visible beneath the sleek canvas of her skin. Stretched out, her legs were taut, her stomach flat to the point of being concave, her breasts beautiful rounds.

"Close your eyes."

She did as I said, without asking why, without considering why. She closed her eyes and kept her hands over her head and let her long hair fall free in a thick golden wave down her naked back.

I got on my knees before her, extremely aware of Jack's eyes on us both, and I pressed my face to her panty-clad pussy, nuzzling forward with my mouth and chin, breathing in deeply. Smelling her. She sighed and lowered one hand to the back of my head, pressing me firmly against her. I heard Jack's low intake of breath behind me, and I kept going, now bringing my hands to her hips and sliding her panties down her legs, helping her to step out of them. To step free.

"Is this okay?" I murmured, my face against her. "Do you want this?"

"Oh, yes..."

I didn't need additional permission. I slid my thumbs into her wet slit and parted the lips of her cunt, lapping quickly at the drops of her juices that fell free. I'd never tasted a woman before, never thought of doing this with anyone outside of my beautiful English composition professor. I hadn't fantasized about Elaine, hadn't ever considered her as anything but a friend. And a sometimes bitchy friend, at that. Still, as I ate her, as I continued nibbling on the lips of her pussy, thrusting my tongue deep inside her warm, wet cunt, I realized that nothing had ever seemed quite so normal.

She was divine, ripe and ready for me to dine on. I visualized what I would have a woman do to me, and I did that to her, gently spreading her pussylips even wider apart. Opening her. Moving back a little and observing the gradation of color within her sex. Pale outer lips, darker inner lips, rich pink in the very center. Her clit poked out at me, and I nipped at it and made her moan and say my name again.

"Alexandra..."

After a few moments of dining, feasting, I felt a hand on my shoulder and Jack, his nerve revived along with his cock, was behind me, entering me. His powerful body felt solid as he slid in deep, and soon the three of us were rocking with the motion of his thrusts. He fucked me and I fucked Elaine. The three of us were joined in a way I'd never imagined. A way that was never discussed afterward—never mentioned again.

At one point, I looked up at Elaine, watching her as a different expression flickered over her pretty face. One that was raw and amazing and real. One that I hadn't seen since until I walked in on the two guys fucking.

Staring at her, watching that look on her face, I had a need to feel it myself. I pulled away from Jack, shooing him back from us. He was good-natured about it, standing against the wall with his hand wrapped around his come-glistening cock, watching. I spread my dress out on the roof, had Elaine lie down on her back, and straddled her quickly in a sixty-nine. She knew just what to do, mimicking the rhythm of my tongue on her, the waves of my body as I started to reach my peak.

When Jack couldn't hold back, he came close to us again and stood over us, shooting his come all over my back, suddenly talkative as his balls were emptied onto our moonlit skins.

"Oh, yeah, I can feel it coming…." His voice growing louder with each word. "It's rising up inside me, it's gonna…it's gonna…ohhhhh!"

Somehow the sound of his voice and the feel of Elaine's tongue and the rhythm of the night took me over the top. For the first time, I came without help from my hand. For the first time, I came with a lover.

Elaine and I never spoke about that evening. She pretended that she didn't remember it, blaming her lack of memory on the beer, blaming the pot we'd smoked earlier, stating only that she and Jack had had a wonderful time together on the roof and that it was too bad I'd had to leave the party early. She said this with her radiant blue eyes so wide and innocent that I questioned whether I'd made the whole thing up in my head. Had I fantasized about it? Had I created an image so realistic that I still had tar from the roof on my dress the next day?

I didn't think so. It was only Elaine, and her need for "normalcy" that kept me from teasing her. That kept me from walking right up behind her in the halls and saying, "You tasted sinful, Lainie. You tasted as fresh as a spring peach, as sweet as a sip of good red wine. I'd like to feel you on my tongue again...."

There was a hush in her eyes when she looked at me, as if she were begging for me to forget the evening, too. If I brought it up, I'd force her to deal with it, to deal with herself. Force her to decide whether she wanted to re-create the moment, whether she wanted to invite me to her bed, to take her further, to take her away.

I relished the confusion I'd created for her. I'd never wanted to compete with her, never wanted to win anything over her. The faux competitions have been alive in her eyes only. But now, at her own request, I had sent her into a tailspin in which she had to make up a fantasy to exist. Had to erase the image of me on my knees in front of her, pleasuring her, of her on her back sixty-nining with me.

She had the taste of come on her tongue, as well.

Jack may or may not have told his buddies—I didn't really care since I graduated soon after. I never saw him again.

Later I wondered, would it really have ruined my reputation if other people had found out? Or would it have given me one?

You have entered Ether. There are 2 people present.

Omen: Have you fulfilled your assignment, slave?

Venus: Not yet, Mistress.

Omen: I want a full report; you know that.

Venus: Yes, Mistress. I know.

Omen: I want to hear all about what it felt like to have a cock in that virgin ass.

Venus: Yes, Mistress. I promise. I'll tell you.

Omen: I'm counting the days, you know.

Venus: I know. I just haven't yet. I'm not sure who...

Omen: You'll find someone.

Venus: Yeah...

Omen: I have a question for you, slave.

Venus: Ask me anything, Mistress.

Omen: Have you been with a woman? Off-line, I mean. Real-time.

Venus: Yes, once...

Omen: When?

Venus: In college...it's funny—you know it?

Omen: What's funny, slave?

Venus: I consider my friend, Raina, to be a bisexual, and yet...

Omen: Yes?

Venus: I've eaten a woman before, but never considered myself bi or gay. Does that make sense? It's as if my experience doesn't count because it happened only one time.

Omen: What do you consider yourself?

Venus: Repressed.

Omen: You've had so many different experiences—at least, from what you've told me. And yet you still consider yourself repressed? Are you talking only sexually?

Venus: No...sexually and nonsexually. Repressed in all the

ways a person can be. Repressed in everything but my innermost thoughts.

Omen: But you do admit you've been, well, released in your experiences, don't you?

Venus: They've all been just one-time flings, bits of fantasy turned reality. But I don't live my life outwardly, the way Raina does. I don't express myself very well.

Omen: You express yourself well to me.

Venus: Yeah, I guess so.

Omen: Have you lied to me? Have you made things up?

Venus: No, Mistress. Of course not. I just meant that it's just easier to tell you things than it is to tell other people. My conversations with you are not indicative of the way I talk with my friends, or coworkers, or lovers.

Omen: So why do you find it easier to "talk" with me than with other people?

Venus: It's just different...

Omen: How?

Venus: The online arena makes it different, I guess. It's a nameless, faceless environment.

Omen: Then send me your picture.

Venus: I can't.

Omen: It's not a request.

Venus: I can't be rejected. Not again. Not by you.

Omen: I won't reject you.

Venus: <shaking head>

Omen: Do not disobey me, young one.

Venus: <silent>

Omen: I will never leave you. I will never hurt you as you've been hurt in the past. I will only hurt you in the way you long to be hurt. The way you need to be hurt.

Venus: I don't know. I don't know you.
Omen: What do you want to know?
Venus: Are you a dominant in real life, or only online?
Omen: Do you really need to ask?
Venus: Please...tell me, reassure me.
Omen: In real life, too, young one. I am always, always in control. In charge.
Venus: Are you in a relationship?
Omen: No...not now.
Venus: Why not?
Omen: I've been celibate for the past six months. This was my own choice. My own way to clear out my mind.
Venus: Have you been only with women?
Omen: I've been with both. The expending of power doesn't require one to choose one sex over another. However, when making love, when fucking, I prefer to be with women.
Venus: Do you hurt your lovers?
Omen: Hurt, but not harm.
Venus: What's the difference?
Omen: I do not cause permanent damage, either mental or physical.
Venus: What...what do you look like?
Omen: <smiling> Is it important, slave?
Venus: You want my picture.
Omen: What do you think I look like?
Venus: <softly> I think you're coldly beautiful, like the queen in Sleeping Beauty.
Omen: That's a pretty good guess, slave.
Venus: What color hair do you have?
Omen: Midnight.

Venus: What color eyes?
Omen: The darkest brown you can imagine.
Venus: Skin?
Omen: Pale.
Venus: What type of body do you have?
Omen: Tough, corded, powerful, sleek.
Venus: You're a panther....
Omen: Another good guess, young one.
Venus: How tall are you?
Omen: Six feet. Even.
Venus: And you want me?
Omen: Yes, very much.
Venus: Tell me your address.... I'll send you my photo.

CHAPTER SIX:
Shame?

On my fire escape, looking out at the lights of the city, I breathe in deeply and think of those men again, in a clinch in the Zuni bathroom, fucking with the power and the...anger—was it anger?—of a lust I've never known, never imagined.

Why don't guys fuck me like that? I wonder. Why haven't I ever been bent over a sink at a local hot spot, panties down, skirt up, panting as my lover ravages me from behind? Why haven't I ever been taken, hard and forcefully, even painfully, gritting my teeth at the intrusion, white-knuckling it as a man discovers my secret inner workings and makes them his own.

I look at my reflection in the window, wondering if I simply don't possess the type of charm, the sexual quality that would make someone want to FUCK. The word screams in my head. Fuck. FUCK. *FUCK!* A naughty word, my mother always said when we heard neighborhood boys shout it at each other. A bad word. A dirty word.

Fuck.

I'd had my mouth washed out with soap when I screamed it at my sister in a flare-up of beyond-the-fringe preteen anger.

"Fuck you, Janet! Fuck you!"

She'd yelled it right back at me, "Fuck you too, Alexa!" But my mother had heard me say it first, and I was the one punished. Dragged by the arm into the bathroom and forced to stick my tongue way out while she lathered the insides of my mouth with foul-tasting soap.

Now, saying it, I feel rebellious—in a puerile, childish way. "Fuck...fuck me...oh, please, please fuck me...."

I lift my hair up, twisting my curls in a bed-tousled look and giving my reflection my best "come-hither" expression, my 1920s movie-star expression. Soulful. Sultry. But, after considering the pose, I decide that I just look silly. I let my hair back down and reach for my cup, taking a sip of the now-lukewarm coffee and thinking—again—about the men.

They hadn't minded me finding them. They had even seemed to enjoy my visit, my startled expression, my embarrassment. I now envision a scenario in which I'd stayed, locked the door behind me and sat down on the closed lid of the white porcelain john to watch. Piping up with questions:

"Um, does it hurt when his cock is up your ass? Do you like it?"

Making up my own answers.

Deep grunt. Then: "It hurts, but in a good way..."

Could I grasp that? I must be able to, since I created the answer myself.

"In a good way...does that mean that you like pain?"

"Yeah...isn't there a new Chili Peppers song about that?"

Shrug on my part. I don't usually listen to the Peppers.

"Do you ever switch?" was my next question. "Do you take turns fucking or being fucked?"

Heavy breathing, followed by "No, he fucks me. I like it that way."

I close my eyes as I build up this imaginary conversation. Taking it further—now setting the vision on the stage of a TV talk show. This would be the type of extreme situation I could really tune into. Two men, nude, bent over, answering questions from the audience while they work each other. But maybe there are places like that in the city that I just don't know about—underground sex clubs that Raina might be able to describe for me if I asked her. I know there are theaters, around Columbus, where you can go to watch two women fucking—so why not men?

Visualizing the scenario made me completely soak my long johns at the crotch. Without really realizing what I'm doing, I slip one hand under the waistband and feel myself. Right there, in the open air of my fire escape, probing, delving.

My panties are dripping, and the smell of my juices mingles with the clean scent of the night air. I drive forward with my fingers, impaling myself, squeezing tightly with the muscles of my pussy, wondering why—why nobody I've ever been with had ever taken the time to do just this. Just what I am doing. Exploring. Revealing.

I remove my hand and bring my musky scent-filled fingers under my nose and inhale deeply. Suddenly, I open my eyes and realize that someone in the building across the way is watching me. Standing in the window a few floors up and looking down at me.

I freeze, unsure of what to do next. How long has the stranger been standing there? Before I stuck my hungry paw into my panties, or after?

It doesn't really matter. There's not much to be done about it. But I can't stay outside, now, not with my heart beating so fast from shame. From confusion. From want.

I look back at the window. The person waves. I think it's a man from the stance, the square shoulders, and the height…but he's too far away for me to make out his features. I wave back—what else can I do? What other response do I have? Then climb in through my window and lower my shade.

Mortified enough for one evening.

You have entered Ether. There are 2 people present.

Omen: Have you sent me your photograph?

Venus: <eyes down> Not yet, Mistress.

Omen: What's the problem? Don't you have a photograph of yourself?

Venus: Nothing recent. Nothing I like.

Omen: I understand that. I want you to send one that you like…but I want one soon.

Venus: I do have a Polaroid with a timer.

Omen: Then take a picture and send it tonight.

Venus: It's late.

Omen: I know what time it is, slave. I own a clock. Is there a mailbox nearby?

Venus: On the corner. But it's dangerous outside.

Omen: I want you to take your picture, slide it in an envelope, walk to the corner and mail it. Now.

Venus: But, Mistress…

Omen: Are you back-talking me?

Venus: <eyes lowered>

Omen: Do as I say, slave. Do not anger me.

Venus: What if you don't like the way I look?

Omen: Haven't we been through this before, young one? Do you need further reassurance? I want to see you, and I will not reject you. I promise you that.

Venus: I can't, Mistress. I can't.

Omen: You're begging for it now, aren't you? Begging…

Venus: No, Mistress…

Omen: Begging for punishment. Begging for pain. Don't worry, young one. You'll get it all. You'll get it all and more. But don't disobey me.

Venus: I'll do as you say, Mistress.

Omen: Of course you will.

Venus: But I have to go now. I have to—

Omen: I want a picture of you, naked. I want your hands crossed behind your head and your eyes lowered. I want an image of pure submission. Send me that, slave. I won't contact you until I receive it.

Venus: But, Mistress...please.

Omen: I'll E-mail you when I receive it. I won't contact you again until then.

Venus: Please, Mistress. Don't leave. Talk to me some more. Please.

Omen: You know what you have to do. Do not fail me, slave. Do not let me down.

Venus: Mistress...

Good-bye to Omen. There is one person present.

CHAPTER SEVEN:
The Search Begins

My class at SFSU is two nights a week. I go straight from work, my notebook stashed in my black leather satchel, my typed assignment stapled neatly and tucked inside. I do my work for this class conscientiously, as I always have at school. But now I work even harder than I did when I was in college. I want a way out, a way to live that doesn't depend on numbers.

I don't mean that I want to be a writer full-time, that I'd ever quit my job at the bank. I want a means of expressing myself, the way Raina does with her performance art and Julia does with her paintings. I want a way to let go, to expose my inner thoughts, my deepest feelings. To unwind the stale linen cloths from my mummified emotions.

The class is a small one—only twenty people—and I sit in the back and stare straight ahead, enjoying my anonymity. I do not mingle with the other students, rarely even offering a friendly hello or a smile at the beginning of class when we all file in. It's the one place where I don't have to be phony. The one area in my life where I am not called upon to be polite. To be happy.

The teacher, Ms. Greene, is a youngish woman, most likely only a few years older than I am. She has a casual appearance but a serious demeanor. She wears faded jeans and oversized oxfords and she captures her shoulder-length blonde hair in a short ponytail. It whips around her face when she writes on the chalkboard.

Although she is attractive—I tend to find simplicity attractive—I do not stare at her as I stared at Ms. Longstreth. I focus on my work, instead. I take careful notes when she lectures, notes which I study diligently during my lunch break at work and in the evenings when I'm at home.

This professor teaches in a way that I can grasp easily. She gives examples and has us mimic her. She doesn't discourage creativity, but she helps us hone our rambling prose. In her class, we have confines within which to work—much different from the way Ms. Longstreth taught.

Ms. Greene collects our papers at the beginning of each class and hands back our assignments from the week before at the end. I'm doing better in this world than I did at college. Most likely it's because I don't know anyone, don't have to perform for anyone, am not going for a grade.

Last week's topic was adventures and I wrote about my Zuni men. After her lecture, the teacher asks me to stay after class. She grips my double-spaced paper titled "Two Men Fucking." She says, "This isn't a class in pornography, Ms. Van Horne."

"I know."

She stares at me for a moment, then asks, "Did this really happen?" I nod and shrug at the same time, blushing.

"All of your papers seem to be about sex."

"I know," I tell her. I'm well aware of the fact. "But I try to fit the assignments. I do try."

This makes her grin. She leans back in her chair and sets her head against the wall, looking up at me. "I like the way you write," she says, and I feel a heat within my chest, a rushing fire of pleasure. "You make me laugh, sometimes," she says, "and you turn me on, too."

I don't know what to say to that, so I look down, feeling young and insecure.

"I think you should submit this somewhere," she tells me. The word "submit" echoes in my head. I don't hear the rest of her sentence.

"I'm sorry.... What?"

"I think you should send it to one of the erotica magazines—*Fringe* or *Off Beat*."

I don't know what to do with my hands. I shove them deep into the pockets of my gray suit jacket and continue to look down at the floor, saying, "I'm not that good. I've never been able to write."

"That's why you're taking this class, isn't it?"

I nod.

"What *are* you good at?"

Is she coming on to me? I look at her, stare at her, then look back at the pockmarked wood floor and say softly, "Numbers."

"You are good, take my word for it. Polish this up, if you like. I wrote some suggestions in the margins. Then send if off. You can find the addresses in one of the writer's-marketplace resources at the library."

She hands me back my paper and continues to stare at me. "You're shy," she says, "I'd never expect it from the way you write."

"I get tired of it…."

"Tired of what?"

"Being shy. Being unable to say what I think, to do what I want."

"You're good," she says again, now leaning over her desk and putting her hand on top of mine. I get a burst of excitement throughout my body, a licking flame of heat that flickers through me and then settles in my cunt.

I say, "Thanks," and then pull away, heading to the door.

She says, "Read through my comments, Alexa. Let me know if you have any questions…."

I promise her that I will, and then I flee.

You have entered The Dangerous Café. There are 25 people present.
Venus: Have any of you seen Mistress Omen?
Elijah: Not lately.
Vanilla Girl: Uh uh. We've missed her.
Jo: Missed her bad.
Verruca: But we've missed you, as well, Venus. Where have you been hiding?
Venus: <blushing> Just been busy. That's all.
Vanilla Girl: You've been hiding. Admit it. We turned you on last time. We turned your world upside down. We rocked you, and now you're scared and confused.
Venus: Yes....
Dameron: Why don't you E-mail her?
Venus: I did...
Evil One: Did you two have a falling-out? Are you looking for a new dom?
Venus: No.
Vanilla Girl: Will you play with us tonight, Venus? We were just setting Jasmine on the rack...about to tighten her up a bit.
Venus: No...
Justine: You don't even wanna watch? See another girl cry? Watch another girl come?
Venus: What's the rack?
Dameron: Ahh, we've piqued her interest.
Justine: <sweetly> It's my favorite form of torture, Venus... stay awhile. Watch.
Elijah: Don't you think Jasmine looks pretty all bound up?
Venus: ::nodding::
Justine: Don't you like how tightly she's tied? She can't move at all. Can you, baby?
Jasmine: <softly> No, Mistress.

Evil One: Don't you wish you were up there, too, Venus? Don't you wish it was your turn to be punished? You've been a bad girl, haven't you?

Venus: Yes...

Evil One: Yes, yes, you're always bad, aren't you? In your twisted, haunted mind, you're always naughty. Always deserving punishment.

Venus: Yes...

Master X: See how lovely Jasmine is? All naked and exposed.

Jo: With the clamps on her nipples...

Elijah: And the clothespins on the lips of her pussy...

Evil One: And that riding crop nearby, ready to be put to use.

Dameron: Stay awhile, Venus.... Just watch...just listen.

Justine: ::lifting the crop:: Are YOU ready, Jasmine?

Jasmine: Yes, Mistress.

Justine: Have you been a bad girl?

Jasmine: <eyes lowered> Oh, yes, Mistress.

Dameron: Confess your sins to us.

Jasmine: There are too many, Sir. Too many to be listed....

Justine: ::raising the crop up high::

Jasmine: <eyes closed> But I've sinned...sinned often. Sinned with pleasure.

Jo: Are you listening, Venus? Are you listening to her? You could be next.

Evil One: Yes, child, you could be the next on the rack, bound on your belly instead of your back, exposing your ass for the punishment you so deserve.

Justine: ::cutting the first stroke, hard, across Jasmine's naked thighs::

Jasmine: Ohhhh...
Dameron: Look how pretty the welt is, all red and puffy.
Vanilla Girl: Can I touch?
Justine: Go ahead, 'Nilla, be my guest.
Vanilla Girl: ::pinching the crimson welt::
Jasmine: ::sighing::
Venus: I have to leave.... I'm sorry...
Good-bye to Venus. There are 24 people present.

CHAPTER EIGHT:
In My Dreams

Carolyn teases me, says that I'm not really a bona fide insomniac, says that if I stopped drinking coffee, I'd sleep like a baby, the way she does. Eight hours a night —seven days a week. We've had the argument often, since college. I say that I'm an insomniac who has come to terms with the situation. I say that since I'm already awake, why not drink coffee and enjoy the night? Why not have that clear head that coffee brings, that vibrating feeling of excitement that caffeine induces when taken in large quantities?

She's on me again this weekend. We're out shopping, and I have my normal purplish circles under my eyes. Since it's a day off, I haven't bothered with the concealer I usually smudge on. (I ought to buy stock in the stuff: In case there are other insomniacs out there who need that special fix, Prescriptives has the most complete, fast-acting cover up.)

Carolyn gives me her pouty look and says, "But when do you sleep, Lexi? How do you function? How can you count out money for the customers when you're not acting with all of your brain cells."

"People use only 8 percent of their brains anyway," I tell her.

"Is that a fact," she asks me as she drags me into Victoria's Secret to go shopping for bras and panties and all things fluffy. She and Jason have recently made up—again—and she wants some "frilly stuff" to tease him. As she fingers a yellow lace, underwire satin bra she says, "Only 8 percent?"

I shrug. "I'm not sure. I think I heard something like that once. But maybe I made it up…in my dreams."

She play-punches me and says, "I'm concerned, though. You need to watch it. A sleep debt isn't something to take lying down."

I look at her.

"Or something like that," she amends, pointing me over to a pair of white cotton pajamas with navy blue piping that she knows are my speed. "I mean, if you were to take a sleep debt lying down, then I guess you'd be asleep, and then—" She'd continue, but we're both laughing, so it doesn't really matter.

Actually, I do get some sleep every night. Simply not as much as most people need. I worked for an actor in Hollywood during summer break one year, a famous actor whom I will not name. He functions on two hours of sleep a night while working on a movie. He told me that during production his mind is awake and ready to do things, and he just can't stay in bed.

I'm like that, except that I don't have anything to do. At least, I didn't until I signed up for the writing course at SFSU. I sleep an average of four hours a night, and I do use a lot of concealer under my eyes. On weekends, I can sleep my preferred hours—snooze during the day, prowl at night—but I don't think I ever really catch up on my sleep debt.

"I'm trying this on," Carolyn says, holding up something black that's barely wrapped around a floral sachet-hanger. She heads toward the dressing rooms without another word. I snag the pj's without checking the size and follow her.

"What is it?" I ask naïvely.

We're let into side-by-side dressing rooms by a snotty young salesperson. There's a long silence from Carolyn's. Then she says, "Um, I'm not really sure."

"Is it underwear?" I call back helpfully.

"Well…"

"A thong?" I suggest.

"Nope…there are too many little strappy things. But I have a thong in here with me."

"A garter belt?"

More silence. I pull on the pajamas and give myself the once-over in the mirror. I look like a little kid. The outfit's too big, especially since I'm used to the skin-hugging feeling of leggings. I leave the dressing-room cubicle and knock on Carolyn's door. She opens it up while standing behind it, so I don't see her immediately. When I do—

"Wow!"

"I know." She grins, blushing, then turning to admire herself in the mirror. She's not wearing her panties under it, which she's supposed to. But I don't call her on it.

"What is it?" I ask.

She shrugs. "A bathing suit?"

"No way. That doesn't cover enough of any part of you. And Victoria's Secret sells bathing suits only through their catalog."

"A merry widow?"

I shake my head, unsure. "I don't think that it's the right configuration. They have that corsetlike piece in front that fits really tight, and then garters." I stare at her. There's sort of an underwire bra, but her rose-hued nipples are exposed above. Ribbons run down her flat belly and attach to what I realize must be garter fasteners, but are hard to discern because of the bows. She'd be naked aside from that, but she has slid on a thong—out of modesty's sake. The whole thing's done in black satin, with the bows in a vibrant purple and the thong in turquoise.

It's hideous.

"Let's ask the salesgirl," I suggest.

"No way! I'm not going out there like this."

I look her over more closely. "Okay, maybe it *is* a merry widow. They've just left off most of the fabric."

"Whatever you call it, I'm getting it," she says, peeling the thing off.

"Are you sure?"

"Jason will die!"

I want to agree with her, but for the wrong reasons.

"Hold on," I say. "Let me look around for you, just to

see if there's anything else that might work. You know something… classy."

She blocks the door and shakes her head, her auburn hair whipping back and forth. "Lexi, I know it's beyond tacky, but that's what I want. Jason likes tacky. It turns him on to act as if I'm some sort of white-trash slut that he's picked up, ready to fuck."

She's serious. I stare at her. We've never talked like this before.

"Didn't I ever tell you?"

"Uh-uh."

I have to admit, I'm suddenly thinking about Jason in a whole new light. I've known him since freshman year at college, and I've always written him off as somewhat of a nerd. He's tall and blond with all-American features, but he's nondescript in the personality department. When he and Carolyn have broken up in the past— which has been often—I've heard her say only bad things about him, skewing any perspective I might have created on my own.

"Look," Carolyn continues, seating me on the puffy violet velvet cushion in the corner. "I know that Jason doesn't look like he's that wild…."

I nod, agreeing.

"But, really, he is. He likes to do all sorts of crazy things. I just never really thought you were into that…."

Obviously, Elaine has never shared her story of the night on top of the frat house. Still, I'm delighted that Carolyn is confiding in me. Suddenly she seems like more of a total person and less of the banking android I've thought of her as in recent years. I wonder fleetingly whether she sees me in the same light.

"Tell me something wild." I want the moment of sharing to continue.

"I don't want to shock you, Lexi." She's dead serious and mildly embarrassed. I feel bad for her. I smile broadly and assure her she won't.

"But you never really date," she says, trying to be tactful. "I mean, you're so, I don't know…proper about everything all the time."

Have you ever had someone hold a mirror up to you and force you to confront yourself? I tilt my head at Carolyn, wondering what I could say to her to convince her that I'm not coldhearted, not Victorian-repressed. That I have emotions. That I like hearing raunchy, nasty fuck-details.

I swallow hard, searching my brain for something to say. Wondering where to start.

She says kindly, "I'm not trying to offend you, Lex. I know you did a lot of guys when we were in the sorority. But since college, you don't really go out, do you?"

I shrug. "That's not a crime."

"No," she admits. "It's not. But I just sort of thought that you didn't like sex, or guys, or something."

What can I tell her? I close my eyes, then say, "You know, the other night…at Zuni…"

She nods, still admiring her lithe body and flat stomach. She's got a great figure, which she keeps great by constant aerobics workouts at the gym in her apartment building. I stare at her ass for a moment, then continue.

"When I went downstairs, to the bathroom…"

She nods again, as if to hurry me on.

"I saw two men fucking," I blurt out, unsure of the

polite way to say it. She turns to look at me. And I realize that I shocked her.

"Are you serious?"

It's my turn to nod.

"What'd you do?"

"Apologized and left."

"Was it weird?"

I know that she wants me to say "yes, it was weird, it was icky. I was disgusted." Instead, I say, "I don't know. I was sort of…intrigued." She begins to unfasten the multiple straps on her newfangled contraption, holding my gaze all the while.

"Tell me," she says, and I can tell that she's interested.

"If you tell me…" I respond, like a kid egging a friend on a dare.

She's got most of the thing off now, and she peels the thong down her long legs and kicks it into the corner. "Sure," she says, "Over lunch. I promise."

So I tell her of my bathroom adventure, of the way the men looked and the way it made me feel. She's rapt, fixing totally on me. Awed.

"You mean, you've never done it like that?" she asks.

"Been a man fucked by a man?"

"No!" She glares. "Had anal sex."

I shake my head so hard that the combs holding my curls in place go flying. Carolyn retrieves them and hands them back to me. As I refasten my marmalade mane, she says, "It's sort of…fun."

"I wouldn't know."

"Jason likes it…"

"Do you?"

"When we're in the tub, I do." She's blushing, but she keeps talking. "It feels good that way, better that way, and then we can clean up right away." That's the Carolyn I know. Clean and neat and nice.

"Have you ever done it out of water?" I ask. She shakes her head.

I think I'd want to do it somewhere away from my house, bent over something, unable to get clean immediately. I think I'd want someone to take me, force me, hurt me with the roughness of it. With the speed. Later we could shower, of course; later we could wash it all away. But in the moment, I'd like it to be as raw, as real as the men I saw together. Unconcerned about appearances. About being seen. About being clean.

"Actually..." Carolyn says, and I turn to look at her, broken from my fantasy world. "There was one time..."

"Yeah?" I hope that I don't sound too eager. But I do, and she gives me a look. I take a deep breath, then say in a more normal tone, "What happened?"

Carolyn closes her eyes, obviously picturing the scene. After a moment, she says, "Remember when I went to Greece with Jason? After graduation?"

I nod.

"We stayed in this little seaside town, and every day we walked to an open air market to buy produce. And there was this amazing guy who worked at one of the vegetable stands. I mean, he was truly beautiful. He had thick, black hair and burnished skin.... amazing."

I nod again, so she'll continue.

"Jason got really jealous because he thought I was flirting with the vegetable seller."

"Which you were…"

She shrugs sheepishly. "Well, yeah, but I didn't mean anything by it. He was simply too…dreamy. Anyway, near the end of the trip, Jason and I got into this out-of-control fight. He accused me of wanting to sleep with the veggie man, and I denied it—lying through my teeth, of course. So Jason said he was going to punish me for lying to him and for flirting with the man."

The word "punish" sends a shiver through me, but I try to keep a calm expression on my face—I don't need to give Carolyn any insights into my personal psyche. Luckily, my friend is so involved in her own story that she doesn't seem to notice my reaction.

"Jason went down to the market by himself and bought a long, ripe zucchini and a bottle of extra-light, virgin olive oil."

This is starting to sound familiar to me, as if I've read it in the letters column in one of *Penthouse*'s mini-magazines. I hold up my hand and say, "Wait a minute. You're about to launch into a bit of urban folklore, aren't you?"

She assures me she's not. "This really happened, Alexa. I swear."

"C'mon…"

"Why would I make it up?"

I think that over for a minute, then motion with my hands outspread for her to continue.

"He came back to the cottage we were renting and said, 'Strip and lay over that bed.' I just looked at him, not believing that he seriously was going to punish me…I mean, for a moment, I thought he was planning on giving me a spanking, or something, as if I were a naughty little kid who'd disobeyed him."

I laugh weakly, as she seems to expect me to do.

"Instead, he brought out the zucchini and said, 'You want that big, handsome man to fuck you. Admit it.' But I didn't. I mean, I did sort of have that fantasy, but I would never in a million years have admitted it to Jason. So he came over, pulled up my sundress, pushed me down on the bed, and tore off my underwear."

"You're serious?"

She nods.

"And you let him?"

Now she looks at me for a moment, as if weighing whether she should trust me with an important secret. Finally she says, "Yeah, Lexi. I liked it. He had the bottle of oil open in a flash, and he spread the cheeks of my ass with one hand and drenched me with the oil, working it into my asshole, getting me all lubed up. Then he picked up the zucchini and started working it into me. I was struggling, crying out. I mean, it *hurt*...but he kept going, saying the whole time, 'Think of him fucking you, Carrie. Pretend this is him....'"

"Wow!" I say, stunned.

Carolyn's blushing out of control, her normally even-toned skin a pure fuchsia. "You can't tell anyone," she says. "I never told Elaine, never told any of my friends."

I'm still in shock-mode. I nod, tell her that of course I won't spill her secret, and then continue to stare at her in awe.

"Did he ever do anything like that again?" I want to know.

"Well, we fuck a lot…but not like that. It was base. He was so angry, and it was as if his manhood was at stake. He had to prove something to me, and to himself. After he used that big vegetable on me, he tore off his own jeans and fucked me there himself. Claiming me. It was …unreal. I came from it."

My eyes must be huge, 'cause Carolyn laughs, still embarrassed, and says, "I'm gonna go buy this. Then we can find somewhere to eat…." She hesitates before adding, "And I'll tell you some more."

Before I can respond, she takes her flimsy number to the cash register. I trail along behind her. After she pays, we cross the mall courtyard and choose a French café for lunch. We sit in a booth in the back, secluded from the rest of the diners, within earshot only of the waiter. I guess that both of us are hoping that he speaks mostly French.

Once we order, Carolyn leans forward, ready to reveal herself even further to me. I can see that she's dying to—that now that she's started, she doesn't want to stop—and I'm thrilled to hear it.

"All right," she says, "but you can't tell anyone anything I tell you."

"Promise," I say, drawing in a cross over my heart with my fingers.

"Jason likes to talk dirty."

I lean forward, now, too. Ready to listen.

"He's always done it, ever since high school. He was really advanced that way compared to other boys I dated."

"I never knew you dated anyone but him," I tell her, astounded.

"Sure," she says. "I was on the cheerleading squad. I dated football players, basketball players…"

"What sport did Jason play?"

She grins broadly, "Badminton."

"Did you cheer for him?"

"No, cheerleaders didn't go to badminton matches all that often. But I saw him around campus and I thought he was cute, if sort of serious. He was in all the science clubs and chess clubs. A regular brain." She raises her eyebrows. "And I was definitely not in his intellectual league. I've always been a bit of a ditz."

I'm about to tell her that she's not at all. She's a math wizard, which is why she is in banking. Still, she stops me.

"I know I'm good with numbers, but he's got a brain for all things scientific. Our first date wasn't even a date—he was tutoring me in chem."

"That's cool," I say.

"What was cool is the way he kissed me at the end of the study period, as if it *had* been a date. And then he pressed his lips to my ear and whispered, 'All the boys talk about your hungry little pussy.'"

"Are you serious?"

She nods. "I was going to slap him, but then I realized he was somehow teasing me. I mean, I'd dated a lot of boys, but I hadn't slept with anyone—I was still a virgin."

"Really?"

"Yeah. So I said, 'You wanna find out?' Sort of calling his bluff."

"And?"

"And, he called mine right back. Took me by the hand

around the back of the science portables. There was this little bit of space between the two buildings, but you had to wriggle through some bushes. We got behind there, and he ripped down my panties and just put it in me."

I'm dumbfounded. "On campus?"

She nods, gleeful.

"And you'd never been on a date?"

"Nope."

"Why'd you let him do it?"

"I wanted to. I don't know. He seemed like the right guy and I was tired of waiting, and the whole time we were doing it he kept whispering, 'I'm gonna tell your brother what a dirty, little fuck you are.'"

My mouth falls open. I close it and just stare at her.

"'I'm gonna tell your brother what a dirty, little fuck you are.' Over and over. My back pressed up against the wall, his cock lifting me with each stroke. And over and over, his voice crooning, 'I'm gonna tell. I'm gonna tell.' It made me come."

"Wow…" I say, in awe, in jealousy. "That's really wild."

"Especially since he didn't even know whether I had a brother or not. He just guessed."

"Lucky guess."

"Mm-hmm." She takes a bite of baguette, then asks, "Have you ever had anyone talk dirty to you?"

"No, not really."

"It's great," she says, "he always surprises me. And just hearing him say these really nasty things makes me so wet. I'm sure it's one of the reasons we stay together."

I wait for her to explain.

"I mean, we fuck so well."

"That's a good reason, I guess," I say. "As long as everything else is there, too."

"Meaning?"

"Friendship, compassion, I don't know. Never really having been in a true relationship, I just don't know what it encompasses."

Our food arrives, and the dark-haired waiter winks at me.

"Why haven't you?" Carolyn asks when he moves away.

"Haven't found the right person," I say honestly.

"Maybe you will at Raina's Party," Carolyn says, digging into her salad niçoise.

I steal an olive from her plate and ask, "Are you going?" I'm stunned. She never goes to Raina's parties.

"Jason's out of town that night on business. I thought if you'd let me go with you…"

I nod enthusiastically. "Sure. That'll be fun. We could even get ready together." A beat. "You can wear your new…whatever." She just gives me her patented "Carolyn" look, and we leave it at that.

CHAPTER NINE:
Raina's Party

Carolyn and I decide to dress in black. I have one T-shirt style dress I bought in New York on my last vacation. I went trolling through the thrift stores in Greenwich Village, trying on vintage clothes, worn-out jeans, sweaters from the 1950s that were gossamer-soft with wear. My friend Tristan, who works as an editor on a criminally hip New York 'zine, took me to all of her favorite haunts. I found this dress in the last one.

It's actually not a pure black. Under some lights, it has a pale indigo hue to it, a vague shimmer that I love. In high school I dyed my hair the same exact color, once, freaking out my mom beyond belief. She went ballistic, reaching for my hair, running her fingers through it, all the while whimpering, "What have you done? What have you done?"

The stuff washed out in a few weeks, dyeing our bathroom tub a dark blue-black, staining our towels every time I washed my hair. I thought I looked amazing, and I always wanted to ask my mom why she'd gotten so upset when there were so many worse things I could have done. Shaved my head completely. Used permanent dye. Tattooed my skull. But it wouldn't have been worth the fight.

The dress is short, miniskirt length, but it's cut with lovely lines—not too tight or too loose. The material is soft and it swirls around me when I walk, revealing even more of my thighs, more of my ass, than when it lies flat against my body. I paid nine dollars for it, which somehow adds to the charm.

With it, I wear black hose with seams up the back and my favorite pair of boots, lustrous black leather with laces and heels that are high for me. I'm showing a lot of leg tonight, but Carolyn promised she'd do the same, that we could be partners in our sexy outfits. And I know that in Raina's crowd I'll never be the one to shock. Anything that Carolyn or I wear will be tame compared to the way her friends will dress.

Raina's guest lists always include other writers who work for the same underground sex-positive magazines that she does. And there are always other "actors" from the theaters where she does her performance art. I've been to her parties before, and things tend to get a bit wild—though I always hug the walls and leave early.

Carolyn has made me promise to stay until at least 2:00 A.M. and since the festivities don't start until midnight, I figure I can make it. Anyway, having Carolyn with me eases my mind. I'll have someone to talk to, someone to hide with if the night gets too outrageous.

We take a cab. The party's being held in the warehouse section of town and I don't want to ride a bus dressed the way I am. During the ride, Carolyn tells me about the success she had with her new Victoria's Secret purchase.

"It's in tatters," she says smugly.

"A one-time use only?" I ask her. "Disposable lingerie?"

She nods.

"It's not even recyclable?" and she shakes her head.

I catch the cabbie's eye in the rearview mirror. He looks interested in our conversation and I lower my voice.

"Let's change the subject," she says.

For a moment, I'm silent, thinking. Then I say, "I'm sort of on an assignment tonight."

"What do you mean?"

I debate about filling her in regarding my online Mistress, but I chicken out and decide not to. "It's been a long, long time," I start, and she grins and gives me a knowing look.

"A long time since you were bedded, huh?"

I nod.

"I know the feeling," she says. "Whenever Jason and I break up, I go through such withdrawal at not having him in my bed." She lowers her voice further. "I even bought a vibrator last time."

"Really?" My interest is piqued. "Is it good? Do you like it?"

She's blushing, but she continues, "I guess. I mean, it makes me come. But I sort of feel like I'm cheating when I use it."

"That doesn't make sense," I assure her. "You deserve to come whenever you want to."

"Jason likes it, too," she says, still confiding. "He uses it on me, uses it on his balls, too."

That's an image I'm not sure I need, but I swallow and say, "Really?" again, as if I want her to tell me more.

"They have a ton of vibrators at Good Vibrations," Carolyn says knowingly. "I went in and asked the different salespeople which ones they recommended. They were extremely helpful. Each woman told me her own favorite tool."

"Is yours very big?" I ask just as we're pulling in front of the warehouse. Carolyn spreads her hands about a foot apart, and I see the cabby's eyes widen in the rearview mirror. We get out and I pay the man, but don't tip. He speeds away, snarling at us. Carolyn is oblivious to the interaction.

The outside of the warehouse is almost frighteningly bare, but we can hear music. We walk up the short flight of steps to the steel-plated door and knock. Raina is the only person I know who has bouncers at her parties. The one who opens the door is a spiky-haired female bodybuilder. She looks us over, then takes the invitation from my hand and looks us over some more.

Luckily, Raina is nearby. She waves to the bouncer to let us in.

"Whew!" Carolyn says. "I didn't think we were going to pass." When I look around the room, I see why the bouncer had hesitated. The warehouse is decorated in a 1970s disco style, replete with a glittering silver ball above the dance floor. Hundreds of female couples are gyrating to the fabulous music of the Bee Gees.

Carolyn presses against me, as if she's scared. "I didn't know—" she starts to say, but then Raina walks up to us and kisses my cheek.

"Glad you could make it, Lexi," she says, before turning her attention on Carolyn, "You, too," she adds. "You've never been to one of my parties before, have you?"

Carolyn shakes her head. She's gone pale beneath the rainbow of lights. I've been to many of Raina's parties. She usually holds them in conjunction with one of her shows, and so cohosts them with other artists. This one is her own, a bash for her thirtieth birthday. I want to ask her where she got the money for the decorations, for the live deejay, for everything, but she beats me to it.

"Trust fund," she grins gleefully. "My mother disowned me when I came out to her, but my grandmother left me a huge amount of money. I received it yesterday" her smile broadens—"just in time to pay for this." Now she stretches her hands wide apart, all-encompassing. Carolyn looks as if she might pass out. I am supporting her entire body weight, but then Raina puts her hand on my shoulder and asks, "Dance with me, Alexa?" and I nod and help seat Carolyn in a nearby chair.

We wend our way to the center of the dance floor, just as a slow song begins to play. It sounds like Maria Muldaur, but I'm not sure that even Raina would go that far to be kitschy.

"Happy birthday," I whisper to her as she takes me into her arms. Her long hair is braided with beads at the end, very "10," and she makes music when she moves her head.

"Thanks," she says. "I'm really glad you came." We turn together, under the glowing lights, and she waves to Carolyn.

"I didn't really warn her," I say. "She asked me if she could come."

"You're the only one of the group who accepts me, Lexi. Why is that?"

We're swaying together, and it feels really comfortable. I'm at ease and I tell her, "You accept me, as well, don't you?"

"What's not to accept?"

I'm quiet for a moment, rolling my hips against hers, swaying to the music. It *is* Maria Muldaur: "Midnight at the Oasis." How could I have doubted that?

"If I were to tell you anything," I begin, "I believe you'd accept me."

She nods. Then, obviously intrigued, she asks, "What do you want to tell me?"

"Nothing…"

"Come on, Alexa, spill it."

We move gracefully apart as the next song starts up. It's Andy Gibb: "Shadow Dancing." I can't get the grin off my face. I say, "Why didn't you tell me it was a disco party?"

"I did…didn't you read the invitation?"

"Yeah," I nod.

"It was on the front, in plain English."

I shrug. "Guess I was in my dreamworld again."

"Anyway," she said, "I would've reminded you. I just didn't think you'd come."

We dance some more, mingling with the women around us. Raina moves closer and says, "So, what were you going to tell me?"

"Soon," I promise her. "I'm not quite ready yet."

She stares at me. "You're blossoming, though, aren't you, Lex? You're about to burst free...."

"You know what, Raina? You might be right." And then I weave through the crowd to where Carolyn is perched on a chair, her face a wash of confusion, and I lift her forward and bring her with me onto the dance floor.

She says, "No...I can't..." but I override her protests, forever shattering her image of me as repressed, conventional, or a-sexual.

Shattering that image for myself, as well.

You have mail. Sent today, at 9:07 P.M. EST

Venus.

Got your photo, my love. My slave. My toy. I cannot wait to get my hands on you, punish you. I will fulfill all of your fantasies. Are you ready for me, sweetheart? Are you ready?

I hope so.

I'll come to you when you least expect it. I'll arrive in your world with the suddenness of a summer storm, with the force of a hurricane. Don't bother bolting your door, darling, I'm already inside.

I have another request. Before I meet with you again online, I want you to send me your panties. A real pair. Don't buy something special; don't try to fool me. I want to know you. I want to cup the fabric in my hands and envision your ass filling the seat.

I want to press the fabric to my nose and inhale deeply, learning your smell.

Put on your favorite pair of panties, lie down on the floor, and make yourself come. Then put the panties into an envelope and send them to me.

I'm waiting.

—Omen

P.S. Has your sweet ass been reamed yet?

CHAPTER TEN:
A+

Although I carried my paper in my satchel with me all week, I didn't dare to read my teacher's comments. I didn't even remove the paper from my bag until the weekend, after the party, a bit drunken from Raina's champagne celebration. Now, that I'm in the privacy of my apartment without anything pressing to do, I pull out the paper and page through it.

Ms. Greene's written simple notes in the margin, offering advice to help me smooth a sentence, to express myself more clearly. Her summary is at the end, below my last paragraph. In a curling, feminine hand, she's penned: "A sexy tale, Alexa…You've described a scene so well that I can see it in my mind. Your use of dialogue is subtle, yet very powerful. Give me a call…" and then her number.

My hands tremble so badly that the paper shakes and I set it down. She wants me—she likes what I like. I can't decide what to do. If I call her, what will happen? What do I want to happen?

I have another assignment, entirely, one that I haven't forgotten. One that my Mistress has commanded me to complete. Do I dare approach my teacher? What will that do to our relationship as student and professor? (I've envisioned this scenario often enough...I shouldn't even have to question it.)

I lift the phone.

But what if she's sleeping? I ask myself. *What if she's dreaming away and I wake her up.*

I put the phone back down.

It's too late to call, I tell myself. *I'll disturb her.*

But she wants me—it says so—in ink, right there on my paper.

I lift the phone again. Put it down.

Weakling! a voice screams in my head.

A final time. On this try, I dial.

Ms. Greene answers, and her calm tone puts me at ease instantly. When I tell her who it is, she says, "I was hoping you'd call. In fact, I've been waiting for your call."

"Thanks," I say, but I don't know what to say next.

"This isn't very professional of me," she admits, "Still, I couldn't stop myself...."

I like the way she talks. I like the way she isn't coming on too strong in the role of the dom.

"I'm sorry it's so late," I tell her, looking at the clock on my desk. Insomniacs forget that other people sleep at night.

"I was up," she assures me. "I was reading."

I take a deep breath and say, "Could we meet? Would that be okay?" And I can tell that she's smiling as she gives me her address and directions how to get there.

You have entered Ether. There are 2 people present.

Venus: Did you read my E-mail, Mistress?

Omen: Yes, I'm proud of you. Now I want details.

Venus: I did as you said—I found someone who would fuck me like that.

Omen: Details…

Venus: I went to her house. She lives near the Haight in one of the refurbished Victorians.

Omen: Yes?

Venus: I dressed simply—she's always casual—in ripped jeans and a man's oversized oxford shirt. She greeted me at the door, totally surprising me. She had on full makeup and was dressed in black leather.

Omen: Was she pretty?

Venus: Beautiful. She had her hair slicked back off her face, and her eyes positively glowered at me. I went to my knees as soon as she opened the door. I didn't know how else to show her that I understood. That I accepted the situation.

Omen: What did she do?

Venus: She hardly spoke. Simply said, "Your story was mostly fantasy based on a bit of reality, right?" And I nodded. She said, "Strip and bend over the sofa."

Omen: And you did?

Venus: I obeyed, unbuttoning my jeans in a flash, losing a few buttons as I tore off my shirt. I started to lower my panties, but she shook her head and shoved me forward.

Omen: Did she beat you?

Venus: No.

Omen: Spank you?

Venus: No.

Omen: What did she do?

Venus: She slid my panties aside, exposing my asshole and my cunt. She licked one finger and then slid it between my rear cheeks, probing me.

Omen: Did you like it?

Venus: Oh, yes. She took her time, making twirling circles inside my ass, moving forward and back, a little at a time. She said, "How does that feel?" And I sighed and said, "Amazing…"

Omen: Finger-fucking doesn't count, slave. Did she do more?

Venus: Yes, Mistress. She stood back and undid her leather pants. I looked over my shoulder and saw she was wearing a strap-on cock, harnessed to her body. I'd never seen anything like it.

Omen: Did she lube it up, first? Or drive in raw?

Venus: She pushed me down on the sofa, pressing my face into the cushions, and she slid the synthetic cock into my pussy, fucking me hard and fast and deep. Making my insides swell around it.

Omen: And then?

Venus: She pulled back and parted the cheeks of my ass, holding me open wide, and then she pressed it in me. Fucked me with it. Hurt me with it.

Omen: Did you like it?

Venus: Yes…

Omen: A lot?

Venus: Oh, yes.

Omen: How did it make you feel?

Venus: Dirty….

Omen: But you liked it.

Venus: Yes.

Omen: I have another assignment for you.

150 | Rosebud Books

Venus: Whatever you want, Mistress.
Omen: First, have you sent me your panties?
Venus: <blushing> Yes...I did that as soon as I got your E-mail.
Omen: Good...now, my second assignment for you is this: I want to meet you.
Venus: I can't...I can't mix reality and fantasy.
Omen: You do it all the time, don't you, lovely one?
Venus: Yes, but—
Omen: I'm going to tell you a secret, young one.
Venus: Mistress?
Omen: You've already met me. Often.
Venus: I don't know what you mean, Mistress.
Omen: I'm not speaking in code...Alexa.
Good-bye to Venus. There is one person present.

CHAPTER ELEVEN:
She Knows Me...

What do I do now? She knows me. I hide, I always hide. it's what I do best. I spin layer on top of layer, like a caterpillar inside a silken cocoon. And she knows me.

Just when I was beginning to break free, to throw off my disguises, she beats me to it. She reveals me before I'm ready.

My fingers stop on my keyboard. Without a thought, I unplug the computer and watch the screen flicker to darkness. Then I head to my kitchen, turn off my coffeepot, and take my emergency bottle of vodka from the freezer.

She knows me. I don't know her.

I sit back on my bed in darkness, drinking straight from the bottle, wondering, drawing lines in my mind from her to him to her. Guessing. Failing. I drink more. I drink until I pass out.

It's easier that way.

My last thought is this: She Knows Me.

Book Two:
OMEN'S WORLD

CHAPTER ONE:
Swoon Scent

Alexa Van Horne's money always smells like pussy. Alexa is a teller at the Bank of ———, and the bills that she carefully extracts from her drawer have that dangerous, tangy odor—or aroma, I should say—of sex. *Alexa's sex.*

I know that smell as I know my own body, the curves and the dips, the hard places of bone and soft places of flesh. I've had my nose against enough women's cunts to recognize even a fraction of a scent from far off. But Alexa's fragrant bills aren't far off, they're close, in my hand, and they are steeped in the nectar of sex.

I always stand in Alexa's line, whether there are other tellers open or not, whether there are ten people ahead of me…or more. I stand in her line with my head down, as if in thought, while actually I am taking deep breaths, trying to pull her smell from the air.

In my dreams, I am bathed in her scent, am saturated from the ends of my blue-black hair to the tips of my glossy, sapphire-polished toes. In my humble opinion, heaven would be an existence drenched in Alexa's heady perfume, in her swoon-scent. Draped in it. Drenched in it. Dream-filled, wondrous.

Alexa, I want to make you mine.

"Good afternoon," she says. "A withdrawal?"

I nod, leaning forward and breathing in.

"Are twenties okay, Ms. Niles?"

"Actually, if you could break it down…"

You wouldn't guess Alexa's seductive nature by looking at her, not from the visage she puts on for the rest of the world. She's pretty—there's no doubt about that. She's got a ferocious figure that she hides discreetly beneath well-cut gray business suits. But you can tell what she'd look like naked, if you have even one percent of perverted imagination. You can read the lines of her body beneath those suits. Though I believe she'd be attractive in a Hefty bag—and I'll tell you this; I've imagined her in stranger things than that.

Her hair is a magic shade of auburn, a tortoiseshell color. I once had a cat with fur the same exact hue, a sleek tabby whose coat looked reddish orange in some lights, brownish gray in others. I drew that cat almost-daily, from different positions, under different lights. I had a showing in a gallery once, when I lived in Greenwich Village, filled only with pictures of Zach the Cat. And I let Zach roam loose in the gallery during the show, in case people didn't believe that a creature could exist with fur that shade.

Life imitates art, they say, but it doesn't have to exactly replicate it. And yet, Alexa's hair is the same color as my cat's was. And isn't that life imitating art, in a way?

Alexa's thick mane is ever-changing, and she wears it pulled back in a loose twist at the nape of her neck, kept in place with a few silvery barrettes. It's done casually, but always perfect. That's my girl, never one to let down her guard, *or* her hair. I would expect that much from one so obviously repressed.

Her skin is pale—no tanning salons for her. She's got a Pre-Raphaelite, translucent quality to her skin, as if you might be able to see right through her under an ideal light. I've thought about that often: stretching my beauty out on my hard wooden drawing table, fastening her wrists above her head, her legs spread wide apart. Cutting through the fabric of her good girl skirt with my ready craft knife. Beaming a bright light down on her and seeing how sheer the canvas of her skin really is. Could you see her bones if you looked hard enough?

Could you see her heart?

Alexa's lips are curved into a smile for every customer. A secret smile. A hidden smile. How I adore it when she smiles for me. Her lips are naturally rose-colored, the palest pink, and she wears only a subtle hint of sheer gloss to make them shine. I imagine a moment in which she stands in front of her bathroom mirror, slicking her lips with a fiery red stick and then wiping them clean and shaking her head. I imagine her trying on Chanel's Vamp, bloodying her lips with that dark blackberry stick and then grimacing at her reflection in the mirror.

Marring her perfect features with the pretense of looking sexy. It wouldn't work. It couldn't work. She doesn't need a color from a tube.

She needs *me*.

I want to kiss her lips until they are bruised with my force. I want to bite her bottom lip until it swells in my mouth. I want to devour her mouth the way one would feast upon a piece of ripe fruit. Juicy plum lips. Sweetest peach lips.

Yes, Alexa, I want to make you mine.

I've watched her move as she pulls the money from her drawer, handing over the crisp bills, the tens, twenties, hundreds. She counts them silently to herself, then again to me aloud.

"Five, ten, fifteen, twenty…"

I watch the way she fingers the bills, seems to caress them. She must love the money, must love the bills she counts. Why else would she spread her scent so casually upon the dollars she gives to strangers?

Why else would she give away the aroma of my dreams?

I don't like to spend the money I get from her. At least, not right away. I keep it confined in my wallet until I get home. I walk the ten blocks to my apartment in a daze, noticing almost nothing, barely aware of my surroundings. I'm certain that I appear mildly frightening as I stalk my way home, my eyes straight ahead, my body moving in a fast-paced gait. People have commented that I always walk as if I'm going somewhere. Even when I'm only out for a casual stroll, I walk as if I have a purpose.

If I have Alexa's money in my wallet, though, I *am* going somewhere. Home. Fast. And when I do catch another's eyes by accident—male or female, doesn't matter—passing pedestrians lower their gaze, as if out of respect. I command respect. I always have.

Once safely ensconced in my apartment, I strip, spread out on my four poster bed, and drip the money over my naked body. As I writhe and sweat, as the glistening beads begin to form on my body, the money sticks to me and her smell rises.

How does it get like that? How does she do it?

I ponder the question at night, before I go to sleep. I think about it over my morning's first cup of coffee. I look into her gray-green eyes when I stand in her line and I come up with a new set of hypotheses every single time.

Perhaps, she is simply so sexual that her scent oozes out of her pores. That would explain it, wouldn't it? But I'm a sexual creature—intensely so—and I've never had that occurrence, or recognized it in a lover or friend. So maybe she gets fucked on her break by one of the lucky tellers. At this, I scan the marble counters, looking jealously at each banker, wondering: *Who? Who? Which one of you?*

If she made love on her breaks, she wouldn't have the time to shower afterward, and the smell of sex would still linger in the air around her. But that would be a lot of fucking, wouldn't it? And something would show for it: a rumpled collar, a flush to her throat. There's none of that in Alexa's flawless demeanor. So I watch her and come up with ever more outrageous ideas.

I'll confess this to you: It's not easy to watch a teller at a bank without arousing suspicion, without making the near-retirement rent-a-cop a little nervous. And I have been known to make many people nervous, even when my slightly neurotic stare is not in place. So I tell myself to "cool it," to "calm down," to "relax."

I make myself stare out the window when she counts the money for me, not even paying her the slightest attention. That's a hard one for me; but if I command myself to do it, I can. If it's a really bad urge, if I need to drink in her scent more than usual, I order myself to stand in another teller's line, or even switch my finances to another bank. But that's something I can't comprehend, cannot obey even my own instruction. For how could I leave Alexa? Even in this ever-more-progressing world, where one is encouraged to use the ATMs, where human contact is downplayed and computer interactions are on everyone's list, I can't leave her. I can barely tear my eyes off her.

She's kind to me, but she's kind to all those who stand in her line. She's friendly as she talks about the weather, or the cable cars, or where she buys her coffee. But it only makes me spin ever-more-dangerous erotic fantasies in which she stars as the sole actress. And I am Cecil B. DeMille.

Despite efforts to cease and desist, still, I watch her.

Alexa wears white shirts beneath her simple gray suits. Crisp white shirts like the crisp bills she handles. I imagine that she irons the shirts in the morning, and then at her coffee break, and again at lunch. How else could they stay so stiff, so smart? Why don't the collars wilt in the occasional heat waves that hit San Francisco?

I consider asking her, think about leaning in toward

her across the safe little divider and saying in a low, whispery voice, "Where do you buy your shirts? What type of starch do you use? Do you carry a portable iron with you in your handbag?"

But she'd think I was insane, just another of San Francisco's crazy people wandering in with the fog. So I keep quiet, and I watch her count my money, and I return to my apartment to smell the bills.

Maybe I *am* crazy. Maybe I am totally insane. But isn't she, perhaps, slightly unbalanced as well? She must be on the lunatic fringe to dip her clear, well-manicured nails into her sweet honey pot before counting the bills out to the customers.

Shaking my head at the mystery, I go home. I walk the steps to my studio apartment, feeling an ache in my legs as I do. I lock the door behind me, greet my tomcat who winds his lithe body around my ankles, and I disregard the blinking red light on my answering machine. No one is more important to me at this moment than Alexa. And Alexa didn't call. So why bother listening to the messages?

I stride down the hall, pulling my black cashmere turtleneck sweater over my head and dropping it in a rumpled heap. My thin, ribbed white T-shirt is next. My breasts are free. Small, molded handfuls of flesh tipped with pale nipples that are already erect. I reach the room that serves as both my living room and bedroom, and I step out of my long, slim black skirt and stand, in black pumps and hose, in front of my windows.

The streetlights are already on at five o'clock. Daylight savings has kicked in. The night is here.

My body is reflected back at me, and I admire my image. I run the flats of my palms along my hips, turning, checking out the curved swell of my ass. I stand on my tiptoes, flexing my calves. I relax, take off the shoes, slip off the hose, and reach into my handbag for my wallet. Nearly naked, I lie down on the hard wood floor, wallet clenched in my hand, and I pop the closure on the worn eelskin. Just that little bit of freedom lets her scent waft out, surrounding me, bathing me. I slip one hand beneath the waistband of my pearl-gray satin panties, and extract the first bill with the other hand. My cunt is wet; the seam of my underwear is a sopping, dripping mess.

I slide out a five and wave it in front of my nose, inhaling deeply. Her scent flows freely through the room, tickling my nose, taunting me with sinful images. I play with myself with my other hand, spreading the lips of my carefully shaved pussy and rubbing two fingers around my clit. Gently at first, just teasing, just right.

I know how I like it, and though I rarely pleasure myself, on bank days I simply cannot help it.

I let the first bill flutter down to my breasts and reach for a second, a ten this time. I place it outside of my panties, but right on the crotch. It sticks to me. Now we are one—Alexa and I—her smell and mine mingling together. How I would love to have her slicked down on top of me, instead of one of her magic bills. How I would love to position her, take her in my arms and line her body up with mine, cunt to cunt, breasts to breasts, skin to naked skin.

I remove my sticky-fingered hand and spread my own come along the edge of the third bill. I am so hot, so wet, ready to lose myself in her body, in her mind, in her milky pure honey come.

I want to know what she's like beneath that gray suit shield. I want to cut apart the tweed and reveal her. Explore her. Devour her.

Another bill, another place to stick it. My inner thigh this time. I wet it, get it nice and sloppy, then glue it to my trembling flesh. And another bill, a high-scented one. A prize. She must have been really turned on when she touched it, and I place this one over my lips. My mother always told me that money was dirty. That I should wash my hands after handling it. "You don't know how many people have touched that bill," she'd say.

But I know the last person who touched it. And I know what she touched before she touched it. And I want to touch her.

I close my eyes and begin a familiar, well-run movie on the back of my lids. Alexa, in her DKNY knock-off suit, cuffed to my drawing table, legs spread wide. I lift my craft knife and run it along her inner thigh, watching her body quiver as I cut through the seam of her skirt and rip it in two with my hands.

"Don't worry," I tell her. "Don't be scared. I won't hurt you."

Not yet, my darling. Yet, my angel. The key word is "yet."

"I won't hurt you," I repeat, and I realize, somewhere deep within myself, that I'm talking out loud. "Not yet, Alexa. Not yet."

You have entered Ether. There are 2 people present.

Omen: You know me, young one. You don't want to admit it to yourself. You don't want to believe that you let down your guard to someone within your inner circle. But you know me. And you can't stay away.

Venus: Please tell me who you are. What you want. Please.

Omen: The same as it's always been. The same as we've always said.

Venus: You've taken advantage of me, of the situation.

Omen: You haven't done anything you didn't want to, have you? I haven't forced you to tell me anything you didn't want to say. Be honest with yourself, Alexa. I've taken only you where you needed to go.

Venus: But you have the upper hand.

Omen: <grinning> Of course. Would you respect me if I didn't? Would you accept my power over you if I didn't exercise it?

Venus: <angrily> Tell me who you are.

Omen: Angrily? Are you angry, submissive one? Are you raising your voice to me? Even online that's a dangerous thing to do. Unless you have the power to back it up, I'd suggest you rethink your approach.

Venus: <eyes lowered> I don't know what to do. Please, Omen. You've destroyed me.

Omen: Not destroyed. Confused. Confounded. But, Alexa, I'll give you everything you've ever wanted.

Venus: Please...tell me.

Omen: I'll meet you, if you want. But I won't reveal myself online

Venus: Why?

Omen: My choice. My rules.

Venus: <softly> I can't sleep.

Omen: You never sleep. You're an insomniac, just like me.
Venus: How do you know so much?
Omen: You've told me some, I've figured out the rest. I'm not stupid, Alexa.
Venus: It's too freaky when I see my name on the screen.
Omen: Then quit hiding and meet me. We won't have to communicate in this mode for much longer. We'll be person to person. Body to body. It's what you want, isn't it...slave?
Venus: Yes.
Omen: But you didn't realize you were going to have it so soon. Is that the problem?
Venus: Yes, I guess. <deep breath> You know me. That means you like the way I look.... I've passed your test?
Omen: I'm laughing out loud. I wish you could hear me. <serious> Don't you know how unreal you are? I have sketch books filled with your body, your face...
Venus: Do you honestly? Do you think I'm pretty?
Omen: Insecure one, you are breathtaking....Truly. What happened to you to make you doubt yourself.
Venus: I've told you...
Omen: And I'm telling you that you are unbelievably beautiful.
Venus: Mistress, I'm scared.
Omen: Then we'll take our time. We'll go slowly. And when you're ready, we'll meet.
Venus: Except that we've already met...
Omen: True.
Venus: I should know you, shouldn't I?
Omen: Yes...
Venus: I'm sorry I don't.

Omen: That's all right, Alexa. That's just fine. I prefer it that way.
Venus: Will you meet me tomorrow night? Online?
Omen: Of course, young one. Of course.

CHAPTER TWO:
The Cave

I show up in the morning to collect more dough, but she's gone today—taken a sick day or on a holiday or maybe a day off. I'm not allowed to ask. I'm not supposed to know. In my world, she is simply gone. I get my cash from the instant teller outside—sorry to have missed Alexa, but glad to have money I can actually spend. I walk down the street to my favorite coffee shop, The Cave, and choose one of the wooden chairs outside. Nina saunters up to me in her feline way and takes my order: double espresso, as always.

"Anything to eat?"

I shake my head.

"You on a diet?" she jokes, knowing there's no spare on my beyond-slender, frighteningly hard-boned frame.

Nina and I have scaled walls together at Rock Solid, an indoor climbing gym on the fringe of the Castro. She's seen me in nylon tights and a racer-back bra. She knows my body. "Diet" is not a word in my vocabulary.

I shake my head again. "Not hungry."

Nina shrugs, flicking her recently dyed, emerald-streaked bangs away from her eyes, then heads back into the café. I cross my legs and stare at my shoes: gleaming black loafers with square four-inch heels. I cross my legs the other way and stare down again. My mind is elsewhere. My mind is on the fact that I don't know what type of shoes Alexa wears. This puzzles me, stuns me. It shouldn't be so. I should know everything about her.

Nina comes back with my tiny white porcelain cup of coffee and a bit of lemon rind.

"A penny…" she offers. She's always offering.

"Not worth it."

She seats herself casually on the chair at my side, tossing back her waist-length mane of thick aquamarine hair and cocking her head at me, expectantly. "No sketchbook today?"

"No."

"They have a sale on monosyllabic words?" she asks next, fucking with me. Oh, she's daring today.

I just stare back at her, with my standard dominant expression in place. One that says; "Think about it. Think about where you're going with this. And make sure you really want to go there."

She lowers her eyes and shrugs. My expression remains cold. But, after a mere moment of silence, she looks back at me and asks, "What will you do with your hands?"

I'm nervous a lot. I move a lot. I drink way too much coffee; I'll admit it readily. Nina's watched me spend hours sketching, losing myself in my artwork. She's watched me fiddle with my pencil when I have no inspiration, smearing charcoal smudges with my thumb like the fog cover that shrouds our bay-hugging city. But she's never seen me without something to keep myself busy. It's dangerous when I don't have a pencil in my hands to play with.

"You're not drawing your girl today?"

"My girl?"

"The pretty one, the one with the hair." She gestures, although *she's* the one with the hair. The ever-changing hair. "You know," she insists, "the one you *always* draw."

I nod. Of course I know who she's talking about, but I play cool, I play dumb. "She's not my girl."

Nina grins and tosses her hair again, standing up as she does. Regaining her confidence as she smiles at me.

"You draw Alexa, don't you?" she asks, and I nod without wondering how she knows this. Nina knows everyone. I look up at her, understanding that she wants more information, but unwilling to feed her hungry mind.

She thrusts her hands in her deep jeans pockets and looks down at me. "Alexa will be your girl, won't she? You'll get her, Omen. I know you will."

I continue to stare at her, continue to not answer, and Nina stares right back. Her body forms a question mark, the way she tilts her head, the way she swivels her hips. She's like a cat in more than one way, stealing from a cat's style of curling its tail into an upward curve. Asking questions with its body alone. Nina asks many questions with her body. She is all limbs and skin, Aztec eyes that fill with sunlight and turn a warm golden brown when she looks at me. She has a flat belly shown to perfection in a cutaway linen vest. A new piercing winks at me from her navel. It's passé—she's admitted it herself—but she likes the way it glints in the sun.

"She will be," Nina says again, this time not asking. "She'll be yours. I'm sure of it."

I take a sip of my espresso and tell her how good it is. Nina doesn't change the subject, though. She's not one to let me off so easily.

"You'll get her, Omen. If you want her."

I give up the charade. "I want her."

"Then you'll get her."

I shrug this time. Nina strikes a pose with her hands crossed at the back of her neck and her elbows up. Sometimes, when she moves like that, I draw her, capturing her quick body motions with a few lines of charcoal on my page. But I don't have my pad today, and I don't have the patience or the will to try to possess her untamable spirit. Not today. Not when my mind is so owned by Alexa.

Nina turns, showing off her perfect ass, then returns to The Cave, and I return to staring at my shoes, imagining Alexa in six-inch spikes—black ones with tiny straps at the ankles. I'd have to hold her to keep her steady, especially walking the San Francisco hills. I'd have to throw her over my shoulder when she stumbled, carrying her that way back up to my apartment. I'd have to take care of her, make sure that she didn't hurt herself in the treacherous heels that would look so pretty on her slim ankles.

I'm wet at the thought. I stare at my shoes some more.

You have entered Ether. There are 2 people present.

Omen: You're not at work today.

Venus: Yes, how did you know?

Omen: I looked for you.

Venus: <eyes lowered> Oh.

Omen: Are you sick?

Venus: No, but I took a day off.

Omen: Why?

Venus: Because...because I can't handle this.

Omen: Try, Alexa. You need to try to handle it. Because I need you.

Venus: Tell me who you are.

Omen: No. I'll meet with you, but I won't reveal myself online. Don't ask me again. Do you understand?

Venus: Yes, Mistress. I'm sorry.

Omen: Relax, Alexa. Think about the things you want. The things we've talked about. I can give you all those things. I can give you all those things and more. So much more.

Venus: I know...

Omen: I can make it all come true. Why are you fighting me?

Venus: I'm scared. I don't mean to fight you, but I'm scared.

Omen: It *is* scary. I agree with you. But it's worth it.

Venus: Tell me...tell me how it was for you...the first time.

Omen: The first time I dominated someone?

Venus: Yes.

Omen: <thinking> Not sure. I've always been in control.

Venus: Tell me about the first time you dominated someone sexually.

Omen: <still thinking> Let me see...

Venus: Was it a man or a woman?

Omen: A woman. My first girlfriend right after high school graduation.

Venus: Really? You were out that early?

Omen: To a select few.... I've always been with women, but I choose to dominate some men, as well. For me, the domination is sexless. However, I prefer to fuck women.

Venus: Tell me more.

Omen: Her name was Mira and she was lovely. A raven-haired lynx. Sleek. She was on the cheerleading squad, if you can believe it.

Venus: I was, too.

Omen: <grinning> Really...that's interesting. Do you still have your uniform?

Venus: No.

Omen: No problem, we can get you one.

Venus: Tell me more, please.

Omen: Her parents thought we were just friends, of course. No one ever put it together that we were lovers.

Venus: And what happened?

Omen: We'd made love often, in her room, sixty-nining. Making sweet, naughty love. But then one time I came over in the afternoon, and her father was asleep in the living room. He worked the night shift, and he was just crashed out on the sofa.

Venus: Yes?

Omen: He was snoring away, and I grabbed Mira and threw her down on the floor in the living room, pressing her face toward her father, making her stare at him while I used my fingers to fuck her. I tore her panties aside, and I violated her cunt, and her asshole, probing her.

Venus: And she let you?

Omen: Let?

Venus: She didn't cry out?

Omen: If she had made a noise, her father would have woken up and seen us.

Venus: Quietly, then, did she fight you?

Omen: Very quietly, she begged me to stop. Whispering "Please…"

Venus: And you did? Then?

Omen: No.

Venus: What else did you do?

Omen: Put my tongue on her hungry little clit and made her come.

Venus: Right there? On the floor?

Omen: Yeah, sweetheart. Right there. In front of God, and her dad, and everyone.

Venus: He could have woken up.

Omen: But he didn't.

Venus: You didn't know that. You didn't know he'd stay asleep.

Omen: I'd seen him sacked out like that before. He was one of those ultra-sound sleepers. I wasn't worried. Plus, I liked how wet it made her. It turned her on immensely. And it turned me on even more.

Venus: And that was the first time you overpowered her?

Omen: Yes.

Venus: What else did you do?

Omen: That night?

Venus: Or any other night. What else did you do with her?

Omen: Everything. From then on, we did everything I wanted to.

Venus: Which included…?

Omen: You're feeling me out, aren't you? You want to see if I'll give you what you need. Alexa, rest assured that I will. I will possess you and make you mine. I will fulfill your wildest, dirtiest, vilest fantasies. When you come, you will sob with relief. Release.

Venus: <begging> Tell me more. Please.

Omen: You don't even have the slightest idea how to beg, Alexa. You think you do, but you don't.

Venus: Teach me.

Omen: Of course. Of course I will. You'll be on your knees, young one, looking up at me, needing what I have to give you. And suddenly it will all be perfectly clear. You'll know exactly how to speak, exactly what tone of voice to use. It will be unreal.

Venus: Tell me more, please, Omen. Don't tease me, tell me more.

Omen: It is teasing you. That's what this whole conversation is. Foreplay. You'll go and come after we get off, won't you? You'll slide your fingers into your panties and go rubby on your clit. Won't you? Tell me honestly, Alexa.

Venus: Yes.

Omen: Then watch this. Watch me deny you. I want to meet with you. In person. I don't want to play any more games.

Venus: Please…

Omen: No.

Good-bye to Omen. There is one person present.

CHAPTER THREE:
Cruel Shoes

After checking my E-mail from The Cave's computer, with Nina hovering too close for comfort, I get a coffee to go and walk to work. Instead of drawing in my own apartment, or in an office, I rent a studio apartment, a small room on the top floor of a building on California Street. I don't like working where I sleep—it makes me even more of an insomniac than I already am. It's important for me to get dressed and leave my own space for at least a few hours at a time. Of course, there are exceptions to the rule. I have pads of drawing paper at home. And I have a sofa bed in my studio. But, for the most part, I attempt to keep my worlds separate.

In my studio, I stare at the colored folders lined up on my drawing table, each one indicating a different assignment.

I've been hired to draw art for two book covers, plus an advertisement for a local gallery, and a few other bits and pieces that I've taken for fun. To fill the time. It's easy work for me. With a pen in hand, I am at complete ease. But instead of doing any of the work that awaits me, I draw shoes. I draw the most amazing, most terrifying pair of spikes—and then I draw Alexa's ankles in them.

I could be a conceptual artist for Frederick's of Hollywood—I've thought about this often. I have a brilliant imagination when it comes to footwear, and the product of my twisted mind is spread out on my drawing board. Ten different pairs of spikes—some slingbacks with feathers on the toes. Others done in shiny vinyl with a zipper running the entire length. I draw boots with even taller heels. Then I sit back and stare at the page before me.

I think that I might be going insane. I look hard. I can almost imagine Alexa's calves curving up from the ankles, her slender knees, her shapely thighs, her whole womanly body right here, on my drawing table.

I shake my head to lose the image, but I can't. No matter how strong I am when I dominate another, I almost always fail when I attempt to dominate myself. At least, where Alexa is concerned.

I reach for my purse—despite the fact that I promised myself I wouldn't—and I pull out my wallet, unzipping the change part where I keep *her* money. I take out a crisp ten and sniff it. I wonder, for the millionth time, perhaps how she gets her scent spread so evenly on all the bills. I've watched her. I've studied her. And suddenly, after all this time, all these months, I know the trick—at least, it's the best guess so far.

In S.F., people often stamp bills with gay or lesbian icons, proclaiming to the masses that homosexuals spend money, too. (We do, ya know.) Alexa has her own way of marking dollars. She uses one of those fancy rubber finger covers they sell in stationery stores. It's nubby, like a French tickler, and makes it easy to turn pages of a book or extract money from a drawer. She must masturbate with it on her breaks, I decide. She must take handfuls of those naughty finger covers and go into the restroom and play with her sweet little button, getting the rubber utensil all covered in her honey scent. And then, as she peels off the bills to one happy customer after another, she spreads her scent—and joy—to the world.

I stand and look down at my drawing of shoes and ankles. Then I take my wallet and keys and leave my studio, walking the seven flights down to street level and then striding the four blocks to the nearest office-supply store. I don't even know the name for the device that Alexa uses. I'd be much more at ease at Good Vibrations or the Pleasure Chest or even the raunchier stores in the Castro. I'm known at those places. They'd help me find what I'm looking for. I could walk in and ask for the latest in anal toys, the hippest thing in monster dildos, the meanest clamps on the market. Instead, I have to wander the aisles of the office-supply store like some deranged, stationery-psychopath, poking around by the paper clips, rustling through the racks of miscellaneous supplies.

One thing's for certain: I get lots of good ideas. Special clips to hold papers together, the ones with the steely bite—how pretty those would look on Alexa's pert nipples, I think. One clamped on each rosy-hued point of flesh. The clips are made of metal, but covered in thick, glossy paint. Even better than the clothespins every dominant woman I know currently favors. And over on the next aisle, brand-new rulers. Clear plastic ones. Thick wooden ones. I pick up a yardstick and smack it against my hand. It's got a good feel to it, and I tuck it under my arm to add to my purchases.

If I had a cock, I'd be getting a hard-on now. But I don't have one and I don't pack. Anything that can be done with a cock can be done with fingers or a tongue. Just as good and just as satisfying. No penis envy, here... or *here*, as I find what my heart desires and scoop up ten—one for every finger. Don't need or want a cock. At all. What I want is this: to tie her down and probe her with these infinitely interesting rubbery devices. Stretch one over my thumb and wedge it into the tight opening of her ass.

The finger covers (they aren't named at the stationery store, either) are twenty cents each. What a bargain. I resolve to order a box next time I buy art supplies. How I never have thought to use office equipment for sex toys is amazing to me. I've spanked with spatulas, bound with nylons, blindfolded with table runners...but here's a world that's totally new to me.

And Alexa was the one to introduce me to it.

I decide to E-mail her immediately and see if I've guessed right. But then, of course, I'll have given away a bit more of myself. I can't believe she doesn't know who I am. My obsession must be better hidden than I think. I suppose as a dom, I should be happy that my emotions are shielded.

At the same time, I wish she would hurry up and guess my name. Then we'd be over that Rumplestiltskin-esque bridge and I could move on to the next... which is taking her.

You have entered Ether. There are 2 people present.

Omen: How's my frightened doe of a slave, tonight?

Venus: I'll meet you this weekend, Mistress.

Omen: You will? What changed your mind?

Venus: I can't sleep...more than normal. Less than normal, I mean. I can't sleep without knowing who you are. And it's beyond that.

Omen: What do you mean?

Venus: I can't think about going in to work. I'm a mess. A wreck.

Omen: I'd like to see that. I'd like to see you lose control. You keep yourself so tightly bound, don't you?

Venus: Yes, Mistress.

Omen: Has that always been the case? I mean, ever since you first told that imbecilic high school boy what you wanted?

Venus: I don't know. I think that over the years I've gotten better at hiding it.

Omen: Like an oyster, carefully wrapping the strands of iridescence around and around a painful grain of sand to make a pearl.

Venus: What do you mean?

Omen: I mean that the concept that gives you pain to think about, that upsets your balanced life, is the same concept that makes you beautiful to me.

Venus: You're serious.

Omen: I don't lie to you.

Venus: I know, Mistress.

Omen: And I know something, too, Alexa.

Venus: What do you mean?

Omen: I know your secret, young one.

Venus: I don't understand.

Omen: I asked you once to tell me your darkest secret. You lied. You told me that nonsense fluff about a boy in London. A one-night stand.

Venus: That happened, Mistress.

Omen: I'm sure it did. But that's not your darkest secret, Alexa.

Venus: What do you know?

Omen: I'll tell you when I see you, slave.

Venus: Friday night?

Omen: At your place.

Venus: You know where I live? Have you been watching me?

Omen: I know.

Venus: I'm scared. Oh, God, Mistress Omen, I'm scared.

Omen: Then meet me at The Cave. That'll be easier for you, I'll bet.

Venus: All right…I can do that. What time?

Omen: Midnight.

Venus: How will I know you?

Omen: You'll know me, Alexa. When you see me, you'll know me.

Venus: Will you meet me before then? Online? Tomorrow night?

Omen: No. I won't contact you until Friday. And I'll see you there. Don't be late, Alexa. You don't want to make me wait. Not after I've had to wait so long already.

Venus: I promise, Mistress O. I promise.

Omen: And I want you to do something for me until then.

Venus: What, Mistress?

Omen: Sleep on the floor. Every night between now and Friday.

Venus: Yes, Mistress. I promise.

Omen: No sheets, no blankets. On the floor, without comfort.
Venus: Yes, Mistress, I understand.
Omen: Until then...
Venus: Wait, Mistress?
Omen: Yes?
Venus: What should I call you?
Omen: You'll know what to call me when you see me.
Venus: All right. Friday, then.
Omen: Midnight.

CHAPTER FOUR:
Love is the Drug?

Withstanding pain is an addiction. Giving it is a drug. I'm not sure if that makes sense, but that's how it has always seemed to me. When Dante wants pain, his eyes get wild and hungry. The pupils shrink down to the tiniest black dots, swimming frantically within the pools of thick molasses-brown irises. When he needs it, he comes sidling up to me like a kid on the playground, promising to be my best friend if I share my dessert with him. Pain is the sweet stuff he craves.

He says, "Please," in a voice that is difficult to deny. He says, "Mistress Omen, please…I need."

We all need.

"I want…"

And want.

"I…" Just lost words, empty words, trying to explain why he's dying for me to take him home and beat him until he comes. He aches to feel the heat of my power. More than simply feeling the pain, though, is his need to withstand it. He wants to take it. He wants to take it unyieldingly. Not bend. Not break. Not cry out his safe word to me.

It's a game. And somehow it doesn't seem to matter who's playing. We both win. So, yeah, I think that needing pain is like being a drug addict. And bestowing the pain is dispensing the drug. Or working magic. I make all of his dreams come true. I make all of his little insecurities fade away. Though, by the time you've reached this point in your life, where you can go up to another human being and confess the things that get you off…well, then, you have graduated to a different level. And there aren't too many insecurities at all to face in the mirror in the morning.

You just have to face yourself. The way I hope Alexa is standing in front of her bathroom mirror and facing herself. She must be. Must be practicing, looking deep into her beautiful eyes and whispering to herself, "Hurt me, please…." She's my needling, and she doesn't even know it. She's my match, my other half.

Dante is simply an appetizer to the main feast. Something to fill me up in the interim until Friday rolls around. I wouldn't let him know that I think of him as that, but it really doesn't matter. As long as he gets what he needs, he's satisfied.

Dante works at The Cave. He is one of those waiters who is only waiting tables while writing the Great

American Underground Angst-Ridden Masterpiece. But he hasn't decided yet if he's a poet or a novelist, or perhaps a performance artist; so he pours coffee for a living and comes up to my apartment to let me hurt him.

The Cave suits me at any time of day. Whether I've just gotten up, or I don't want to go to bed. Whether I've been up for days and want a bit more of the bean to keep me up a few more days. It always suits me.

There's something about the dark interior, with the vibrantly painted walls that glow under a violet light; something about the way the waiters and waitresses all look as if they might be part-vampire, or part-alien. Dark hollows beneath their eyes that I find infinitely attractive. Thin, junkie-looking, all after the same thing I want: not caffeine, not pure adrenaline, but that satisfied feeling that you can find only when sex is molded with love.

Though sometimes just the rush of sex will have to do.

They serve drinks in "Vaseline glass" at The Cave. It's a type of material manufactured in the 1950s that glows bright green under the violet light, borrowing from the atmosphere of Disney's Haunted Mansion. I like that ghostly quality. It makes me feel normal—it makes me blend in.

I'm dressed down tonight, a pair of black velvet slacks and matching black velvet T-shirt, short boots tucked in under the pants. I have my hair slicked back off my face and wound tightly in a knot at the nape of my neck. I didn't bother with too much makeup—only a little powder to accentuate my pale skin and the same dark lipstick I always wear. My eyes are large enough and deep enough not to require any extra dressing up, but I have on eye shadow anyway. Just for show.

I wander into the dimly lit interior in what is a slow-paced gait for me. I need more coffee to rev up my system, but I relish the dreamy quality I get in the moments before a cup of the brew. It's like walking through water. I don't need any other drugs to enhance the effects of no sleep. The dreams start to come when I'm awake—that's the most amazing feeling.

I nod to people as I make my way through to the back. It's always hard to tell the time in The Cave—the café's open twenty-five hours and they don't have any clocks on the walls—but I can tell the approximate hour by which waiters are working and which customers are seated at the counter and in the sofas at the front of the room. The Cave is decorated in an avant-garde, yet comfortable fashion. There are tables and chairs for the clients who want to sit and nibble on something while they drink. But there are also velvet-draped lounges and huge, soft pillows to sprawl upon.

I like the thronelike wooden chair at the very back of the room. It's in Dante's section and I make my way to it and sit down, crossing my long legs and waiting to catch Dante's eyes. He spots me immediately and brings me my sinful potion without even waiting for my order. As he sets it down in front of me, he asks, "How do you drink this stuff at night, Omen?" It's a joke. I know he lives on the same orgasmic French roast fumes as I do.

"Night?" I ask, looking around. "How do you know what time it is in here?"

He grins his beautiful, tie-me-down smile, then pulls

up a chair at my table and makes himself comfortable. My waiters and waitresses know me at The Cave. They always join me. I hate to drink alone.

"You on a break?"

"I am now."

We flirt easily, and occasionally I take him up to my apartment and give him what he needs. Deal out the pain he so craves desperately.

"I'm off in an hour," he tells me, innocently slipping one hand over mine. I let him. I'm in a forgiving mood.

"Yeah?"

"Well, I just thought…"

"Yeah?" I ask again. "You thought what?"

"Are you free?"

That brings a smile to my lips. I lean back in my chair and regard him under my half-closed lids that are well-shaded in my favorite hue: Bruise. I make him sweat. It's almost too easy.

"I'm never free," I say, as is expected in the script between us. "I always exact a price."

"I'll pay, Mistress Omen. I'll pay…."

"Yeah," I assure him. "You will." Then I lift my glimmering green shot glass of black espresso and down it while he watches. He flushes at my words, waiting, wanting. "I'll make you pay," I say next, the hot liquid filling my throat, but not burning it. "Tonight. When your shift is over. You may come visit me."

He lowers his head in a quick, humble bow and his gleaming, white hair falls over his handsome face. Then he peeks up at me in a look that's a combination of fear and thankfulness—a look that I understand, but no one outside the SM world ever would. No one who doesn't live the life of pain/pleasure could understand that look of yearning. To me, it's heartrending. To a vanilla lover, it would mean nothing.

When the moment's passed, Dante winks at me, back in his waiter persona, and stands, saying, over his shoulder, "That's on me."

"Then bring me another."

I like being served. In more ways than this. And Dante knows just what I like. I may be dreaming of Alexa. I may draw her feet in torturous shoes, in *cruel* shoes. Visions of her submitting to me may be dancing throughout my sleepless nights. But everyone needs to let off a bit of pent up steam. I'm no different.

And Friday's three days away.

I look around at the crowd. The Cave draws an interesting mix of people. There's a couple clad all in leather standing at the bar. The man, Jeremy, is a photographer; his wife, Sasha, is his model. I watch as they scope out the place, knowing exactly what they're doing: looking for a third. Sasha likes women and Jeremy likes photographing Sasha with women. I scan the room, too, but don't see any promising young models for them.

I recognize a few other regulars and I nod to them, but I don't wave anyone over to join me. If I did, I'd have a whole party in my corner, and I'm not looking to entertain a crowd tonight. I catch the eye of a voluptuous redhead in a skintight red vinyl outfit. She's with a dom I've known for years; looks as if he's slumming tonight. Or maybe she's simply the appetizer of the evening. It's only 1:00 A.M. Plenty of time to play.

Dante brings me my second cup and then bends to whisper into my ear. "Please…"

"What?" I ask in my normal voice. I rarely whisper in public.

He's hungry. "Please, Mistress Omen. Hurt me tonight."

"Of course," I tell him. It's a promise.

I watch him walk away. He's got a fine body, slim-hipped in faded black jeans worn low down to reveal his pale white skin. He's showing off his corded arms in a plain black T-shirt, arms that are well-muscled for one so thin. He has long bleached-platinum hair and dark brown eyes. He's amazing looking, with the fine, cut cheekbones that models envy and diet (unsuccessfully) for, and a jaw that screams defiance, even when he's in a lowly slave's position.

I like to hurt him, which works out well for Dante, since he likes to be hurt. He is the truest masochist I've ever met. He'll bow to a dom, regardless of sex, on the condition that the Master/Mistress can control him. And he's a handful. He wants pain, but there's a filament of fire burning within him that makes him refuse to give himself totally.

I like that. I like mastering that. I like making him beg.

I slip a ten—but not one of Alexa's—under my glass, tap my watch in a motion to Dante that I'll be ready for him in an hour, and then make my way out of The Cave. The street outside is alive with people, moving from the jazz bar on the corner, to the all-night bookstore where a local author is reading, to the competing coffee shop down the street.

I walk back to my apartment to change into something a bit more appropriate for my postmidnight rendezvous: my vinyl catsuit. It's incredible on me, form-fitting, of course, with a zipper running down the back and up the crotch. I special-ordered it from one of the many slutty catalogs that make their way into my mailbox. I special order most of my SM gear. It can be difficult to find what I need in an average mall.

After dressing, I open my antique wardrobe, handed down from my grandfather, and extract a series of pain-producing implements, From the ravenous look in Dante's eyes, I know just what he needs tonight.

Then I brew a pot of extra-strong coffee, retreat to my sofa, and wait.

You have mail. Sent today, at 12:34 A.M. EST
Mistress Omen,

I miss you. This is difficult for me, not being able to meet you online. I am anxious and scared and I feel as if the bottom is falling out of my life. Please respond. Please don't make me wait until Friday to know who you are.

I don't even know if you'll read this, or if you'll return it unread. I am only hoping that you'll take pity on me and write back. Please tell me that you won't reject me. You know what I want. You know more than anyone. And you know who I am. This frightens me beyond belief, beyond anything I ever imagined.

I know...I know...I'm pathetic.

My teacher called me tonight. She wants to see me again. I only met with her because you requested it.

What do you want me to do, Omen? What should I tell her?

—Venus

P.S. I want only to be yours.

CHAPTER FIVE
A Little Tenderness

Dante has a key. At 2:05, he lets himself in without knocking.

"Omen?" he calls from the front, startled by the darkness of the apartment. I've killed the lights and lowered the blinds, setting the mood. My mood. A mood of blackness, tonight. A mood of rage. If I owned any, I'd have screwed red bulbs into my lamps, giving my humble apartment the lighting of Hell. Instead, it's dark, and Dante stumbles as he walks through the doorway.

"Right here," I tell him, giving him my voice to follow.

He comes closer down the hall and then stops in the

entrance to the living room, allowing his eyes to adjust to the blackness. Then, seeing my silhouette on the couch, he drops quickly to his knees.

"Mistress..." he says softly.

"Strip!" I command, standing, circling, moving in for the kill. "I shouldn't have to tell you this shit, Dante. You should have been naked when you stepped into the apartment. Your clothes should be folded neatly in a pile in the hall.

"I'm sorry, Mistress," he whispers, pulling his shirt over his head. I walk to him and jab him with the point of my boot. He nearly loses his balance. Then I step back and watch as he crouches to slip off his own boots and jeans. He's not wearing underwear—he never does.

Like a cat, my eyes are accustomed to the darkness. By now Dante's are, as well. I stalk back to my wall of windows and pull up the blinds. Instantly, Dante's waxen skin glows in the room, caught by the lights in the apartment building across the way. I open each one of my windows to the chill night air, loving Dante for the shiver that runs through his naked body.

"Dante," I say, softly, as if I'm talking to a frightened animal, "Dante, love, do you know why I'm opening the windows?"

He shakes his head, "No, Mistress."

"I want an audience."

He lowers his head.

"You're gonna scream for me tonight," I tell him, assuring him. "By the end of this show, we'll have a curious audience watching from the safety of their own apartments across the way. Watching and listening."

I like being watched.

Dante's head is still down, chin to his chest. He says my name in a low voice, obviously confused, not expecting my wrath. He wants what he wants and he need what he needs, but he doesn't fathom what it does to me to give it to him. He doesn't comprehend what I have to become in order to bestow the pain he desires.

I walk back over and bend to him, press my lips to his ear and whisper, "You understand me, don't you? They'll be listening to your cries. Listening to you beg for me to stop."

He shakes his head—an unconscious move—and his hair falls forward, hiding his face from me. He doesn't want to fight me, but he can't help it. There's something alive within him that refuses to admit that he needs what I give. The pain and the humiliation. He thrives on it. But he can't accept it—not all of it.

"This will hurt," I tell him, because he needs to hear the words. "You know it, Dante. Don't you?"

He gives me a nod, but no verbal response. I slap his face for it—hard. Sometimes it's almost too easy. He makes it hard on himself and easy for me. I backhand him again and he looks up at me with wild, feral eyes. I click my tongue against the roof of my mouth and shake my head at him.

"Answer your Mistress when she asks you a question."

"I forgot the question, Mistress."

Oh, I want to make him pay. I slap him again and he bites his bottom lip and tightens his fists. He wants to strike me back. He doesn't like it when I humiliate him.

He likes only the pain. But it's part of the bargain with me. If he wants to be beaten, he'll take the abuse. It's foreplay to a sadist such as myself. It's simply my way of getting started.

I hiss, "The question was this. I'll repeat it again, once more. Don't fail me, now, Dante. Don't let me down."

He looks up at me, waiting.

"You know it's gonna hurt tonight"—one long, slow beat—"don't you?"

He starts to nod and I almost laugh out loud. I want to get right up close to him and scream in his handsome face, "Don't be such an easy mark! Give me something more. Give me something I can chew on."

But then he catches himself and says, "Yes, Mistress. I know."

"And why?" I ask. "Why, Dante? Why am I gonna make you hurt tonight?"

It's important to keep repeating his name. I've learned this during my many years' experience dominating submissive ones. It's important to keep right on him. Not to give him a fucking inch.

"Because I deserve it," he says, and I know I've got him. Locked him into my game. I'm controlling this ride. I alone know where it will take us.

"Right," I say, stroking his hair, then running my fingertips over the warm surface of his cheek where I slapped him. "That's right, Dante. You deserve it. But now, honey"—oh, he flinches when I say it; he hates when I say it—"...now, darling, I want you to tell me something else."

I get quieter. I get on my knees next to him. I bring my lips against his ear and softly, sweetly, I whisper, "Why, Dante?" In a singsong voice that must drive him mad. "Why do you deserve it, Dante? Tell me, sweetie. Tell your Mistress."

And then, because he's not expecting it, because the power is alive and screaming through my body, I grab his shoulders and shake him viciously. His head rocks back hard, slamming into the wall behind him, stunning him but not damaging him. His eyes open wider than they have all night.

I let him go and rise quickly, moving until my body is pressed against the window. I want a cigarette, something in my hands to calm me down. I know I'm taking out my aggression on him, know I'm doing to him what I want to be doing to Alexa. But it doesn't matter. It's just a way to let off a little bit of energy. But I need to slow down.

When I look back at Dante, he's rocking himself, talking to himself. I didn't really hurt him. I know this. I simply shocked him. I say, "Dante," and he looks up at me, his eyes shiny with impending tears. "What did you do, Dante? Why am I going to beat you tonight."

His body goes on rocking as he quiets himself. He says, "I don't know."

I reach for my paddle and slap it firmly against the palm of my hand. Feeling the weight of it, the sting of it, helps me to regain my sense of control.

"Tell me," I order him, and he looks up at me again, helplessly, and he swallows hard.

"I don't know." He's begging. "I just need it. Please,

Omen. Please. Don't make me say it. Don't keep asking me questions. I just need it. Just hurt me. Please. Just…"

Now there are tears in his voice.

"Tell me."

He covers his face with his hands, still rocking, still soothing himself with the motion. He's naked and exposed on my floor, ready to be hurt, to be punished physically, and I'm mentally giving him a beating first.

"I'm just bad," he says, as if that will satisfy me, when it only whets my appetite further. "There's something inside me that's bad."

"And the pain…" I start, helping him out.

"The pain makes it go away."

"Forever?"

He shakes his head. "Only while it lasts."

"Not after…?"

"The bruises," he says, admitting it. "The bruises help. When I see them. When I look at them in the mirror or press my fist into them, I can remember what it was like. Taking it. Submitting to you."

"The pain…" I prod him again.

"The pain clarifies it all for me."

"Clarifies what?"

He shakes his head and takes a deep, tremulous breath. His body twists uncomfortably, and now he's begging me physically as well as vocally. Just the way his body moves on the floor, the way his left shoulder comes forward, the way he arches his neck…he's begging. I want to give it to him.

"Clarifies what?" I repeat. I need more. This is what gets me ready, what revs me up.

"Not clarifies," he amends, "but purifies…"

It's what I was waiting for. A definition I could fathom and swallow. It's different for me. I think that as I begin. It's so much different. My need to overpower. To hurt. The intense rush of pleasure I get at the first sign of his impending tears. The even larger burst of fire in my belly at the first sob he lets escape. And then—as the games begin—I can stop thinking.

He lets out a sigh of relief when he sees me step forward. Then he lowers his head and gives himself to me. Totally.

Sometimes it's like art, when we're together. I put one hand on his chest and push him backward. I lift his legs and press his feet over his head. He's in a yoga position, now, one that I think is called "the plow," one that his body contorts into effortlessly. He's a flexible boy, but I press him to the full limit of his abilities, and he moans.

"Come on, Dante," I croon to him, "give it up."

I use my thick wooden paddle to heat his ass for him. It makes him semi-hard in only a few strokes. I paddle him with about half of my strength. It gives him a huge erection.

"Oh, dear," I say, as if sadly. "You're going to come from this, aren't you? You're not even gonna need me to bring out the harder stuff. You're just a little boy tonight, aren't you, Dante? A little boy in need of some stern punishment."

No response. He's trying too hard to hold in the tears. Crying from a spanking is something he cannot allow himself do.

I drop the paddle and reach for my discipline stick, a thin piece of metal encased in hand-tooled black leather. I bought it at Good Vibrations and I love the action of it. When I first checked it out in the store, two other customers stopped what they were doing to watch me swing it. I whip Dante with the stick while his cock grows larger. I punish his ass and his thighs. It's been much too long.

"No…" he says finally, but it's not the right word to use if he wants me to stop. "Please, Omen…"

I shake my head, lean my weight on the backs of his bent legs, and decorate his ass with the side of the stick, using it like a cane. The weapon makes thin, red stripes on his ass and thighs. I can see them even in the streetlight that dimly illuminates the room. I like the way they look. I add some more.

"No…" Dante says again.

"That's not the magic word." I'm not even breathing hard.

"Oh, God…"

He's going to come. This is one of my favorite moments: watching a sub come from pain alone. No sexual stimulation. No heavy-duty role playing, or acting. No nothing. Just pain.

His body tenses. His face is a picture of pure agony. I stand back while he shoots. Then I slip on a pair of rubber gloves, sit at his side, lower his legs to the floor, and rub his come into his chest with my hands. He's breathless. His mouth is open, his breathing hard.

"Mistress O." He looks up at me, wanting to say more.

I nod, then let him lick my fingers clean. When he's finished, I tell him to get dressed.

"I can't stay the night?" he asks.

"I'm not going to sleep." I shrug. "Got work to do."

"Can I at least…"

I wait.

"…satisfy you?"

"You just did," I assure him.

"Physically?" He sits up and gets ready to move toward me, to unzip my catsuit and reveal my throbbing cunt.

"Not tonight."

"Please, Mistress?"

"Not tonight," I repeat more firmly. He lowers his eyes, lowers his head, and says, "I'm sorry."

"Don't be. It's not about you."

He waits for a moment to see if I'll explain any further or if I'll change my mind. When I don't, he stands and walks nude to my bathroom to get cleaned up. I admire the blush to his ass, the lines cutting across that pale skin in a near perfect pattern.

Artwork, I think. *My* work. I take more pride it in than in much of the art that pays my bills. An odd thought—sex gives me more artistic pleasure than drawing with pen and ink, with charcoal smudges. I consider a whip my pen, a paddle my crayon. I consider Dante my work of art.

I hear the shower running, and I wonder, fleetingly, if I should let him pleasure me. He knows the right way to use his tongue, the perfect way to bring me to climax. I've taught him well, helped him to perfect his technique.

But it's not what I want. Not now. What I want is Alexa. This was simply my way of waiting for her. Then, if I get to her soon, if I win her honestly on Friday, I won't scare her off immediately.

I realize that I've pegged her as a deer, a frightened little wood creature who will flee at the first sign of my dominant personality. But until she proves me wrong I will continue to picture her like this. It's safest.

Dante sings to himself in my shower. I recognize the song; Otis Redding's "Try a Little Tenderness." Dante's got a beautiful voice. But I don't want to try tenderness. I want to take Alexa.

I want to make her mine.

Mail. Composed at 3:09 A.M. EST. Sent to Venus at 3:10 A.M.
Slave,

Do not see your teacher privately again. If you do, then do not meet me on Friday. If you are going to be mine, then be mine. Otherwise, I do not want you.

I will not contact you again.

I will return anything you send me, unread.

Be faithful to me, Alexa, and I will make all of your wickedest fantasies realities. I will make your dreams come true.

And your nightmares, too.

Your Owner.
Omen

P.S. You can meet me online Thursday night. At 1:00 A.M. In Ether. If you need to.

P.P.S. I will be wearing my belt on Friday night in The Cave. You'll recognize me by that if by nothing else.

CHAPTER SIX
One Dungeon or Another

There's light coming in my window, but it could be dawn or dusk. It doesn't really matter to me. I sit at my computer and log onto my online server, wanting to check my E-mail, wanting to write to Alexa again, but denying myself that pleasure. I have friends with whom I correspond regularly. None have written me today.

I've got time to kill, and I don't feel like venturing to The Cave. I'm not up for a replay with Dante. Not without drawing blood, and he and I haven't reached that point in our relationship yet.

He thinks he wants pain. He doesn't even begin to understand the concept, the true meaning. For him, he needs pain until he comes. And then he needs it to stop. For me, when we're together, it's all I can do to keep from continuing, from taking him where *I* need to go. Beyond the fringes of his boundaries, his imagination.

Instead, I cruise the menu of chat rooms that are available and end up in one of the dungeons—just to "listen," I tell myself. Not to play. Honestly, I am a voyeur at heart. The fun of watching other people play and talk and fuck and cry is immense. Online, being a wallflower, hugging the perimeters of the rooms, I am able to observe without being approached.

The words go by quickly on the screen, come-dripping images between strangers. It's child's play compared to what I prefer, but sometimes I like the Peeping Tom quality that one can only find in cyberspace, or in the very raunchiest theaters in North Beach. And I don't feel like getting dressed and going to watch a show.

You have entered The Dungeon F for F. There are 17 people present.
Jasmine: Yes, Mistress…whatever you want…
Mistress X: On your knees, slave. Kiss my feet.
Althea: Can anyone play?
Vagabond: Althea, Dom or sub?
Althea: Which are you looking for…?
Vagabond: Check my profile if you're interested.
Althea: You won't just tell me?
Vagabond: Can't you read?

I drag down the profile bar. I am interested in Vagabond's attitude. I like to keep up on the players, and when a new name is featured, I do my homework. Perhaps it's the artist in me that attempts to match a face to the creative online tags. Whatever the reason, the game works for me late at night.

Vagabond's profile is vague, at best. There is no sex listed, though one would have to assume that Vag is a "she," being in the F for F dungeon. And if not a she, a wannabe-she, which serves as the same thing in cyberspace. Vagabond is a Dominant, with a penchant for blondes. I shrug and return to the session in progress.

Mistress X: We'll give them a little show tonight; won't we, Jasmine?

Jasmine: What do you mean, Mistress?

Mistress X: A little display, a little informative lesson about what happens when a slave misbehaves.

Jasmine: But...Mistress..

Mistress X: Are you back-talking me? Am I hearing your words correctly?

I decide to cruise through space, to come back when the chitchat is over and the pain/pleasure session has begun. Because that's what I want. That's what I need. The rest isn't interesting anymore. At least, it's no longer interesting to me.

You have entered Demon Lounge. There are 25 people present.

Vampire: Won't anyone play?

Elijah: Play what, Vampire?

Vampire: Rough...

I decide to talk, though I don't know why. I type in.

Omen: What do you consider rough?

Vampire: Make me cry...?

Omen: Of course.

Vampire: Private room?

I instant-message her/him. I type: Meet me in Fire, and then quickly create a private room of that name.

Then I wait, like a spider at the edge of a sticky web, to see if Vampire really is in the mood. Two seconds later:

You have entered Fire. There are 2 people present.
Vampire: Male or female?
Omen: Female…and you?
Vampire: Same. Do you want to play?
Omen: Is that what you call it? Do you "play" for real?
Vampire: Of course…it's just hard to find people willing to online.
Omen: Describe yourself.
Vampire: Pale skin, dark hair, red lips.
Omen: Tattoos?
Vampire: A blue rose on my inner thigh.
Omen: Bruises?
Vampire. What do you mean?
Omen: Have you been whipped lately?

   I tell myself to go slower, but I can't.

Vampire: No, Mistress.
Omen: How old are you?
Vampire: I'm legal.
Omen: Good to hear… When were you last beaten?
Vampire: A year ago.
Omen: What happened?
Vampire: I…I liked it too much…
Omen: You were afraid of what?
Vampire: Dying…
Omen: Ah…then you didn't choose your partner very carefully, did you?
Vampire: I thought I did.
Omen: Be aware. Subs need to read between the lines.

Vampire: Yes…and you? What do you like?
Omen: Power.
Vampire: Over?
Omen: You…others…submissive women.

In my head, her name is SCREAMING: ALEXA, ALEXA, ALEXA…

Vampire: I'm at your service.
Omen: What are you wearing?
Vampire: A sheer black dress, garter belt, stockings, no bra, no panties.
Omen: Take off your dress.
Vampire: Yes, Mistress…
Omen: Stand in front of the mirror. Let me admire you. Keep your eyes down.
Vampire: Yes, Mistress.
Omen: Yes, lovely, let me admire you. Turn around. Face me.
Vampire: Yes, Mistress.
Omen: Bend over. Part the cheeks of your ass. I want to see.
Vampire: ::following the command::
Omen: ::walking closer, licking my thumb:: Do you know where this is going, slave?
Vampire: <haltingly> In my ass?
Omen: Yes. ::pressing my thumb into the opening of your anus::
Vampire: ::sighing::
Omen: How does that feel, slave?
Vampire: It hurts…too dry…
Omen: But I got it all wet for you.
Vampire: It still hurts….
Omen: <grinning> And you like it. That's a fact. I see the drips of come already coating your thighs.
Vampire: Yes, Mistress. I like it.

Omen: ::thrusting harder, filling you:: So, you like pain?
Vampire: <breathless> Yes, Mistress.
Omen: ::slapping your ass, hard:: That kind of pain?
Vampire <trembling> Yes, Mistress.
Omen: But more, right? Harder?
Vampire: Oh, please, harder. Much harder.
Omen: ::extracting my thumb and bringing it to your mouth:: Clean me up, slave.
Vampire: ::sucking::
Omen: You do that well, don't you?
Vampire: <mouth full> Yes, Mistress...
Omen: How much harder do you like it? A belt? A paddle? A strap?
Vampire: A belt, Mistress.
Omen: I have a nice belt, a heavy one.
Vampire: I'll kiss the buckle for you, Mistress.
Omen: Get down on all fours.
Vampire: <obeying>
Omen: I'm going to whip you now. I want you to count.
Vampire: Yes, Mistress.

I wonder why I'm doing this. I want Alexa. I don't want to fuck with someone else. It's too surreal. I chicken out. And turn my computer off, leaving Vampire on all fours, waiting for the pain that will never begin.

CHAPTER SEVEN:
Alexa Breaks

I decide that I have to get some work done, regardless of whether I want to or not. I can't let my dreaming of Alexa dominate my life completely. Especially since I long to dominate hers.

Besides, it's important for me to work, to draw. Otherwise I'll start to lose clients. It's not so much a financial obligation for me—I have plenty of money—but a need to keep at least one part of my life regimented. To keep one corner of my world in order. I force myself to spend all of Thursday at my drawing table. It's not much punishment, though, because I can go to my window and look down at the building across the way, peering into Alexa's apartment on the third floor. A few times, I catch her sitting on the fire escape, but she doesn't look up to see me watching.

I almost tap my finger against the glass to get her attention. But I stop myself just in time. I want to fling open the window and scream her name. But, instead, I bite my tongue and force myself to go back to work.

Of course, only moments later, I creep back to the window and look down again. I'm not scared she'll recognize me if she does look up. The distance is too great. But I wonder if I'll ever be able to admit to her that I rented this studio after following her home. Maybe it will always be my secret. Or maybe she'll remember the time I caught her touching herself on the fire escape. And she'll know it was me watching.

Between "Alexa breaks," I draw. I lose myself in my work, creating the image for the first book cover in a few hours. My client has requested a piece of art with a 1950s look to it, paying homage to one of those pulp-magazine covers so popular during that era. I have a series of postcards reproduced from actual book covers of the time, and I spread them out on my desk and stare at them. After a drinking them in, I begin to sketch, focusing until I get something I really like. It's definitely pulp—a woman and a man in a tight clinch. And although the woman is faced away from the viewer, it's Alexa. Anyone who knows her would recognize the line of her body, the curves of her hips.

I send the pencil drawing through the fax machine to get approval before starting the final. I'm sure my client will approve—she likes my style—but I always wait for feedback before wasting my time with ink. After another "Alexa break," I begin the next project; a second book cover with an entirely different look. This one is for an anthology of women-written erotica, and I have been given free-rein to do whatever I want.

I draw Alexa.

Of course.

I draw Alexa in a silky negligee, sprawled on a chaise longue, reading. The book covers her face—I don't want to get sued. But again, it's Alexa, and anyone who's ever seen her would know it. I laugh as I fax this cover to my second client. Then I go to the windows and look down again, hoping for a glimpse, but she's nowhere in sight.

I'm almost to the point of calling her and hanging up when I hear her voice. I feel like a little kid making prank calls. Like someone completely out of control, which is what I am. She said she was a wreck, and, although I wish I could deny it, I realize that I am, as well.

I imagine what will happen when we meet, the fireworks of emotions exploding between us. All of my imaginary scenarios are positive, controlled by me. I can't allow myself to wonder what will happen if we don't click. I can't even fathom a scenario in which she doesn't even come to The Cave, which is definitely possible. My frightened child. If that happened, I'd have to come get her. I shake my head to erase the thought. Instead, I plan what we will do, what I will do to her. How we will be together.

And over and over, I walk from my drawing table to the window and look down.

But for the rest of the afternoon, she's not there.

You have entered Ether. There are 2 people present.
Omen: You slept on the floor last night—correct, slave?
Venus: Yes, Mistress.
Omen: And every night since we last spoke?
Venus: Yes, Mistress, as you instructed.
Omen: Nude?
Venus: Yes, Mistress.
Omen: No sheets, no blankets. You slept naked on the cold wood floor.
Venus: Yes, Mistress. Just as You said.
Omen: I think that you're lying to me.
Venus: ...Mistress?
Omen: Never lie to me, slave. Never do that.
Venus: ::eyes lowered::
Omen: I'll find out. <dark laugh> I always find out....
Venus: Please believe me, Mistress.
Omen: Make me believe you. Describe the sensation to me.
Venus: <haltingly> I showered before bed and dried my hair. I didn't put on my nightgown or a T-shirt. I just lay down on the floor at the foot of my bed...
Omen: And?
Venus: And I cried myself to sleep.
Omen: Why, slave?
Venus: Because I was cold and alone. Shivering on the floor. With no one to care, no one nearby.
Omen: You didn't feel me with you?
Venus: <shaking my head> No, Mistress.
Omen: But you will, slave. You will. You will feel my hands on your body. You will feel my warmth around you.
Venus: I know, Mistress.
Omen: Tomorrow night, Alexa. It's only hours away.
Venus: Yes, Mistress.

Omen: You will do what I say for my pleasure...
Venus: Yes, Mistress. I promise.
Omen: ...for my pleasure...and yours.

Book Three:
SIMULTANEOUS STORIES

CHAPTER ONE:
Almost Midnight at The Cave

Omen's Voice

I arrive at 11:30, knowing that she'll be early, too, and wanting to have the upper hand. This is the first time in years that I've been nervous about anything, and I need to be completely at ease when she walks through the door. I need to be completely prepared. I want to have a drink before she arrives, and I want to feel its effects inside me. Working through my body to still my soul.

I plan on ordering my favorite caffeine-alcohol concoction, a little number that the bartender, Sera, invented just for me. She calls it Omen's World, and it's a blended icy drink that has more ingredients than I care to name. I hope that it will give me the power not to leap out at Alexa and tie her down to the table when she first approaches. I'm praying that it will give me the strength not to strip off her clothes and whip that little ass of hers in public, making her whimper and beg for mercy. That wouldn't draw too many raised eyebrows among the clientele of The Cave, but it might scare off my doelike slave before I've truly possessed her. I can't take that chance.

On weekends, The Cave is decorated in different themes. Last Friday, I wandered unknowingly into the era of the Renaissance. Waiters and waitresses, stripped down and spray-painted gold, stood as still as marble statues until someone required a drink. Between 8:00 and midnight, a trio played period pieces on the outdoor patio—which was something to be avoided.

Tonight, The Cave has been transformed into an island paradise. Red and turquoise paper tiki lanterns hang over the bar and pink plastic flamingos reside in planters around the room. Two huge palm trees stand at the entranceway leading into the café, and a few well-waxed surfboards hang overhead menacingly. I resolve not to sit beneath one as I make my way through the café. We live in earthquake central and I'm not in the mood for risks.

People greet me as I brush past them, some calling me Olivia, most calling me Omen, a few brazen ones addressing me as "Mistress." I nod to the different groups, but don't stop in my path, heading directly toward the back of the club.

At The Cave, everyone drinks some sort of coffee drink. That goes without saying. But at night the menu features creative blends of coffee and hard liquor. To stay with the evening's island mood, Kona coffee drinks are listed as half-price on the chalkboard over the bar. When I look, I see that even Sera, the handsome butch girl bartender, is wearing a grass skirt with her usual man's tank top. When she turns to reach for a bottle of Absolut Peppar vodka, I can see her naked ass through the flimsy green leaves.

Others can see it, too, and some can't take their eyes off her.

I've been with the bartender, and when she turns to hand off a drink, she winks at me. I nod back at her. Even tops need to bottom sometimes. When Sera and I were together, I took her down—hard—gave her just what she needed. I made her whimper by the end of the night. It wasn't easy. I had to pull out chains, a riding crop, a bamboo cane. But I took her where she needed to go. That's a rush, I'll tell you. Converting a top into a bottom, even for a solo evening, even for one impassioned moment, can be an explosive interaction. It's like two lionesses fighting in the wild. Untamed. Untamable.

I pass Dante, who shoots me an up-from-under look with his amazing brown eyes. His expression is cowed when he sees me, but he gives me a look I immediately recognize. His look says that he wants more. I stop and motion for him to approach, and when he reaches me I press one palm against his bruised ass and ask him how it feels.

"Good, Mistress O," he says. "I mean, it still hurts. Especially when I sit down."

"Then I did my job right," I tell him. He grins sheepishly and returns to his work. I watch him walk away.

He's dressed in the island theme, too, as are all the waiters and waitresses. He has a vibrant lei made of magenta flowers looped around his neck. The scent is overwhelming, lingering even after he's gone. I stare at him as he serves a nearby table. He's clad in a Hawaiian shirt worn open over nothing and tight white slacks hanging insolently loose on his skinny hips. He's a plasticine-dream—so pale, so perfect.

I continue to make my way through the café, choosing a seat in Nina's section at the far end of the room. Nina works most days during the week and Friday nights. I sit with my back to the wall, Mafia-style. As soon as Alexa comes in, she'll scan the place, and then her eyes will meet mine and she'll know.

While I wait, Nina spots me and comes forward, settling herself at my side and staring at me as if reading my fortune. Or trying to.

"She's coming tonight, isn't she?" Nina asks me after a long moment.

I say, "Yeah, I think so." Not putting a whole lot into the answer. Not giving away my cards. Nina's wearing a short blue sundress cut from a gaudy printed fabric emblazoned with huge golden flowers. The dress hardly covers her cunt when she crosses her legs, which she does. It's obvious that she knows I'm watching, and she gets a smug look on her face.

"You're gonna make her your own, aren't you?" she asks. "You're not going to need anyone else anymore, will you?"

"We've had this conversation before, haven't we, Nina?" I enjoy answering questions with questions, and

I think that my powerful tone should quiet her, but it doesn't.

The jukebox at the front of the café has apparently been programmed to play tropical songs and, up until now, the Aqua Velvets have been the chosen musical entertainment. When their final song ends, Elvis comes booming out of the speakers: "Blue Hawaii." I grimace, but Nina begins to move her body to the beat.

"You'll claim her tonight, won't you, Omen?"

I stop myself from answering right away. I can tell that the words on the tip of my tongue are going to come out too fast, too viciously. Nina doesn't deserve my anger. I take a deep breath, silencing the voice that wants to respond. While Nina waits patiently, I turn my attention to a duo seated two tables away. The man is wearing a screamingly loud Hawaiian shirt whose print makes Nina's dress look tame. He's wearing sunglasses and what appears to be zinc oxide on his nose. His date is a woman wearing frayed cutoff shorts and a tummy-baring halter. I can smell the suntan lotion they've slathered on their bodies from where I'm seated. Some people get way too into a theme.

Nina's still waiting for a response. After a moment, I sigh and ask her, "When did you become a mind reader?"

"What do you mean?"

"Why are you so interested? Why do you care? Are you afraid I'll damage her?" I'm teasing Nina, but not giving her the information she's searching for. She looks at me with her hungry eyes and then twists her newly dyed mane of streaked goldenrod-yellow and sunburst-orange hair and pins it up into a bun. I find it immensely sexual to watch women play with their hair. Nina knows this.

"Where are you gonna take her?" she asks me. "You're not going to stay in The Cave, are you? You're not going to fuck her here." It is a statement, not a question.

I look around the room. There's an attractive drag queen holding court at the bar. He's feminine in his movements—nearly passable—but he's got a loud voice that carries. Even over Elvis. He's not someone I'd want to be next to while courting my future slave.

In the front of the café, at a high table, a man surreptitiously strokes his girlfriend's thigh under the table. I watch with mild interest from my vantage point, and as the woman spreads her legs I can see that she isn't wearing panties. Her date parts her thighs further apart and then slips his fingers inside her.

At the small, round table closest to mine, a man is handcuffed to his Mistress's wrist. He squirms away from her every few moments, and she looks sharply at him, then eyes the bone-handled cane at her side.

"No," I tell Nina finally. "I won't fuck her here. I picked this spot only because it's where she comes to buy her coffee. She knows the location. She's comfortable with it. She won't get lost on her way over. After we chitchat for a few minutes, I'll take her for a late meal somewhere in North Beach. At least, that's the plan for the moment. If she's not hungry, I'll have to think of something else."

"You won't take her back to your place?"

"Not tonight, Nina."

"Oh." She looks down.

She's not expecting me to move, and I quickly lean over and cup her chin in my hand, looking deep into her mesmerizing eyes. Catching her off guard. "Why all the questions?"

She flushes and pulls away violently, nearly upsetting the table.

"Are you jealous?"

"No!" She tries to leave, but I grab her wrist and pull her back down.

"You are," I say, laughing at my stupidity. I've been too overwhelmed with my own many needs to concentrate on hers. "How come I never knew that?"

"You don't read minds as well as I do," she tells me, trying to grin with her wide mouth, but not quite achieving it with the rest of her face. I wonder if those are tears making her eyes shine in the colored light filtering from the tiki lantern overhead. She stands and says, "I'll bring you another espresso if you'd like, Omen. A celebratory one. On me."

"You're okay?" I ask her, meaning it.

She tries for a smile again, this time forcing her face to follow her command. "Sure," she says, "I always knew she was right for you. I mean, the way you draw her, every single detail." She shakes her head, and a few tendrils pull free of the bun. "I'll get that drink."

I nod my thanks as Nina turns toward the doorway and stops. I follow her gaze, knowing, somehow, just who it is she's looking at. Only one person could capture Nina's attention like that tonight.

Alexa stands in the doorway to The Cave, squinting into the room.

"Your Cinderella's here," Nina tells me, as if I didn't know. "Better get into Prince Charming mode."

I don't have the heart to tell her that I'm the evil queen.

"Make that two espressos," I tell Nina. Then I turn my attention on Alexa, watching as she makes her way through the throng of people. She's dressed entirely different from the way I've seen her at the bank, which makes me happy. She knows that much, at least, knows a gray flannel suit would be inappropriate after midnight at The Cave. Instead, she has on a long black jersey dress that hugs her slender form. Her hair, usually up in pins or a French twist, swirls casually loose past her shoulders in a shimmering halo of fire and heat.

I stop myself from putting my hand up and waving to her. I simply lean back, regarding her, waiting for her to look my way. Waiting for her to notice me. She bumps into Nina, who greets her coolly. I see Alexa's eyes widen, wondering if the waitress is the one she's looking for—but knowing, at the same time, that Nina is a sub, Nina's not her match.

She continues in my direction and suddenly lifts her eyes to mine. I don't smile, don't move. I watch the recognition flood through her. I watch her perfect lips curve upward. I watch relief fill her troubled soul.

Elvis finishes singing. "One," a song from U2's *Achtung Baby* album, comes on. Not in the island motif at all, but perfect for the moment. I catch Nina standing by the jukebox, leaning against it and staring at me, and

I smile my gratitude to her. She ducks her head, then wanders back behind the bar. I catch her pouring herself a shot. Then I return to watching my prize.

Alexa's quick now, pushing forward, arriving at my table with rose-flushed cheeks and so much nervous energy crinkling around her that it's nearly audible.

She says, "You…"

And I nod.

She says, "Oh, God, thank God, it's you."

And I stand and open my arms, and take her in.

CHAPTER TWO:
12:10 at The Cave

Alexa's Voice

I want to explain it all to her, and I want to ask too many questions in too short a time. In no time at all. For the first time in my life, I wish that I were psychic, able to send her the questions telepathically and have the answers back in a nanosecond. But I'm not, and I end up tripping over my tongue, repeatedly. I start to speak at least seven different times, stuttering and losing my train of thought.

Omen hushes me, tells me to slow down.

I stare at my fingers, painted a glossy crimson for the evening. Then I take a deep breath and try again, saying, "How...I mean, when...?" She puts her hand on mine and tells me quietly, "Shh, sweetheart, don't rush it. We have all the time in the world. Relax." An easy, warm smile to let me know everything's all right, then softly, "Relax."

"I'm sorry," I say, meaning it, but she shrugs my apology aside.

"You don't have to be sorry for being nervous, young one." She brings my hand to her lips and kisses my fingertips. "Later I'll make you sorry for many other things."

Heat rushes to my face I look around, wanting a glass of water, a shot of hard liquor, something to calm me down. Omen nods to a waitress, and within moments I have a glass of ice water in front of me. That helps, until the man at the table to my right stands abruptly. The lady he's with yanks hard on his wrist, throwing him over her lap with unexpected force. Unexpected by me, anyway. The man moans as his date begins smacking his ass in hard, thrilling strokes. I am spellbound.

The woman says, "I told you, James. I told you not to mess with me tonight."

I stare, wide-eyed, until Omen, showing zero interest in the scene, says "Drink up, Alexa. We're leaving."

I down my glass in a few swallows and set it down on the table, my eyes never leaving the show at my side. Nonplussed, Omen takes me by the hand and leads me from the place. As we walk, she continues to speak to me in her comforting voice, "Didn't you know, Alexa? Didn't you know it was me?"

Omen's power emanates from her. Others, sensing it, step aside—the crowd parting almost down the middle to let us through. And then suddenly, we're on the street, walking, I don't know where. I don't feel in control of my body at all and I let her make all the decisions. She's fine with this unspoken agreement, keeps up a monologue, calming me down with her melodic voice. She says, "Who did you think I would be?"

"I didn't know."

"Who did you want me to be?"

"I didn't even let myself imagine," I tell her.

"But who, if it could have been anyone…?" And I understand what she wants to hear.

"You…" I promise her. "Only you." I pause for a moment and then make sense of her name. I say, "Miss Niles. I always call you Miss Niles."

"Sometimes you call me Olivia," she reminds me.

"Olivia…what?" I need to know.

"Olivia Marina Niles. OMN. Omen. It's how I sign my artwork."

I nod, understanding, and then look her over, wanting to memorize her appearance. She seems to know everything about me. Now I want to know her.

She's wearing black, too. A pair of the sleekest black leather pants I've ever seen and a long-sleeved velvet top tucked in. With a belt. A *belt*—she assured me she'd have it on, and there it is. Oiled leather coiled sinuously around her slender waist. Mocking me. I snake my fingers out to touch it, but Omen grabs my hand again and holds me steady.

"Plenty of time," she assures me. I can hear the humor in her voice. "Plenty of time for everything you want to know and everything you need to feel."

I say, "I know…I know…" and continue my observation of her. She has her hair pulled back off her face and it's slick with some sort of gel; it shines beneath the streetlights. Her eyes, when she turns them on me, are savage. Her body language screams. But when she speaks, her voice is sweet and low. And though the sound of it soothes me, it frightens me, too.

"Are you angry?" I ask, swallowing hard over the lump in my throat, swallowing hard over my anxiously beating heart, "Have I disappointed you? Do you want me less—I mean, now that I'm here?"

She stops walking, pushes me back against the wall of the nearest building, and nearly lifts me off the ground with her strength. I am pinned, frozen, in her power. She says, "No," her voice a hush, a quiet rumble. She says, "I need you. Do you understand that? I have always intended to make you mine. I'm not in this for the thrill of the chase. That's not my style, Alexa."

I tremble. I do not know how to respond.

"Can you fathom what I'm saying, Alexa? Do you understand?"

Finally, finding a reserve of power somewhere deep within myself, I say, "Yes..." She releases me and steps back, seeming to regain control. She takes my hand, and we keep walking.

After a few moments of silence, I say, "Did you know me at the bank before you knew me online?"

She nods.

"When did you know who I was online, then? When did you put my two personalities together?"

"Right away," she says, not looking at me.

"But how?"

"You don't have two personalities," she explains. "You might think you do, but you don't. You have just one. I knew your bank persona. I just sensed it was you online. And when I checked your profile and found that you lived in San Francisco, that simply sealed the deal. It was too much of a coincidence...especially after hearing about your hair. You described yourself extremely well to the throng in The Dangerous Café that night. No one has hair like you do, Alexa." She grabs a handful of it and we stop walking again. I wait for her to kiss me, but she doesn't.

"What's my secret?" I ask then, testing her. She glares at me, her dark eyes flashing, and I realize that there's never a moment with her when I am not afraid. Even when she assures me she's not angry or displeased. It's been this way online, as well. Fear controls each one of my actions. It makes me hesitate before I speak, makes me worry about the response I'll get when I do.

I realize one other thing, as well: I want to be hers. It's all I want in the world.

She says, "You know that I know, Alexa." (Oh, I love the way she says my name.) "You know that I know, but you want me to say it. You want me to whisper in your ear all the things I know about you." And in my head I can suddenly hear her talking dirty to me, can visualize just what it will be like when we make love, when we fuck.

She laughs indulgently, and then explains simply, "You spread your come on the money, Alexa. I don't know why you do it. I could make something up if you want me to. I've dreamed a million reasons why you do it. Maybe you wanted to lure a particular lover into your trap. Maybe you thought you were being daring, being naughty. I don't know why you do it, my young one, but I know just what you do."

And, magically, she reaches into her pocket and pulls out one of the textured tools I use to extract the money cleanly from my drawer at the bank. It's a finger cover—I don't know its name—and it has nubs all around it.

"Am I right?" she asks, moving close.

I nod.

"Are you surprised?"

"You're the only one who ever guessed the source of my perfume," I tell her, and she stops walking again, takes me into her arms, presses her lips to my neck. I think she's going to kiss me, am certain of it, am dying for it. But she doesn't, and after a moment I realize that she's inhaling deeply. Her words are muffled in my hair, but I still hear her. She says, "Your smell. I need it. I can't get enough."

And then we're walking again, and she tells me about my money—money she's withdrawn from my line. And she tells me she'll show it all to me. That she's kept every bill.

"You've been withdrawing money from me for months," I say, stunned.

"Um-hmm." She doesn't look at me when she answers. "That's right."

"But…that must be thousands of dollars…."

She nods, waiting for me to continue my thought process, to make sense of it all—but I can't.

"You're mine," she tells me. "You are mine, Alexa."

And suddenly I understand that everything's going to be all right. And for a moment, at least, my fear leaves me and a warmth fills my body in its stead.

CHAPTER 3:
North Beach Night

Omen's Voice

I take her to my favorite all-night, Italian restaurant in North Beach. It's perfect for a romantic meal, with red-and-white checkered cloths and candles burning in red jars in the center of each table. I order us each a plate of pasta smothered in rich marinara sauce and a glass of red wine. Alexa seems pleased that I have taken control. She needs me to. She has no hold over herself.

Once the waiter has attended to us, I wait for Alexa to have a few sips from her glass of wine. I want her to calm down. I want her to focus on me. Just as she needed to test me, I need to ask her questions, need to hear the answers.

After a few moments, I look at her and ask, "Why did you go online?"

"I bought a computer when I went back to school. I had to have one for compositions—at least, that's what I told myself. The modem was built-in, and it took me only a few weeks to sign up for an online service."

She laughs at herself, and my heart races at the sound. She is beautiful, beyond a level that I realized watching her at the bank. Every motion she makes is dreamy; the way she lifts the wineglass to her lips, the way she tilts her head to the side when she's embarrassed. I want to reach out and grab her by the shoulders. Want to tattoo my name on her heart to let her know just how mine she is. But first I need to pay attention to her story.

Alexa continues, "In the very beginning, I simply looked at the online arena as the neatest form of procrastination I'd ever seen. But then I realized that there were other night owls in the world, and that I could kill an evening listening to them talk, piping in occasionally, myself."

"How long did it take you to talk?"

"A few nights."

"How did you find the rooms you were looking for?"

"I just scanned the lists. I had the time. I don't sleep much, as you well know. I spent hours doing detective work, visiting one location after another. Asking questions. Reading the different profiles until I found like-minded players."

"Did you use more than one name."

She lowers her amazing fire-hued lashes. I want to kick myself as I hear her tell me something I should have known. I thought I was such a fucking good dom, and she's outwitted me. She says, "Vampire," and then waits, thinking I'll be angry. Thinking I'll leave her.

I laugh louder than I have in a long time. The waiter, across the room, turns to stare at me. I say, "That was you? Ohhh, I'm gonna punish you for that one, sweetheart."

She's trembling, but I think that I've put her at ease momentarily. She says, "I couldn't handle you talking to other people. I signed on and saw that you were cruising the rooms, and I made myself available."

"Yes, you did, didn't you?"

"But you left…"

"…wanting you," I explain. "Frustrated beyond belief."

She's proud of herself. I can tell it from her demeanor. I let her bask in the glory of it for a few seconds before leaning forward and drinking in a deep breath. "You're wet," I tell her and her smug smile clicks off and she becomes my doe-eyed sub again. "You gave me the power to know that," I say. "You gave me the scent of your sex; and now, forever, when I smell it on you, I'll know that you're turned on."

She lowers her eyes, which is exactly what I want her to do. I push her wine forward, and when she doesn't take it, I lift her hand and place it on the stem of her glass.

"Drink," I command. She does, still without meeting my gaze. "Now, listen to me," I tell her.

"Yes, Omen," she says.

"If you try to trick me again, in any way, I will discipline you. Severely."

She shudders. It makes me love her all the more.

"I will punish you often, Alexa. Don't worry about

that. I will punish you all the time, little one." Another pause, to watch her face lose its color, to watch her translucent skin become a chalky white with impending shame. I go on, "But in particular, Alexa, if you fuck with me, I will discipline you severely. I will embarrass you."

"Please, Omen..." she says, and I don't know if she wants me to stop, or if she's asking me to do it to her now.

"Can you guess how I'll discipline you?"

She shakes her head.

"Not even one guess?"

Her hair falls forward and frames her lovely face as she shakes her head more drastically, more dramatically.

"Do you know where I'll take you?"

"Where...?"

"Down to the seedier part of North Beach, just a few blocks from here, in fact, where the triple-X theaters are, where the whores walk back and forth, looking for tricks. I'll take you right up to one of them and make you lift your skirt and lower your panties, and then I'll ask her how much she thinks I can get for you. For your cunt."

"You're not serious...." Now she's begging.

"Oh, yes," I tell her. "Oh, yes I am, Alexa. Wanna try me?"

Her mouth is open, and I reach over and shut it for her. Then we stare into each other's eyes, sizing each other up.

"You *are* serious," she says finally.

I nod.

"You'd really do that to me, wouldn't you?"

I nod again.

Oh," she says, then stops as our food arrives.

"Does it shock you? What I just told you. Does that shock you?"

Now it's her turn to nod.

"But you don't doubt me, do you? You don't doubt that I'd do that."

"No, Mistress," she says, the words out of her mouth before she realizes it. She's called me everything but this tonight. She's called me Miss Niles. Olivia. Omen. But not Mistress. And now my heart begins to beat faster with the scent of victory in the air.

"It shocks you, but you're not afraid of me anymore, are you?"

She shakes her head.

"Because you understand that this is how it is between us. What I say will happen, will happen. You can trust me. And when I promise you something, I will never let you down." I take a sip from my own glass of wine. "You want what I have to give, don't you, Alexa?"

"I need it," she says, again seemingly startled by the fact that she's speaking. That she's confessing her secret thoughts aloud, to me. Knowing that I will make them all come true. "I need it, Mistress."

"Anything you need," I say, nodding, motioning for her to eat. "Anything you need, little one. You shall have. All of it, as I promised you. All of it…"

And more.

You have entered Ether. There are 2 people present.

Omen: How do you feel, young one?

Venus: I'm all right.

Omen: Just all right?

Venus: I'm adjusting, I guess.

Omen: To the new situation...?

Venus: To the reality of it all.

Omen: Does your ass still hurt?

Venus: Yes, Mistress. A lot. And it's all red...

Omen: Did you look in the mirror?

Venus: <eyes lowered> Uh-huh. In the bathroom mirror. I stood on the edge of the tub and turned around to see it.

Omen: And you liked what you saw.

Venus: Yes, Mistress.

Omen: Good. I liked it, too. Liked spanking you. That's how your ass should be—raw and red and tender. That's how I'd like to see it all the time...

Venus: <blushing> Did I do okay?

Omen: We weren't playacting, Alexa. You were honest and pure.

Venus: But did I please you?

Omen: You were perfect. You don't have to worry about anything.

Venus: Thank you, Mistress.

Omen: We didn't go too far for you?

Venus: No, Mistress. You made one of my fantasies come true.

Omen: Yeah, I know.... I'm glad to hear it. You'll have to help me out a little, in the beginning. I don't want to move too fast. I want to break you in easy. It's a new world for you.

Venus: When can I see you again?

Omen: Tomorrow night.

Venus: <sighing with relief>
Omen: You *do* want to see me again?
Venus: Don't even joke about it! I need to see you! Please, Mistress…don't make me think you won't let me….
Omen: Shhh…I was teasing you.
Venus: I know, I know. But I'm still shaky. Why wouldn't you let me sleep over? Why wouldn't you let me stay?
Omen: I wanted to give you a little time alone. To think about things.
Venus: Things?
Omen: Your first spanking…
Venus: <sighing> Yes.
Omen: You did like it, didn't you?
Venus: Yes, Mistress.
Omen: Did it embarrass you?
Venus: Yes…
Omen: But you liked it.
Venus: Yes, Mistress.
Omen: What does this tell you?
Venus: I don't know what you mean.
Omen: If this were a lesson in school, you would be able to learn something from it. What would you learn?
Venus: That I get off by being humiliated.
Omen: Did you get off?
Venus: I mean, it turned me on. It made me wet…so wet…my panties were sopping when I took them off.
Omen: Did you come when you got home? Was that the very first thing you did?
Venus: <blushing> Yes, Mistress.
Omen: You blush so pretty, Alexa. I like making you blush. How did you masturbate?

Venus: With my fingers.

Omen: I want you to touch yourself now. What are you wearing?

Venus: My black long johns.

Omen: Pull them down. I'll wait.

Venus: All right, Mistress.

Omen: Slide two fingers into your cunt and squeeze them. You can type with one hand for a few moments. You don't have to call me Mistress while we play this out. You can type in short answers to my questions.

Venus: Yes, Mistress.

Omen: Are you very wet?

Venus: Uh-huh.

Omen: Next time we're together, Venus?

Venus: Yes...

Omen: I'm going to lick your cunt clean with my tongue. Would you like that?

Venus: Ohhh....

Omen: Keep touching yourself. I want you to rub your clit with your thumb. But keep your fingers inside you, all right?

Venus: Yes...

Omen: We'll sixty-nine for a while, I think...but that's not what you need to get off, is it?

Venus: No...

Omen: You need pain, don't you, my girl? Don't you, my sweet thing?

Venus: Yes...

Omen: And humiliation, like when Harley examined you in The Dangerous Café. When he probed you.

Venus: Yes...

Omen: Don't you worry, Alexa. As my property, you will be probed and examined and prodded. I'll slide on a pair of rubber gloves and spread you wide. Check out all your holes. Would you like that? Does that image make you wetter? Tell me honestly, Alexa. Feel deep inside your cunt and tell me if you're wetter....

Venus: I am.

Omen: Good girl...good girl. We are going to have so much fun, Alexa. Our kind of fun. When you walked into The Cave tonight, you saw all sorts of SM couples, didn't you?

Venus: Uh-huh.

Omen: You don't usually go in at night, do you?

Venus: No...

Omen: That couple next to us. The lady spanking her slave boy. That will be you and me, Alexa. You'll be over my lap, getting your ass warmed, and everyone's gonna watch.

Venus: Oh...

Omen: Keep playing with yourself, Alexa...keep it up for me....

Venus: Yes...

Omen: I am going to enjoy showing you off, Alexa. I will take you to all the clubs, to every stage. I will display you and you will bloom in the heat of my power. And Alexa?

Venus: Yes?

Omen: Everyone's gonna see....

Venus: Ohhh...

Omen: Like when you sit on your fire escape, casually playing with yourself. Wondering if anyone's watching you. Just like that. They'll all be watching you.

Venus: Oh...

Omen: Just like I've watched you...

Venus: I'm...

Omen: Come for me, Alexa.

Venus: Yes...yesssss....

Omen: Take a deep breath.... I'll wait while you clean off your fingers.... I mean, I'll wait while you lick them clean.... <sighing> Are you ready, young one? Are you with me again?

Venus: Yes, Mistress. I'm here. That was divine.

Omen: There will be so many lessons, Alexa. You have so much to learn.

Venus: I know, Mistress. I'm a novice. I said so when we first met online. But I really want to learn. I want you to teach me.

Omen: I'm glad...do you have any questions, anything you want to ask me? You were quiet for most of our evening together, weren't you?

Venus: I get shy.

Omen: But you won't be shy with me. Not for long. You'll be subdued. You'll keep your eyes down. You won't disobey me—not unless you want to feel my wrath. But you will get over your shyness.

Venus: Yes, Mistress.... I'm sure you're right.

Omen So, is there anything you want to ask me? Anything you didn't ask tonight, while we were together?

Venus: What will we do tomorrow night?

Omen: Buy you a collar.

Venus: Oh...

Omen: You're mine, aren't you?

Venus: Yes, Mistress.

Omen: Then I want everyone to know.

Venus: Everyone?

Omen: Don't worry, little girl, I'll only take you places where it's acceptable. I won't walk with you down Market Street on a leash...but other places. Clubs. Restaurants. You're okay with this?

Venus: Whatever you say, Mistress?

Omen: Am I going too fast?

Venus: No, Mistress.

Omen: That's good, because I have something else I want to ask you.

Venus: Yes?

Omen: Well, more than ask, I suppose. Tell...

Venus: Yes, Mistress?

Omen: I want you here. In my apartment. I don't want to continue to have to drop you off at night.

Venus: You want me to move in?

Omen: You're mine, aren't you?

Venus: <thrilled> Yes, Mistress.

Omen: Then, yes, I want you to move in.

Venus: Yes, Mistress.

Omen: Do you understand what it means?

Venus: I think so.

Omen: You will obey me, all the time. You will be punished for my pleasure, not only when you misbehave, but when I want to see you cry. I will protect you and love you, and no harm will come to you. I mean that I will not damage you. But I will hurt you. Do you understand?

Venus: Yes, Mistress.

Omen: And do you want this?

Venus: Yes...

Omen: Is there a problem?

Venus: I'd like to address you in a different way. Is that okay?

Omen: What would you most like to call me?

Venus: Omen.

Omen: That's fine. Call me Omen. You and I will understand what it means. If we go somewhere that I want you to address me as Mistress, I will tell you. Is that a deal?

Venus: <grinning> Yes, Omen.

Omen: We speak easier online...at least, you seem to. Can you get over that?

Venus: What do you mean?

Omen: Can you talk to me in person the way you talk to me online?

Venus: I'll try.

Omen: Just because I dominate you doesn't mean I want you to be silent. In fact, the opposite is true. I want you to tell me everything you're feeling, thinking, needing. All right?

Venus: Yes, Omen. Of course.

Omen: I will never leave you, Alexa. That's one thing you don't have to worry about. Do you understand?

Venus: Yes.

Omen: And that should make it easier for you, shouldn't it? If you don't have to worry about me leaving, then you can tell me anything you need, everything you want. Am I right?

Venus: Yes, Omen.

Omen: Then tell me...

Venus: Tomorrow. In person.

Omen: Promise me.

Venus: Yes, Omen. I promise.

CHAPTER 4:
The Collar

Omen's Voice

"You're mine," I tell her. Though she nods as if she understands, I continue. "You're going to be mine. And everyone's going to know." I've told her this much online. I need to tell her in person. I need to make her truly understand the scope of what I'm saying.

She stops walking and gives me a puzzled look, but I override it, pull her hard by the arm and drag her into the leather store. It's about 2:00 A.M., but they're open, of course. They're always open in the Castro. I've waited all day to do this, wondering if she'd ask me about it. She's been silent, though. She hasn't wanted to bring it up. She's frightened.

I scare her a bit more.

"We want a collar," I tell the man behind the counter. Alexa's face couldn't be more red if she painted it. "A thin one," I continue. "To fit her neck."

While we're waiting for the man to find one for us, I turn to Alexa. "I told you I'd buy you one."

She nods and says, "I know."

"But you didn't believe me?"

"I did…I just didn't know how to process the information."

"You don't have to process anything. You just have to wear a collar around your neck, indicating you're mine. Other people will process that information as *they* need to."

In spite of her embarrassment, she grins. I want to explain that the man behind the counter, and the other men in the store, couldn't care less about two dykes buying toys. But I enjoy her discomfort, and I let her wallow in it.

The man looks us both over, completely disinterested, then reaches for a few collars from beneath the glass case. "These will probably fit," he says, "but if you need it tighter, we can add extra holes."

"I can't wear it at the bank," Alexa says in a rush of words.

"Shh." My voice goes cold. "Be quiet."

She's shocked. I haven't spoken to her like this yet. I resolve to shake her up a bit. I'm already coddling her. She needs to know what reality will be like for her now.

"Don't worry," I say, as I fasten the first one around her neck, "I won't make you wear it to work. I told you that last night online. Weren't you listening?"

She lowers her head.

"You were. You just want added assurance, don't you? That's how it is for you, isn't it, Alexa? You need to hear the words from my lips, don't you?"

"Yes," she says softly.

"Well, hear this. You won't wear the collar to work—I don't want to cause you consternation in front of other employees or your bosses. But every night, when you come home, you'll put it on without my reminding you. And every time you and I go out, you'll wear it. Sometimes, I'll put you on a leash."

She shudders.

"I told you that last night. Did you think I was kidding?"

She doesn't know which way to shake her head. She doesn't know what she's thinking anymore. She's mine.

"Does that bother you?" I ask, as I fasten the little buckle as tightly as it goes. I can still slip three fingers between the leather and her skin. Much too loose.

"No." I glare at her to see if she can read the warning in my eyes.

"No, Omen," she corrects herself. Pleasing me.

The salesman watches us, bored out of his mind. I drag Alexa over to him and show him with my fingers under that loop of leather how much tighter it needs to be. He shrugs as I remove it and hand it over. Then, as slowly as is humanly possible, he adds a few extra notches. Alexa is scarlet. I kiss her behind the ear, and then say, in a voice loud enough for all three of us to hear, "When we go outside, I'm going to whip you."

She drags in her breath in a way that makes me fall in love. The man hands over the collar and we try it again. It fits much better. I tell the man we'll buy it. Now Alexa has something new to worry about. She's completely forgotten her need to be embarrassed in front of the salesman. Instead, she's mortified because I'm going to punish her. Within minutes. I've hardly given her any time to "process the information," as she'd say. In a whirlwind of activity, I grab a leash from a rack, pay for both, attach the leash to Alexa's collar, and drag her from the store.

She says, "Omen. Mistress. Please."

I turn on her. "Isn't this what you wanted?"

There are tears in her eyes. Good.

"I—" she starts, completely at a loss.

"You don't know, do you?" I undo the leash, moving forward to take off the collar. Letting her know that once I take it off, we're through. Without realizing what she's doing, she puts her hands up protectively. She wants to keep it on. I have a serious look on my face, but inside, I'm smiling. Inside, I've won.

"Wait," she says, still not realizing what she's done. "I didn't mean that—I just meant—"

"That you're confused," I sound kind again, assuring her.

She starts to smile at me, "Yes," she agrees. "That's it."

"Let me help you," I say, and the nice voice shuts down, and it's the real me. Angry. Harsh. I attach the leash to the loop in the collar and drag her back to my car. I rarely drive it, but I wanted to have wheels tonight. While she stumbles behind me, I let her know exactly what she's in for.

"You're a tease," I tell her. "You teased me. You're going to pay now."

"Mistress," she begs. "Please...I didn't mean to."

"I don't give a shit what you did or didn't mean to do." I press her against the back of my car and lift her skirt. "You behaved in a way that has earned you a whipping."

She doesn't know what she's done. And, in fact, she hasn't really done anything. I warned her I'd do this to her—for my pleasure, at my whim. She didn't believe me. Or she didn't know what it was she was believing in. And now I'm going to show her.

Alexa lowers her head on the cool metal of my car, and she begins to cry. I haven't even touched her yet. I tell her so. "You're crying prematurely, Alexa. You haven't even been punished yet."

She can't speak. She's scared. I decide to go forward, to show her that, yes, it will hurt, but no, it's not the end of the world. I double the leather of the leash in my hand. Alexa's skirt's up, but she still has her panties on. I tell her to lower them and she does, following my orders quickly. Good girl.

Her eyes are shut tightly. Her teeth are clenched. I bring the belt down on her naked skin. She flinches but doesn't cry out. I bring it down again, in the same place, and she moans. I get into a groove, lining up the blows evenly, covering her ass and her thighs, occasionally catching the backs of her knees. After about seven blows, she's crying for real. From pain, not humiliation. I keep going, though, proving to her what she needs to know. That pain will open the door for her, the way giving it opens the door for me. The pain will prove to her that she needs it. That she'll get off on it. That even though she's scared—and I know she's petrified—this will take her higher than she's ever been.

When I finish, she's sobbing. I look at her skin and realize I have taken her a step too far. There are a few drops of blood on the back of her thighs. I bend down behind her and lick them away. I didn't mean to do that—to cut her—and I tell her so.

Her eyes are alight with an inner glow. She can't speak for a moment, and then, choking back a sob, she says, "You marked me."

I nod, stepping away from her, wondering if she'll flee. If I've ruined it when I was only starting.

"Will you mark me permanently?" she asks, and I sigh inwardly with relief. Her face is wet with tears. Her lower lip trembles uncontrollably, as if her teeth are chattering. As if she senses the iciness in my soul. "Will you, Omen? Tattoo me? Brand me? Will you mark me permanently?" There's a longing in her voice that is music to my ears. I take her in my arms and kiss her, lapping at the crystal droplets that drip from her eyelashes. I kiss her, long and slow and deep, and I tell her what I know now to be the truth.

She's mine.

CHAPTER FIVE:
A Lesson in Art

Alexa's Voice:

After the whipping, she brings me to her studio. At first, I think we're going to my apartment, but then she unlocks the outer door to the building across from mine and leads me inside and up seven flights of stairs. As we're walking, I realize that she's the one I've seen watching me. I don't say anything about this—it's as if we've both decided not to mention it.

Once inside her studio, she takes out her books of artwork and spreads them out for me to see. Over the last few months, she has drawn thousands of pictures of me. From every angle, in every style of clothing. I am stunned. I touch the pages, gently, reverently, and then look up at her.

"Why?" I ask her, but she doesn't answer. "Why, Omen? Why did you pick me?"

She shrugs and then helps me up from the sofa and leads me to a wooden jewelry box which stands on the bookcase next to her drawing table. When she opens the box, I get a whiff of a scent that I am more than familiar with. Inside are thousands of dollars. I reach out my hand to them, but Omen takes my hand in hers and brings it to her heart.

"See?" she asks, and I nod. Realizing I'll never really understand how all this happened. I thought I was being outrageous. She's right. She pegged me right on. I thought that I was being dirty, in a way, spreading my come on the bills as I handed them off. Taking my breaks in the bathroom to masturbate. I thought I was sneaky. She caught me. She'll always catch me.

I'm home.

I tell her that I want to see the rest of her artwork, but she says, "Another time, young one," and then leads me to her drawing table.

"What do you want me to do?" I ask.

"Strip."

"What are you going to do to me?"

"Make love to you. That is, fuck you. It's what you need, isn't it, Alexa? I've already whipped you. I know that your panties are sopping. I can sense the changes within your body." She comes forward and takes me in her arms. "I know your scent. And I think I know what each different subtle transformation within your scent means."

I sigh, then move slightly away and peel off my clothes until I'm naked, except for the collar.

"I want you on my table," she says. I climb up onto it carefully and lie down on my back. Her drawing table is made of smooth, sturdy wood. It's larger than any I've seen before; it holds my weight easily.

"Close your eyes," Omen orders. "Put your hands over your head."

I do as she says, and instantly she's captured my hands and tied them together with what feels like a silk scarf. She brings a length of the same fabric over my eyes in a blindfold and ties it at the back of my neck. And then she uses two short pieces of cloth—one for each ankle—to fasten them to the posts of the table.

"I want to make you come," she says. "I've dreamed of the moment."

I swallow hard.

"And I want something else, Alexa..."

"Yes?" I ask.

"I want you to be loud for me."

I feel my limbs jerk against the bindings. My body wants to fold in on itself, but can't.

"I don't know how." I realize I've confessed too much to her. I've told her that I've never moaned, never made noise. Never been fucked. And now she wants to make me go where I haven't, take me to a new level. And I...

"I can't," I say, aloud. She slaps me for it, rocking my head back against the hard wood table.

"You'll do as I say."

"But—"

Another blow makes my head ache.

"You'll do as I say, Alexa."

"Yes, Omen...."

"What I want you to do is relax and enjoy this and let me know that it feels good by the noises you make."

"Yes, Omen," I say, so that she won't slap me again.

The table moves slightly as she climbs onto it and settles herself between my legs. I feel her fingers parting my netherlips. Then there's a long moment while I imagine her observing the way I look. I want to ask if I please her, but I can't make my mouth work.

"You're beautiful," she says softly, assuring me. "Oh, Alexa, so beautiful."

I breathe in deeply as she brings her mouth to my cunt and tastes me.

"I've dreamed..." she says against my pussy, her words vibrating within me. "I've dreamed so often about this moment." And then she stops speaking and begins to work me, her mouth and her tongue, her probing fingers, parting, spreading, dipping inside me. Feasting upon me. And it's all I can do not to scream as her tongue begins to make long, languorous circles. She knows how to do it. She knows everything.

I moan loudly. I can't recognize my own voice. It's low, guttural. I say her name, but she doesn't stop. I wish my hands were free so I could press my fingers to the back of her head and push her harder against me. But it's as if she knows what I was thinking and she begins to play me more powerfully, her fingers thrusting inside me, the flat of her tongue lapping at my clit in wide, voracious strokes.

"Yes," I sigh, swallowing hard, my head thrown back against the table, my hips slamming up and down, as far as the restraints will allow. I can't even feel the heat from the whipping anymore. I'm consumed with need. "Oh, yes. Please, Omen! Please!"

And then she stops, as somewhere inside myself I knew she would. She stops and moves away from my cunt.

"Don't—" I start, before realizing what I've said. She crawls up my body to backhand me.

"You don't give the orders," she says. I sense the smile on her face. This is a lesson. She talked to me about lessons in our online conversation yesterday, and here she is, giving me one in real life. Real time.

"You don't tell me what to do. Do you, Alexa?"

I shake my head.

"But if I ask what you want, you can answer." She strokes my face where she slapped me, feeling the warmth of my skin.

"What do you want, Alexa?" The contractions within my pussy have lessened. The swells of my impending orgasm are receding. I don't know what I want.

I simply say, "Please…"

"Please what, Alexa? How can I know what you want if you don't tell me?"

"You know," I say, without thinking about which words are going to come out of my mouth. I am rocked with the need. My hips slip in wet circles on the table. My entire body is begging. She wants me to beg with my voice. "You know," I say again, slightly louder. "You're teasing me."

"Testing you," she corrects. "Didn't you test me last night? Didn't you ask me if I knew your secret?"

A spark of anger burns within my heart. Self-anger. Why did I test her?

"Yes," I admit, when it's obvious she's not going to

speak again until I do. "Yes, I tested you…and now you're punishing me."

"Punishing?" Her voice is incredulous. "You don't begin to understand the word. Here I am, pleasuring you with my tongue, and you consider it punishment?"

She's fucking with me.

"I don't know," I am confused.

"Then tell me what you want."

"Your mouth on me…"

"Where?"

"On my pussy."

"Wrong answer."

I'm more confused. "What do you want me to say, Omen?"

"Whose pussy?" Suddenly I understand everything.

"Yours." I amend my answer.

"I own you," she says, and my body rocks uncontrollably at the sound of her voice. "I own all parts of you." She cups my cunt with one hand, exerting the slightest bit of pressure. I feel my juices slip between her fingers. "Your head, and your heart, and your pussy. All mine. Do you understand?"

I nod, then answer. "Yes, Omen. Yes."

"Good. Now tell me—what do you want?"

This lesson is too hard. I want only to come. I tell her that. "Please," I say, near tears. "Please make me come. Please let me come. Please…"

She kisses my lips, gently, giving me a taste of myself, and then she relents, sliding down my body, resting again between my legs and releasing me. "Be loud," she says into my cunt. "Be loud for me, Alexa."

And I am so grateful to her that I find my voice. Screaming her name, crying her name, lifting up to meet her mouth with my hips until she grips me to keep me steady. To make me behave.

I have never been unleashed before, never let myself go before. I howl her name as she makes me come. I scream it—"Omen!"—as she makes me come again. And again.

And then, limp and useless, I relax on her table, and…for the first time in what seems like weeks…I sleep.

CHAPTER SIX:
Public Humiliating

Omen's Voice

On Sunday afternoon, I take her to the Baghdad Café in the Castro. No one here minds her leash and collar. In fact, the only glances we get are a few envious ones from a lithe twenty-something lesbian seated at the counter. She can't stop looking at Alexa; and each time she does, she strokes her own bare throat as if wishing for a tight leather choke tag to remind her of her place.

Alexa's eyes are downcast. She hasn't stopped trembling since our morning whipping. I say, "Sweetheart, no one cares about our relationship but us. We're the only people who count. Why are you so embarrassed?"

"I don't know...." Humble, confused. Her fingers flutter to her collar, and I think it must be the daylight hours that are troubling her. At night she has been able to hide.

"Is it the collar?" I want her to be honest with me.

She nods.

"Alexa, there were much more frightening things in the display in the collar store. Didn't you see them? Cock and ball holders, gags, masks, bindings... Other slaves are made to wear much more serious equipment than you. Don't you understand?"

She shakes her head, and her outrageous tortoiseshell hair waves around her face in perfect coils.

"A collar's nothing. The man in the store hardly noticed you as I fit it around your throat," I assure her. "He was much more concerned with the handsome cowboy standing by the lace-up leather chaps."

She sighs, then starts to play with her fork, fiddling with the tines, pressing them into the ball of her thumb to make an imprint, to feel the pain. It soothes her. I know.

"Are you hungry?" I ask my baby, wanting her to snap out of it.

"Just a coffee," she says, her eyes still down. She can't meet my eyes.

"Look out the window." She hears the command in my voice and she turns her head. "Do you see the mountain out there?" I point beyond the stores to a gently sloping hill cresting above. Alexa nods.

"When we're finished here, I'm going to take you up on that hill and whip you. Again."

She looks around frantically, to see if anyone else has heard me. No one has. I repeat it, louder.

"Alexa, when you're finished with your coffee, I am going to take you up on that hill, make you drop your slacks, and I am going to whip you until you cry."

She draws in her breath loudly, then covers her face with her hands. She is nearly crying already.

"Do you understand me? Have I made myself clear?"

She nods, then looks at me, then looks down again, freaked out beyond belief. Finally, in a whisper-soft voice, she says, "Why?"

I grin. "Because you're naughty."

"What did I do?" So soft. So scared.

"Nothing specific. You're just naughty in general." A pause while I regard her. "Aren't you?"

I love the way she blushes. I lift my hand to her cheek and stroke her tender skin. I say, matching her soft tone, "Don't you want me to whip you, Alexa? Isn't that what you've wanted for years and years and years?"

She nods. I want more.

"Tell me," I command. "Tell me that you want this."

"I want this."

"Convince me. Say my name."

"Mistress…" she's guessing.

I shake my head, "Nope. My name."

"Olivia. Omen…"

I nod.

"I want this, Omen. More than anything."

"What makes you come?" I ask, knowing the lawyer's rule. Ask only questions that you know the answers to.

"Pain."

Inside, I tremble for her.

Our waitress comes and I order two coffees, black,

and then sit back and stare at my prize. In the pocket of my leather jacket I have the pair of panties she sent me, still redolent with her scent. In my wallet are bills that were touched with her own juices. I am hungry for her. I will give her what she needs—then I will take what I need. I tell her this and she smiles at me, weakly, for the first time today.

"I want to please you." I hear truth in her voice. "I want to make you happy."

"Subservient one," I call her, reaching across the table to stroke her hair, to play my fingers up and down the ridge of her cheekbones. To learn her features. I will draw her so much better from now on. My pictures will capture the essence of her very soul.

"Have you taken other women up there?" Alexa motions toward the hill with her chin. I want to laugh out loud at her obvious jealousy. I nod.

"Lovers?" I can tell that she is suddenly angry. I nod again.

"Is it your spot, then?" she wants to know. I don't like having things demanded of me, but we're still only beginning, so I let it slide.

"It's hard to find good spots for public punishment," I explain to her, watching her expression change at my words. "People are pretty relaxed about things in the Castro. And up on the hill you can see everything, and everyone who wants to look up can see you. Do you understand?"

"Yes, Omen."

"I won't go too hard on you. I know you've already been whipped this morning. But I want to take you in public. In the daylight. I want you to feel the wind on your ass, cooling you down, while the blows from my belt heat you up."

I think she might pass out. I can't believe my luck in finding someone so pure.

"Now, tell me that you want it."

"I—"

"Alexa." My voice holds a warning that she can't miss. With my eyes I let her know that if she doesn't answer me, I will whip her right here, right now, right over my knee.

"I want it." She sighs as she says it. "I want you to expose me."

That's all I need to hear.

After coffee, we walk up the street to the steps that lead to the hill. On our way, we pass various couples with various pets. Two gay men with long mustaches walking Scottish terriers with matching mustaches. A beautiful redhead with a parrot on her shoulder. Then we pass two dykes on a tandem bicycle—one I recognize from the gym. San Francisco has a fairly-tight-knit community of lesbians. Alexa keeps her eyes lowered, not even looking up when I wave to my gym buddy.

We climb the hill in silence. It's not too steep, but it's a hot day, and we walk slowly. Alexa has a reason to walk slowly. She's scared. Again. I will prove to her, over time, that her fear will fade. But for now, I let her experience it. The prolonged agony that comes with impending doom can only intensify the rush of her pleasure that accompanies pain.

When we reach the top of the first hill, I take her

hand and lead her off the trail. There's a chain-link fence running the length of the hill. At the bottom is a parking lot and a tennis court.

I walk with Alexa a little farther down the side of the hill, taking her directly to the fence and motioning for her to grab onto it with both hands. She does, without asking questions, without offering excuses.

From where we stand, we can see an apartment building several hundred feet away. There are windows open and people standing out on decks. If we look farther, we can see rows of residential streets and houses.

I stand behind Alexa and unbuckle her jeans slowly and lower them down her thighs. She squirms slightly, but then forces herself to stay still. I pull her panties down next and then lift her shirt and tuck it into her bra strap, completely exposing the area from the middle of her back to her knees. Then I take off my belt.

Before I whip her, I place one hand between her legs to feel her cunt. It's wet. I knew it would be. "I could smell you on the walk up," I tell her.

"Yes. I know."

"Count for me," I order her. It will help her keep focused, help her to forget that there are people who can see her, that we could be discovered at any moment.

"Yes, Omen." I start, cutting her low, across the backs of her thighs. She chokes out, "One." I've started hard, and she grips the chain link fence as I line a second blow below the first. "Two," she says, a rush of air, controlling herself. Trying to.

I move closer, doubling the belt tighter in my hand and catching her hard on her still-tender buttocks. She whimpers as she says, "Three." She has a low tolerance. We will work together to strengthen it. I smack the fourth and fifth blows in rapid succession, and her knees buckle. I lean forward, lifting the hair away from her face and whispering into her ear, "There will be twenty. You keep counting."

A deep breath. Then, "Yes, Omen."

And now I lay into her, placing one hand on her lower back, pushing her forward and into the fence, tired of coddling. I give her five quick strokes, let her rest for a moment to hear her sob, and then give her five more. Her knuckles are white from gripping the fence.

"Fifteen," I say calmly. "Only five to go."

She says, "Please...Omen," through her tears.

"Please what? Do you want me to stop."

She doesn't know what she wants, poor thing. She says, "No," while nodding her head yes. I shrug and give her the last five, harder than anything she's felt so far, counting for her because she's crying too hard. Then I motion for her to pull up her pants.

She does, with shaky hands, then crouches in a low squat and continues to cry, loudly, deep sobs that pour from the center of her soul.

"Touch yourself," I command. She looks up at me with haunted green eyes.

"Touch yourself," I repeat. "Put one hand in your jeans and touch your cunt."

She does, then brings her fingertips out and looks down at them. They're glistening with her honey. It makes me laugh. Another lesson for her. I reach down and take her into my arms and she cries even harder. I say softly, "See, Alexa? See, darling? This is what you need."

Then I hold her and rock her and let her cry it all away.

"Are you okay?" I ask finally, concerned that there are so many tears over a mild whipping.

She looks up at me and grins, even though her face is still wet and shiny. And she says one word that makes my heart beat rapidly in my chest: "Paradise."

CHAPTER SEVEN:
The End

Alexa's Voice

It's amazing to me that we're both insomniacs. I believe it must be fate—much more than a coincidence. We are both insomniacs and caffeine freaks. When I get up and check the coffeepot, it's always full. Always. It's as if one of us is perpetually awake, and more often than not, both of us are. Maybe we'll die young because of it. Maybe humans are allotted only a certain numbers of hours to be awake, and we're using them up all at once, but we can't help it.

The dreamy stage that life takes on when you cut back the hours you sleep is transcendent. Yes, it might be hard to string a sentence together, occasionally, but the fucking is unreal. And the pain—it's a higher level. A completely new world.

I've quit my job, which is good. I wouldn't want to be dealing with numbers when I have these few hours under my belt. Besides, Omen says that it doesn't make sense to do something I dislike, and after thinking about it, I realized that I didn't like it at all. Instead, I'm back at school, taking writing classes—but not at SFSU, and not from Professor Greene.

I'm getting better, I think. I'm easier with words, have an easier time expressing myself on paper. I'm fairly certain that Professor Longstreth would be proud of me. Writing is no longer a chore, it's a pleasure. I never thought it would be. Raina read one of my stories aloud in her latest performance piece, and people applauded.

I sat in the audience and looked around me at the others clapping. What a surreal experience. I always knew Raina would accept me.

The piece went like this, in her island way of speaking, making my words a song.

Paradise? Chica, you think you know what paradise is? Let me tell you...let me explain.

Paradise is the look in her eyes in the morning, when she stares down at me in our bed. Paradise is the grin she gives me when she realizes that yes, yes, this is real.

She grabs me around the waist, pulling me to her, pressing her body against mine. She touches my skin and makes me come alive. She kisses my neck and gives me a reason to breathe. She puts her hand on my heart, and it beats at her touch.

Paradise?

Leather on skin in a dimly lit room. Heat and fire and the moisture that clings in glistening beads to her forehead when she whips me.

Paradise is living in her shadow, in her embrace, on the cold stone floor of her heart. It is being a model for her paintbrush, a still life for her charcoal. A canvas for her art.

She paints me all the time. She has a sketchbook in hand wherever we go. Up on our apartment walls are charcoal sketches of my eyes, my mouth, the lines in my skin from her crop. She marks me. She makes me her own. It's all I want to be. It's all I need.

I've dreamed about it, created it in my head for years. I've whispered it to strangers in passing and been denied. She never denies me.

Paradise is residing forever in her embrace.

If Omen approves, I'd like to have that word tattooed somewhere on my body. Just that word, with our initials around it. Symbolizing forever that I've reached it…
Paradise.

You've heard of the writers
but didn't know where to find them

Samuel R. Delany • Pat Califia • Carol Queen • Lars Eighner • Felice Picano • Lucy Taylor • Aaron Travis • Michael Lassell • Red Jordan Arobateau • Michael Bronski • Tom Roche • Maxim Jakubowski • Michael Perkins • Camille Paglia • John Preston • Laura Antoniou • Alice Joanou • Cecilia Tan • Michael Perkins • Tuppy Owens • Trish Thomas • Lily Burana • Alison Tyler • Marco Vassi • Susie Bright • Randy Turoff • Allen Ellenzweig • Shar Rednour

You've seen the sexy images
but didn't know where to find them

Robert Chouraqui • Charles Gatewood • Richard Kern • Eric Kroll • Vivienne Maricevic • Housk Randall • Barbara Nitke • Trevor Watson • Mark Avers • Laura Graff • Michele Serchuk • Laurie Leber • John Willie • Sylvia Plachy • Romain Slocombe • Robert Mapplethorpe • Doris Kloster

You can find them all in
Masquerade

a publication designed expressly for the connoisseur of the erotic arts.

ORDER TODAY
SAVE 50%
1 year (6 issues) for $15; 2 years (12 issues) for only $25!

Essential. —*Skin Two*

The best newsletter I have ever seen! —*Secret International*

Very informative and enticing. —*Redemption*

A professional, insider's look at the world of erotica. —*Screw*

I recommend a subscription to **MASQUERADE**... It's good stuff. —*Black Sheets*

MASQUERADE presents some of the best articles on erotica, fetishes, sex clubs, the politics of porn and every conceivable issue of sex and sexuality. —*Factsheet Five*

Fabulous. —*Tuppy Owens*

MASQUERADE is absolutely lovely ... marvelous images. —*Le Boudoir Noir*

Highly recommended. —*Eidos*

DIRECT

Masquerade/Direct • DEPT BMRB17 • 801 Second Avenue • New York, NY 10017 • FAX: 212.986.7355
MC/VISA orders can be placed by calling our toll-free number: 800.375.2356

☐ PLEASE SEND ME A 1 YEAR SUBSCRIPTION FOR $30 NOW $15!
☐ PLEASE SEND ME A 2 YEAR SUBSCRIPTION FOR $60 NOW $25!

NAME _____
ADDRESS _____
CITY _____ STATE _____ ZIP _____
TEL (___) _____
PAYMENT: ☐ CHECK   ☐ MONEY ORDER   ☐ VISA   ☐ MC
CARD # _____ EXP. DATE _____

No C.O.D. orders. Please make all checks payable to Masquerade/Direct. Payable in U.S. currency only.

MASQUERADE BOOKS

MASQUERADE

ATAULLAH MARDAAN
KAMA HOURI/DEVA DASI
$7.95/512-3
Two legendary tales of the East in one spectacular volume. *Kama Houri* details the life of a sheltered Western woman who finds herself living within the confines of a harem—where she discovers herself thrilled with the extent of her servitude. *Deva Dasi* is a tale dedicated to the cult of the Dasis—the sacred women of India who devoted their lives to the fulfillment of the senses—while revealing the sexual rites of Shiva.

"...memorable for the author's ability to evoke India present and past... Mardaan excels in crowding her pages with the sights and smells of India, and her erotic descriptions are convincingly realistic."
—Michael Perkins,
The Secret Record: Modern Erotic Literature

J. P. KANSAS
ANDREA AT THE CENTER
$6.50/498-4
Kidnapped! Lithe and lovely young Andrea is whisked away to a distant retreat. Gradually, she is introduced to the ways of the Center, and soon becomes quite friendly with its other inhabitants—all of whom are learning to abandon restraint in their pursuit of the deepest sexual satisfaction. This tale of the ultimate sexual training facility is a nationally bestselling title and a classic of modern erotica.

VISCOUNT LADYWOOD
GYNECOCRACY
$9.95/511-5
An infamous story of female domination returns to print. Julian, whose parents feel he shows just a bit too much spunk, is sent to a very special private school, in hopes that he will learn to discipline his wayward soul. Once there, Julian discovers that his program of study has been devised by the deliciously stern Mademoiselle de Chambonnard. In no time, Julian is learning the many ways of pleasure—under the firm hand of this demanding headmistress.

CHARLOTTE ROSE, EDITOR
THE 50 BEST PLAYGIRL FANTASIES
$6.50/460-7
A steamy selection of women's fantasies straight from the pages of *Playgirl*—the leading magazine of sexy entertainment for women. These tales of seduction—specially selected by no less an authority than Charlotte Rose, author of such bestselling women's erotica as *Women at Work* and *The Doctor is In*—are sure to set your pulse racing. From the innocent to the insatiable, these women let no fantasy go unexplored.

N. T. MORLEY
THE PARLOR
$6.50/496-8
Lovely Kathryn gives in to the ultimate temptation. The mysterious John and Sarah ask her to be their slave—an idea that turns Kathryn on so much that she can't refuse! But who are these two mysterious strangers? Little by little, Kathryn not only learns to serve, but comes to know the inner secrets of her stunning keepers.

J. A. GUERRA, EDITOR
**COME QUICKLY:
FOR COUPLES ON THE GO**
$6.50/461-5
The increasing pace of daily life is no reason to forgo a little carnal pleasure whenever the mood strikes. Here are over sixty of the hottest fantasies around—all designed to get you going in less time than it takes to dial 976. A superhot volume especially for couples on a modern schedule.

ERICA BRONTE
LUST, INC.
$6.50/467-4
Lust, Inc. explores the extremes of passion that lurk beneath even the coldest, most business-like exteriors. Join in the sexy escapades of a group of high-powered professionals whose idea of office decorum is like nothing you've ever encountered! Business attire not required....

VANESSA DURIÉS
THE TIES THAT BIND
$6.50/510-7
The incredible confessions of a thrillingly unconventional woman. From the first page, this chronicle of dominance and submission will keep you gasping with its vivid depictions of sensual abandon. At the hand of Masters Georges, Patrick, Pierre and others, this submissive seductress experiences pleasures she never knew existed....

M. S. VALENTINE
THE CAPTIVITY OF CELIA
$6.50/453-4
Colin is mistakenly considered the prime suspect in a murder, forcing him to seek refuge with his cousin, Sir Jason Hardwicke. In exchange for Colin's safety, Jason demands Celia's unquestioning submission—knowing she will do anything to protect her lover. Sexual extortion!

AMANDA WARE
BINDING CONTRACT
$6.50/491-7
Louise was responsible for bringing many prestigious clients into Claremont's salon—so he was more than willing to have her miss a little work in order to pleasure one of his most important customers. But Eleanor Cavendish had her mind set on something more rigorous than a simple wash and set. Sexual slavery!

BUY ANY 4 BOOKS & CHOOSE 1 ADDITIONAL BOOK, OF EQUAL OR LESSER VALUE, AS YOUR FREE GIFT

MASQUERADE BOOKS

BOUND TO THE PAST
$6.50/452-6
Anne accepts a research assignment in a Tudor mansion. Upon arriving, she finds herself aroused by James, a descendant of the mansion's owners. Together they uncover the perverse desires of the mansion's long-dead master—desires that bind Anne inexorably to the past—not to mention the bedpost!

SACHI MIZUNO
SHINJUKU NIGHTS
$6.50/493-3
A tour through the lives and libidos of the seductive East. No one is better than Sachi Mizuno at weaving an intricate web of sensual desire, wherein many characters are ensnared and enraptured by the demands of their long-denied carnal natures.

PASSION IN TOKYO
$6.50/454-2
Tokyo—one of Asia's most historic and seductive cities. Come behind the closed doors of its citizens, and witness the many pleasures that await. Lusty men and women from every stratum of Japanese society free themselves of all inhibitions....

MARTINE GLOWINSKI
POINT OF VIEW
$6.50/433-X
With the assistance of her new, unexpectedly kinky lover, she discovers and explores her exhibitionist tendencies—until there is virtually nothing she won't do before the horny audiences her man arranges! Unabashed acting out for the sophisticated voyeur.

RICHARD McGOWAN
A HARLOT OF VENUS
$6.50/425-9
A highly fanciful, epic tale of lust on Mars! Cavortia—the most famous and sought-after courtesan in the cosmopolitan city of Venus—finds love and much more during her adventures with some of the most remarkable characters in recent erotic fiction.

M. ORLANDO
THE ARCHITECTURE OF DESIRE
Introduction by Richard Manton.
$6.50/490-9
Two novels in one special volume! In *The Hotel Justine*, an elite clientele is afforded the opportunity to have any and all desires satisfied. *The Villa Sin* is inherited by a beautiful woman who soon realizes that the legacy of the ancestral estate includes bizarre erotic ceremonies.

CHET ROTHWELL
KISS ME, KATHERINE
$5.95/410-0
Beautiful Katherine can hardly believe her luck. Not only is she married to the charming and oh-so-agreeable Nelson, she's free to live out all her erotic fantasies with other men. Katherine's desires are more than any one man can handle.

MARCO VASSI
THE STONED APOCALYPSE
$5.95/401-1/mass market
"Marco Vassi is our champion sexual energist." —VLS
During his lifetime, Marco Vassi praised by writers as diverse as Gore Vidal and Norman Mailer, and his reputation was worldwide. *The Stoned Apocalypse* is Vassi's autobiography; chronicling a cross-country trip on America's erotic byways, it offers a rare glimpse of a generation's sexual imagination.

ROBIN WILDE
TABITHA'S TICKLE
$6.50/468-2
Tabitha's back! The story of this vicious vixen—and her torturously tantalizing cohorts—didn't end with *Tabitha's Tease*. Once again, men fall under the spell of scrumptious co-eds and find themselves enslaved to demands and desires they never dreamed existed. Think it's a man's world? Guess again. With Tabitha around, no man gets what he wants until she's completely satisfied—and, maybe, not even then....

TABITHA'S TEASE
$5.95/387-2
When poor Robin arrives at The Valentine Academy, he finds himself subject to the torturous teasing of Tabitha—the Academy's most notoriously domineering co-ed. But Tabitha is pledge-mistress of a secret sorority dedicated to enslaving young men. Robin finds himself the utterly helpless (and wildly excited) captive of Tabitha & Company's weird desires! A marathon of ticklish torture!

ERICA BRONTE
PIRATE'S SLAVE
$5.95/376-7
Lovely young Erica is stranded in a country where lust knows no bounds. Desperate to escape, she finds herself trading her firm, luscious body to any and all men willing and able to help her. Her adventure has its ups and downs, ins and outs—all to the undeniable pleasure of lusty Erica!

CHARLES G. WOOD
HELLFIRE
$5.95/358-9
A vicious murderer is running amok in New York's sexual underground—and Nick O'Shay, a virile detective with the NYPD, plunges deep into the case. He soon becomes embroiled in an elusive world of fleshly extremes, hunting a madman seeking to purge America with fire and blood sacrifices. Set in New York's infamous sexual underground.

CLAIRE BAEDER, EDITOR
LA DOMME: A DOMINATRIX ANTHOLOGY
$5.95/366-X
A steamy smorgasbord of female domination! Erotic literature has long been filled with heartstopping portraits of domineering women, and now the most memorable have been brought together in one beautifully brutal volume. A must for all fans of true Woman Power.

MASQUERADE BOOKS

CHARISSE VAN DER LYN
SEX ON THE NET
$5.95/399-6
Electrifying erotica from one of the Internet's hottest and most widely read authors. Encounters of all kinds—straight, lesbian, dominant/submissive and all sorts of extreme passions—are explored in thrilling detail.

STANLEY CARTEN
NAUGHTY MESSAGE
$5.95/333-3
Wesley Arthur discovers a lascivious message on his answering machine. Aroused beyond his wildest dreams by the acts described, Wesley becomes obsessed with tracking down the woman behind the seductive voice. His search takes him through strip clubs, sex parlors and no-tell motels—and finally to his randy reward....

AKBAR DEL PIOMBO
DUKE COSIMO
$4.95/3052-0
A kinky romp played out against the boudoirs, bathrooms and ballrooms of the European nobility, who seem to do nothing all day except each other. The lifestyles of the rich and licentious are revealed in all their glory.

A CRUMBLING FAÇADE
$4.95/3043-1
The return of that incorrigible rogue, Henry Pike, who continues his pursuit of sex, fair or otherwise, in the most elegant homes of the most debauched aristocrats.

CAROLE REMY
FANTASY IMPROMPTU
$6.50/513-1
A mystical, musical journey into the deepest recesses of a woman's soul. Kidnapped and held in a remote island retreat, Chantal—a renowned erotic writer—finds herself catering to every sexual whim of the mysterious and arousing Bran. Bran is determined to bring Chantal to a full embracing of her sensual nature, even while revealing himself to be something far more than human....

BEAUTY OF THE BEAST
$5.95/332-5
A shocking tell-all, written from the point-of-view of a prize-winning reporter. And what reporting she does! All the secrets of an uninhibited life are revealed, and each lusty tableau is painted in glowing colors.

DAVID AARON CLARK
THE MARQUIS DE SADE'S JULIETTE
$4.95/240-X
The Marquis de Sade's infamous Juliette returns—and emerges as the most perverse and destructive nightstalker modern New York will ever know. One by one, the innocent are drawn in by Juliette's empty promise of immortality, only to fall prey to her strange and deadly lusts.

ANONYMOUS
NADIA
$5.95/267-1
Follow the delicious but neglected Nadia as she works to wring every drop of pleasure out of life—despite an unhappy marriage. A classic title providing a peek into the secret sexual lives of another time and place.

NIGEL McPARR
THE TRANSFORMATION OF EMILY
$6.50/519-0
The shocking story of Emily Johnson, live-in domestic. Without warning, Emily finds herself dismissed by her mistress, and sent to serve at Lilac Row—the home of Charles and Harriet Godwin. In no time, Harriet has Emily doing things she'd never dreamed would be required of her—all involving the erotic discipline Harriet imposes with relish. Little does Emily realize that, as strict and punishing as Harriet Godwin is, nothing could compare to the rigors of her next "position...."

THE STORY OF A VICTORIAN MAID
$5.95/241-8
What were the Victorians really like? Chances are, no one believes they were as stuffy as their Queen, but who would have imagined such unbridled libertines!

TITIAN BERESFORD
CINDERELLA
$6.50/500-X
Beresford triumphs again with this intoxicating tale, filled with castle dungeons and tightly corseted ladies-in-waiting, naughty viscounts and impossibly cruel masturbatrixes—nearly every conceivable method of erotic torture is explored and described in lush, vivid detail.

JUDITH BOSTON
$6.50/525-5
Young Edward would have been lucky to get the stodgy old companion he thought his parents had hired for him. Instead, an exquisite woman arrives at his door, and Edward finds his lewd behavior never goes unpunished by the unflinchingly severe Judith Boston! Together they take the downward path to perversion!

NINA FOXTON
$5.95/443-7
An aristocrat finds herself bored by run-of-the-mill amusements for "ladies of good breeding." Instead of taking tea with proper gentlemen, naughty Nina "milks" them of their most private essences. No man ever says "No" to Nina!

P. N. DEDEAUX
THE NOTHING THINGS
$5.95/404-6
Beta Beta Rho—highly exclusive and widely honored—has taken on a new group of pledges. The five women will be put through the most grueling of ordeals, and punished severely for any shortcomings—much to everyone's delight!

BUY ANY 4 BOOKS & CHOOSE 1 ADDITIONAL BOOK, OF EQUAL OR LESSER VALUE, AS YOUR FREE GIFT

MASQUERADE BOOKS

LYN DAVENPORT
THE GUARDIAN II
$6.50/505-0
The tale of Felicia Brookes—the lovely young woman held in submission by the demanding Sir Rodney Wentworth—continues in this volume of sensual surprises. No sooner has Felicia come to love Rodney than she discovers that she must now accustom herself to the guardianship of the debauched Duke of Smithton. Surely Rodney will rescue her from the domination of this stranger. *Won't he?*

DOVER ISLAND
$5.95/384-8
Dr. David Kelly has planted the seeds of his dream—a Corporal Punishment Resort. Soon, many people from varied walks of life descend upon this isolated retreat, intent on fulfilling their every desire. Including Marcy Harris, the perfect partner for the lustful Doctor....

THE GUARDIAN
$5.95/371-6
Felicia grew up under the tutelage of the lash—and she learned her lessons well. Sir Rodney Wentworth has long searched for a woman capable of fulfilling his cruel desires, and after learning of Felicia's talents, sends for her. Felicia discovers that the "position" offered her is delightfully different than anything she could have expected!

LIZBETH DUSSEAU
THE APPLICANT
$6.50/501-8
"Adventuresome young women who enjoys being submissive sought by married couple in early forties. Expect no limits." Hilary answers an ad, hoping to find someone who can meet her special needs. The beautiful Liza turns out to be a flawless mistress, and together with her husband, Oliver, she trains Hilary to be the perfect servant.

ANTHONY BOBARZYNSKI
STASI SLUT
$4.95/3050-4
Adina lives in East Germany, where she can only dream about the freedoms of the West. But then she meets a group of ruthless and corrupt STASI agents. They use her body for their own perverse gratification, while she opts to use her talents and attractions in a final bid for total freedom!

JOCELYN JOYCE
PRIVATE LIVES
$4.95/309-0
The lecherous habits of the illustrious make for a sizzling tale of French erotic life. A widow has a craving for a young busboy; he's sleeping with a rich businessman's wife; her husband is minding his sex business elsewhere! Sexual entanglements run through this tale of upper crust lust!

SARAH JACKSON
SANCTUARY
$5.95/318-X
Sanctuary explores both the unspeakable debauchery of court life and the unimaginable privations of monastic solitude, leading the voracious and the virtuous on a collision course that brings history to throbbing life.

THE WILD HEART
$4.95/3007-5
A luxury hotel is the setting for this artful web of sex, desire, and love. A newlywed sees sex as a duty, while her hungry husband tries to awaken her to its tender joys. A Parisian entertains wealthy guests for the love of money. Each episode provides a new variation in this lusty Grand Hotel!

LOUISE BELHAVEL
FRAGRANT ABUSES
$4.95/88-2
The saga of Clara and Iris continues as the now-experienced girls enjoy themselves with a new circle of worldly friends whose imaginations match their own. Perversity follows the lusty ladies around the globe!

SARA H. FRENCH
MASTER OF TIMBERLAND
$5.95/327-9
A tale of sexual slavery at the ultimate paradise resort. One of our bestselling titles, this trek to Timberland has ignited passions the world over—and stands poised to become one of modern erotica's legendary tales.

MARY LOVE
MASTERING MARY SUE
$5.95/351-1
Mary Sue is a rich nymphomaniac whose husband is determined to declare her mentally incompetent and gain control of her fortune. He brings her to a castle where, to Mary Sue's delight, she is unleashed for a veritable sex-fest!

THE BEST OF MARY LOVE
$4.95/3099-7
Mary Love leaves no coupling untried and no extreme unexplored in these scandalous selections from *Mastering Mary Sue*, *Ecstasy on Fire*, *Vice Park Place*, *Wanda*, and *Naughtier at Night*.

AMARANTHA KNIGHT
THE DARKER PASSIONS: THE PICTURE OF DORIAN GRAY
$6.50/342-2
Amarantha Knight takes on Oscar Wilde, resulting in a fabulously decadent tale of highly personal changes. One young man finds his most secret desires laid bare by a portrait far more revealing than he could have imagined....

THE DARKER PASSIONS READER
$6.50/432-1
The best moments from Knight's phenomenally popular Darker Passions series. Here are the most eerily erotic passages from her acclaimed sexual reworkings of *Dracula*, *Frankenstein*, *Dr. Jekyll & Mr. Hyde* and *The Fall of the House of Usher*.

THE DARKER PASSIONS: THE FALL OF THE HOUSE OF USHER
$6.50/528-X
The Master and Mistress of the house of Usher indulge in every form of decadence, and initiate their guests into the many pleasures to be found in utter submission.

MASQUERADE BOOKS

**THE DARKER PASSIONS:
DR. JEKYLL AND MR. HYDE**
$4.95/227-2
It is a story of incredible transformations achieved through mysterious experiments. Explore the steamy possibilities of a tale where no one is quite who—or what—they seem. Victorian bedrooms explode with hidden demons!

THE DARKER PASSIONS: FRANKENSTEIN
$5.95/248-5
What if you could create a living human? What shocking acts could it be taught to perform, to desire? Find out what pleasures await those who play God....

THE DARKER PASSIONS: DRACULA
$5.95/326-0
The infamous erotic retelling of the Vampire legend. "Well-written and imaginative, Amarantha Knight gives fresh impetus to this myth, taking us through the sexual and sadistic scenes with details that keep us reading.... A classic in itself has been added to the shelves."
—Divinity

THE PAUL LITTLE LIBRARY

**PECULIAR PASSIONS OF LADY MEG/
LOVE SLAVE**
$8.95/529-8/Trade paperback
Two classics from modern erotica's most popular author! What are the sexy secrets *Lady Meg* hides? What are the appetites that lurk beneath the surface of this irresistible vixen? What does it take to be the perfect instrument of pleasure—or go about acquiring a willing *Love Slave* of one's own? Paul Little spares no detail!

THE BEST OF PAUL LITTLE
$6.50/469-0
Known throughout the world for his fantastic portrayals of punishment and pleasure, Little never fails to push readers over the edge of sensual excitement.

ALL THE WAY
$6.95/509-3
Two excruciating novels from Paul Little in one hot volume! *Going All the Way* features an unhappy man who tries to purge himself of the memory of his lover with a series of quirky and uninhibited lovers. *Pushover* tells the story of a serial spanker and his celebrated exploits.

THE DISCIPLINE OF ODETTE
$5.95/334-1
Odette was sure marriage would rescue her from her family's "corrections." To her horror, she discovers that her beloved has also been raised on discipline. A shocking erotic coupling!

THE PRISONER
$5.95/330-9
Judge Black has built a secret room below a penitentiary, where he sentences the prisoners to hours of exhibition and torment while his friends watch. Judge Black's House of Corrections is equipped with one purpose in mind: to administer his own brand of rough justice!

TEARS OF THE INQUISITION
$4.95/146-2
The incomparable Paul Little delivers a staggering account of pleasure and punishment. "There was a tickling inside her as her nervous system reminded her she was ready for sex. But before her was...the Inquisitor!"

DOUBLE NOVEL
$4.95/86-6
The Metamorphosis of Lisette Joyaux tells the story of a young woman initiated into an incredible world of lesbian lusts. *The Story of Monique* reveals the twisted sexual rituals that beckon the ripe and willing Monique.

CHINESE JUSTICE AND OTHER STORIES
$4.95/153-5
The story of the excruciating pleasures and delicious punishments inflicted on foreigners under the leaders of the Boxer Rebellion. Each woman is brought before the authorities and grilled, to the delight of their perverse captors.

CAPTIVE MAIDENS
$5.95/440-2
Three beautiful young women find themselves powerless against the debauched landowners of 1824 England. They are banished to a sexual slave colony, and corrupted by every imaginable perversion.

SLAVE ISLAND
$5.95/441-0
A leisure cruise is waylaid by Lord Henry Philbrock, a sadistic genius. The ship's passengers are kidnapped and spirited to his island prison, where the women are trained to accommodate the most bizarre sexual cravings of the rich, the famous, the pampered and the perverted.

ALIZARIN LAKE

SEX ON DOCTOR'S ORDERS
$5.95/402-X
Beth, a nubile young nurse, uses her considerable skills to further medical science by offering incomparable and insatiable assistance in the gathering of important specimens. Soon, an assortment of randy characters is lending a hand in this highly erotic work.

THE EROTIC ADVENTURES OF HARRY TEMPLE
$4.95/127-6
Harry Temple's memoirs chronicle his amorous adventures from his initiation at the hands of insatiable sirens, through his stay at a house of hot repute, to his encounters with a chastity-belted nympho!

JOHN NORMAN

TARNSMAN OF GOR
$6.95/486-0
This controversial series returns! Tarl Cabot is transported to Gor. He must quickly accustom himself to the ways of this world, including the caste system which exalts some as Priest-Kings or Warriors, and debases others as slaves. A spectacular unfolds in this first volume of John Norman's Gorean series.

BUY ANY 4 BOOKS & CHOOSE 1 ADDITIONAL BOOK, OF EQUAL OR LESSER VALUE, AS YOUR FREE GIFT

MASQUERADE BOOKS

OUTLAW OF GOR
$6.95/487-9
In this second volume, Tarl Cabot returns to Gor, where he might reclaim both his woman and his role of Warrior. But upon arriving, he discovers that his name, his city and the names of those he loves have become unspeakable. Cabot has become an outlaw, and must discover his new purpose on this strange planet, where danger stalks the outcast, and even simple answers have their price....

PRIEST-KINGS OF GOR
$6.95/488-7
Tarl Cabot searches for the truth about his lovely wife Talena. Does she live, or was she destroyed by the mysterious, all-powerful Priest-Kings? Cabot is determined to find out—even while knowing that no one who has approached the mountain stronghold of the Priest-Kings has ever returned alive....

NOMADS OF GOR
$6.50/527-2
Another provocative trip to the barbaric and mysterious world of Gor. Norman's heroic Tarnsman finds his way across this Counter-Earth, pledged to serve the Priest-Kings in their quest for survival. Unfortunately for Cabot, his mission leads him to the savage Wagon People—nomads who may very well kill before surrendering any secrets....

RACHEL PEREZ

AFFINITIES
$4.95/113-6
"Kelsy had a liking for cool upper-class blondes, the long-legged girls from Lake Forest and Winnetka who came into the city to cruise the lesbian bars on Halsted, looking for breathless ecstasies...." A scorching tale of lesbian libidos unleashed, from a writer more than capable of exploring every nuance of female passion in vivid detail.

SYDNEY ST. JAMES

RIVE GAUCHE
$5.95/317-1
The Latin Quarter, Paris, circa 1920. Expatriate bohemians couple with abandon—before eventually abandoning their ambitions amidst the intoxicating temptations waiting to be indulged in every bedroom.

GARDEN OF DELIGHT
$4.95/3058-X
A vivid account of sexual awakening that follows an innocent but insatiably curious young woman's journey from the furtive, forbidden joys of dormitory life to the unabashed carnality of the wild world.

DON WINSLOW

THE FALL OF THE ICE QUEEN
$6.50/520-5
She was the most exquisite of his courtiers: the beautiful, aloof woman whom Rahn the Conqueror chose as his Consort. But the regal disregard with which she treated Rahn was not to be endured. It was decided that she would submit to his will, and learn to serve her lord in the fashion he had come to expect. And as so many knew, Rahn's depraved expectations have made his court infamous....

PRIVATE PLEASURES
$6.50/504-2
An assortment of sensual encounters designed to appeal to the most discerning reader. Frantic voyeurs, licentious exhibitionists, and everyday lovers are here displayed in all their wanton glory—proving again that fleshly pleasures have no more apt chronicler than Don Winslow.

THE INSATIABLE MISTRESS OF ROSEDALE
$6.50/494-1
The story of the perfect couple: Edward and Lady Penelope, who reside in beautiful and mysterious Rosedale manor. While Edward is a true connoisseur of sexual perversion, it is Lady Penelope whose mastery of complete sensual pleasure makes their home infamous. Indulging one another's bizarre whims is a way of life for this wicked couple, and none who encounter the extravagances of Rosedale will forget what they've learned....

SECRETS OF CHEATEM MANOR
$6.50/434-8
Edward returns to his late father's estate, to find it being run by the majestic Lady Amanda. Edward can hardly believe his luck—Lady Amanda is assisted by her two beautiful, lonely daughters, Catherine and Prudence. What the randy young man soon comes to realize is the love of discipline that all three beauties share.

KATERINA IN CHARGE
$5.95/409-7
When invited to a country retreat by a mysterious couple, two randy young ladies can hardly resist! But do they have any idea what they're in for? Whatever the case, the imperious Katerina will make her desires known very soon—and demand that they be fulfilled... Sexual innocence subjugated and defiled.

THE MANY PLEASURES OF IRONWOOD
$5.95/310-4
Seven lovely young women are employed by The Ironwood Sportsmen's Club, where their natural talents are put to creative use. A small and exclusive club with seven carefully selected sexual connoisseurs, Ironwood is dedicated to the relentless pursuit of sensual pleasure.

CLAIRE'S GIRLS
$5.95/442-9
You knew when she walked by that she was something special. She was one of Claire's girls, a woman carefully dressed and groomed to fill a role, to capture a look, to fit an image crafted by the sophisticated proprietress of an exclusive escort agency. High-class whores blow the roof off in this blow-by-blow account of life behind the closed doors of a sophisticated brothel.

N. WHALLEN

TAU'TEVU
$6.50/426-7
In a mysterious land, the statuesque and beautiful Vivian learns to subject herself to the hand of a mysterious man. He systematically helps her prove her own strength, and brings to life in her an unimagined sensual fire. But who is this man, who goes only by the name of Orpheo?

MASQUERADE BOOKS

COMPLIANCE
$5.95/356-2
Fourteen stories exploring the pleasures of ultimate release. Characters from all walks of life learn to trust in the skills of others, hoping to experience the thrilling liberation of sexual submission. Here are the many joys to be found in some of the most forbidden sexual practices around....

THE CLASSIC COLLECTION
PROTESTS, PLEASURES, RAPTURES
$5.95/400-3
Invited for an allegedly quiet weekend at a country vicarage, a young woman is stunned to find herself surrounded by shocking acts of sexual sadism. Soon, her curiosity is piqued, and she begins to explore her own capacities for cruelty. The ultimate tale of an extraordinary woman's erotic awakening.

THE YELLOW ROOM
$5.95/378-3
The "yellow room" holds the secrets of lust, lechery, and the lash. There, bare-bottomed, spread-eagled, and open to the world, demure Alice Darvell soon learns to love her lickings. In the second tale, hot heiress Rosa Coote and her lusty servants whip up numerous adventures in punishment and pleasure.

SCHOOL DAYS IN PARIS
$5.95/325-2
The rapturous chronicles of a well-spent youth! Few Universities provide the profound and pleasurable lessons one learns in after-hours study—particularly if one is young and available, and lucky enough to have Paris as a playground. A stimulating look at the pursuits of young adulthood.

MAN WITH A MAID
$4.95/307-4
The adventures of Jack and Alice have delighted readers for eight decades! A classic of its genre, *Man with a Maid* tells an outrageous tale of desire, revenge, and submission. This tale qualifies as one of the world's most popular adult novels—with over 200,000 copies in print!

CONFESSIONS OF A CONCUBINE III: PLEASURE'S PRISONER
$5.95/357-0
Filled with pulse-pounding excitement—including a daring escape from the harem and an encounter with an unspeakable sadist—*Pleasure's Prisoner* adds an unforgettable chapter to this thrilling confessional.

CLASSIC EROTIC BIOGRAPHIES
JENNIFER
$4.95/107-1
The return of one of the Sexual Revolution's most notorious heroines. From the bedroom of a notoriously insatiable dancer to an uninhibited ashram, *Jennifer* traces the exploits of one thoroughly modern woman as she lustfully explores the limits of her own sexuality.

JENNIFER III
$5.95/292-2
The further adventures of erotica's most daring heroine. Jennifer has a photographer's eye for details—particularly of the masculine variety! One by one, her subjects submit to her demands for sensual pleasure, becoming part of her now-infamous gallery of erotic conquests.

RHINOCEROS

KATHLEEN K.
SWEET TALKERS
$6.95/516-6
Kathleen K. ran a phone-sex company in the late 80s, and she opens up her diary for a very thought provoking peek at the life of a phone-sex operator. Transcripts of actual conversations are included.

"If you enjoy eavesdropping on explicit conversations about sex... this book is for you." —*Spectator*

"Highly recommended." —*Shiny International*
Trade /$12.95/192-6

THOMAS S. ROCHE
DARK MATTER
$6.95/484-4
"*Dark Matter* is sure to please gender outlaws, body-mod junkies, goth vampires, boys who wish they were dykes, and anybody who's not to sure where the fine line should be drawn between pleasure and pain. It's a handful." —Pat Califia

"Here is the erotica of the cumming millenium.... You will be deliciously disturbed, but never disappointed." —Poppy Z. Brite

NOIROTICA: AN ANTHOLOGY OF EROTIC CRIME STORIES
$6.95/390-2
A collection of darkly sexy tales, taking place at the crossroads of the crime and erotic genres. Thomas S. Roche has gathered together some of today's finest writers of sexual fiction, all of whom explore the murky terrain where desire runs irrevocably afoul of the law.

ROMY ROSEN
SPUNK
$6.95/492-5
Casey, a lovely model poised upon the verge of super-celebrity, falls for an insatiable young rock singer—not suspecting that his sexual appetite has led him to experiment with a dangerous new aphrodisiac. Casey becomes an addict, and her craving plunges her into a strange underworld, where the only chance for redemption lies with a shadowy young man with a secret of his own.

BUY ANY 4 BOOKS & CHOOSE 1 ADDITIONAL BOOK, OF EQUAL OR LESSER VALUE, AS YOUR FREE GIFT

MASQUERADE BOOKS

MOLLY WEATHERFIELD
CARRIE'S STORY
$6.95/485-2
"I had been Jonathan's slave for about a year when he told me he wanted to sell me at an auction. I wasn't in any condition to respond when he told me this..." Desire and depravity run rampant in this story of uncompromising mastery and irrevocable submission. A unique piece of erotica that is both thoughtful and hot!
"I was stunned by how well it was written and how intensely foreign I found its sexual world.... And, since this is a world I don't frequent... I thoroughly enjoyed the National Geo tour." —bOING bOING

"Hilarious and harrowing... just when you think things can't get any wilder, they do." —Black Sheets

CYBERSEX CONSORTIUM
CYBERSEX: THE PERV'S GUIDE TO FINDING SEX ON THE INTERNET
$6.95/471-2
You've heard the objections: cyberspace is soaked with sex. Okay—so where is it!? Tracking down the good stuff—the real good stuff—can waste an awful lot of expensive time, and frequently leave you high and dry. The Cybersex Consortium presents an easy-to-use guide for those intrepid adults who know what they want. No horny hacker can afford to pass up this map to the kinkiest rest stops on the Info Superhighway.

AMELIA G, EDITOR
BACKSTAGE PASSES
$6.95/438-0
Amelia G, editor of the goth-sex journal *Blue Blood*, has brought together some of today's most irreverent writers, each of whom has outdone themselves with an edgy, antic tale of modern lust. Punks, metalheads, and grunge-trash roam the pages of *Backstage Passes*, and no one knows their ways better...

GERI NETTICK WITH BETH ELLIOT
MIRRORS: PORTRAIT OF A LESBIAN TRANSSEXUAL
$6.95/435-6
The alternately heartbreaking and empowering story of one woman's long road to full selfhood. Born a male, Geri Nettick knew something just didn't fit. And even after coming to terms with her own gender dysphoria—and taking steps to correct it—she still fought to be accepted by the lesbian feminist community to which she felt she belonged. A fascinating, true tale of struggle and discovery.

DAVID MELTZER
UNDER
$6.95/290-6
The story of a 21st century sex professional living at the bottom of the social heap. After surgeries designed to increase his physical allure, corrupt government forces drive the cyber-gigolo underground—where even more bizarre cultures await him.

ORF
$6.95/110-1
He is the ultimate musician-hero—the idol of thousands, the fevered dream of many more. And like many musicians before him, he is misunderstood, misused—and totally out of control. Every last drop of feeling is squeezed from a modern-day troubadour and his lady love.

LAURA ANTONIOU, EDITOR
NO OTHER TRIBUTE
$6.95/294-9
A collection sure to challenge Political Correctness in a way few have before, with tales of women kept in bondage to their lovers by their deepest passions. Love pushes these women beyond acceptable limits, rendering them helpless to deny anything to the men and women they adore. A volume dedicated to all Slaves of Desire.

SOME WOMEN
$6.95/300-7
Over forty essays written by women actively involved in consensual dominance and submission. Professional mistresses, lifestyle leatherdykes, whipmakers, titleholders—women from every conceivable walk of life lay bare their true feelings about explosive issues.

BY HER SUBDUED
$6.95/281-7
These tales all involve women in control—of their lives, their loves, their men. So much in control that they can remorselessly break rules to become powerful goddesses of the men who sacrifice all to worship at their feet.

TRISTAN TAORMINO & DAVID AARON CLARK, EDITORS
RITUAL SEX
$6.95/391-0
While many people believe the body and soul to occupy almost completely independent realms, the many contributors to *Ritual Sex* know—and demonstrate—that the two share more common ground than society feels comfortable acknowledging. From personal memoirs of ecstatic revelation, to fictional quests to reconcile sex and spirit, *Ritual Sex* provides an unprecedented look at private life.

TAMMY JO ECKHART
PUNISHMENT FOR THE CRIME
$6.95/427-5
Peopled by characters of rare depth, these stories explore the true meaning of dominance and submission. From an encounter between two of society's most despised individuals, to the explorations of longtime friends, these tales take you where few others have ever dared....

AMARANTHA KNIGHT, EDITOR
SEDUCTIVE SPECTRES
$6.95/464-X
Breathtaking tours through the erotic supernatural via the macabre imaginations of today's best writers. Never before have ghostly encounters been so alluring; thanks to a cast of otherworldly characters well-acquainted with the pleasures of the flesh.

MASQUERADE BOOKS

SEX MACABRE
$6.95/392-9
Horror tales designed for dark and sexy nights. Amarantha Knight—the woman behind the Darker Passions series—has gathered together erotic stories sure to make your skin crawl, and heart beat faster.

FLESH FANTASTIC
$6.95/352-X
Humans have long toyed with the idea of "playing God": creating life from nothingness, bringing life to the inanimate. Now Amarantha Knight collects stories exploring not only the act of Creation, but the lust that follows....

GARY BOWEN

DIARY OF A VAMPIRE
$6.95/331-7
"Gifted with a darkly sensual vision and a fresh voice, [Bowen] is a writer to watch out for."
—Cecilia Tan
Rafael, a red-blooded male with an insatiable hunger for the same, is the perfect antidote to the effete malcontents haunting bookstores today. The emergence of a bold and brilliant vision, rooted in past and present.

RENÉ MAIZEROY

FLESHLY ATTRACTIONS
$6.95/299-X
Lucien was the son of the wantonly beautiful actress, Marie-Rose Hardanges. When she decides to let a "friend" introduce her son to the pleasures of love, Marie-Rose could not have foretold the excesses that would lead to her own ruin and that of her cherished son.

JEAN STINE

THRILL CITY
$6.95/411-9
Thrill City is the seat of the world's increasing depravity, and this classic novel transports you there with a vivid style you'd be hard pressed to ignore. No writer is better suited to describe the extremes of this modern Babylon.

SEASON OF THE WITCH
$6.95/268-X
"A future in which it is technically possible to transfer the total mind...of a rapist killer into the brain dead but physically living body of his female victim. Remarkable for intense psychological technique. There is eroticism but it is necessary to mark the differences between the sexes and the subtle altering of a man into a woman." —*The Science Fiction Critic*

GRANT ANTREWS

ROGUES GALLERY
$6.95/522-8
A stirring evocation of dominant/submissive love. Two doctors meet and slowly fall in love. Once Beth reveals her hidden desires to Jim, the two explore the forbidden acts that will come to define their distinctly exotic affair.

MY DARLING DOMINATRIX
$6.95/447-X
When a man and a woman fall in love, it's supposed to be simple and uncomplicated—unless that woman happens to be a dominatrix. Curiosity gives way to desire in this story of one man's awakening to the joys of willing slavery.

JOHN WARREN

THE TORQUEMADA KILLER
$6.95/367-8
Detective Eva Hernandez gets her first "big case": a string of vicious murders taking place within New York's SM community. Eva assembles the evidence, revealing a picture of a world misunderstood and under attack—and gradually comes to understand her own place within it.

THE LOVING DOMINANT
$6.95/218-3
Everything you need to know about an infamous sexual variation—and an unspoken type of love. Warren guides readers through this world and reveals the too-often hidden basis of the D/S relationship: care, trust and love.

LAURA ANTONIOU WRITING AS "SARA ADAMSON"

THE TRAINER
$6.95/249-3
The Marketplace includes not only willing slaves, but the exquisite trainers who take submissives firmly in hand. And now these mentors divulge the desires that led them to become the ultimate figures of authority.

THE SLAVE
$6.95/173-X
The second volume in the "Marketplace" trilogy. One talented submissive longs to join the ranks of those who have proven themselves worthy of entry into the Marketplace. But the delicious price is high....

THE MARKETPLACE
$6.95/3096-2
The volume that introduced the Marketplace to the world—and established it as one of the most popular realms in contemporary SM fiction.

DAVID AARON CLARK

SISTER RADIANCE
$6.95/215-9
Rife with Clark's trademark vivisections of contemporary desires, sacred and profane. The vicissitudes of lust and romance are examined against a backdrop of urban decay in this testament to the allure of the forbidden.

THE WET FOREVER
$6.95/117-9
The story of Janus and Madchen—a small-time hood and a beautiful sex worker on the run from one of the most dangerous men they have ever known—examines themes of loyalty, sacrifice, redemption and obsession amidst Manhattan's sex parlors and underground S/M clubs.

BUY ANY 4 BOOKS & CHOOSE 1 ADDITIONAL BOOK, OF EQUAL OR LESSER VALUE, AS YOUR FREE GIFT

MASQUERADE BOOKS

MICHAEL PERKINS

EVIL COMPANIONS
$6.95/3067-9
Set in New York City during the tumultuous waning years of the Sixties, *Evil Companions* has been hailed as "a frightening classic." A young couple explores the nether reaches of the erotic unconscious in a shocking confrontation with the extremes of passion.

THE SECRET RECORD: MODERN EROTIC LITERATURE
$6.95/3039-3
Michael Perkins surveys the field with authority and unique insight. Updated and revised to include the latest trends, tastes, and developments in this misunderstood and maligned genre.

AN ANTHOLOGY OF CLASSIC ANONYMOUS EROTIC WRITING
$6.95/140-3
Michael Perkins has collected the very best passages from the world's erotic writing. "Anonymous" is one of the most infamous bylines in publishing history—and these steamy excerpts show why! Includes excerpts from some of the most famous titles in the history of erotic literature.

LIESEL KULIG

LOVE IN WARTIME
$6.95/3044-X
Madeleine knew that the handsome SS officer was a dangerous man, but she was just a cabaret singer in Nazi-occupied Paris, trying to survive in a perilous time. When Josef fell in love with her, he discovered that a beautiful woman can sometimes be as dangerous as any warrior.

HELEN HENLEY

ENTER WITH TRUMPETS
$6.95/197-7
Helen Henley was told that women just don't write about sex—much less the taboos she was so interested in exploring. So Henley did it alone, flying in the face of "tradition" by writing this touching tale of arousal and devotion in one couple's kinky relationship.

ALICE JOANOU

BLACK TONGUE
$6.95/258-2
"Joanou has created a series of sumptuous, brooding, dark visions of sexual obsession, and is undoubtedly a name to look out for in the future."
—Redeemer

Exploring lust at its most florid and unsparing, *Black Tongue* is a trove of baroque fantasies—each redolent of forbidden passions. Joanou creates some of erotica's most mesmerizing and unforgettable characters.

TOURNIQUET
$6.95/3060-1
A heady collection of stories and effusions from the pen of one our most dazzling young writers. Strange tales abound, from the story of the mysterious and cruel Cybele, to an encounter with the sadistic entertainment of a bizarre after-hours cafe. A complex and riveting series of meditations on desire.

CANNIBAL FLOWER
$4.95/72-6
The provocative debut volume from this acclaimed writer.
"She is waiting in her darkened bedroom, as she has waited throughout history, to seduce the men who are foolish enough to be blinded by her irresistible charms.... She is the goddess of sexuality, and *Cannibal Flower* is her haunting siren song."
—Michael Perkins

PHILIP JOSÉ FARMER

A FEAST UNKNOWN
$6.95/276-0
"Sprawling, brawling, shocking, suspenseful, hilarious..."
—Theodore Sturgeon
Farmer's supreme anti-hero returns. "I was conceived and born in 1888." Slowly, Lord Grandrith—armed with the belief that he is the son of Jack the Ripper—tells the story of his remarkable and unbridled life. His story begins with his discovery of the secret of immortality—and progresses to encompass the furthest extremes of human behavior.

THE IMAGE OF THE BEAST
$6.95/166-7
Herald Childe has seen Hell, glimpsed its horror in an act of sexual mutilation. Childe must now find and destroy an inhuman predator through the streets of a polluted and decadent Los Angeles of the future. One clue after another leads Childe to an inescapable realization about the nature of sex and evil....

DANIEL VIAN

ILLUSIONS
$6.95/3074-1
Two tales of danger and desire in Berlin on the eve of WWII. From private homes to lurid cafés, passion is exposed in stark contrast to the brutal violence of the time, as desperate people explore their deepest, darkest sexual desires.

SAMUEL R. DELANY

THE MAD MAN
$8.99/408-9
"Reads like a pornographic reflection of Peter Ackroyd's *Chatterton* or A. S. Byatt's *Possession*.... Delany develops an insightful dichotomy between [his protagonist's] two worlds: the one of cerebral philosophy and dry academia, the other of heedless, 'impersonal' obsessive sexual extremism. When these worlds finally collide...the novel achieves a surprisingly satisfying resolution...." —*Publishers Weekly*

For his thesis, graduate student John Marr researches the life of Timothy Hasler: a philosopher whose career was cut tragically short over a decade earlier. On another front, Marr finds himself increasingly drawn toward shocking, depraved sexual entanglements with the homeless men of his neighborhood, until it begins to seem that Hasler's death might hold some key to his own life as a gay man in the age of AIDS. Unquestionably one of Delany's most shocking works, *The Mad Man* is one of American erotic literature's most transgressive titles.

MASQUERADE BOOKS

EQUINOX
$6.95/157-8
The Scorpion has sailed the seas in a quest for every possible pleasure. Her crew is a collection of the young, the twisted, the insatiable. A drifter comes into their midst and is taken on a fantastic journey to the darkest, most dangerous sexual extremes—until he is finally a victim to their boundless appetites. An early title that set the way for the author's later explorations of extreme, forbidden sexual behaviors. Long out of print, this disturbing tale is finally available under the author's original title.

ANDREI CODRESCU
THE REPENTANCE OF LORRAINE
$6.95/329-5
"One of our most prodigiously talented and magical writers."
—NYT Book Review
By the acclaimed author of *The Hole in the Flag* and *The Blood Countess*. An aspiring writer, a professor's wife, a secretary, gold anklets, Maoists, Roman harlots—and more—swirl through this spicy tale of a harried quest for a mythic artifact. Written when the author was a young man, this lusty yarn was inspired by the heady days of the Sixties. Includes a new introduction by the author, detailing the events that inspired *Lorraine*'s creation. A touching, arousing product from a more innocent time.

TUPPY OWENS
SENSATIONS
$6.95/3081-4
Tuppy Owens tells the unexpurgated story of the making of *Sensations*—the first big-budget sex flick. Originally commissioned to appear in book form after the release of the film in 1975, *Sensations* is finally released under Masquerade's stylish Rhinoceros imprint.

SOPHIE GALLEYMORE BIRD
MANEATER
$6.95/103-9
Through a bizarre act of creation, a man attains the "perfect" lover—by all appearances a beautiful, sensuous woman, but in reality something far darker. Once brought to life she will accept no mate, seeking instead the prey that will sate her hunger for vengeance.

LEOPOLD VON SACHER-MASOCH
VENUS IN FURS
$6.95/3089-X
This classic 19th century novel is the first uncompromising exploration of the dominant/submissive relationship in literature. The alliance of Severin and Wanda epitomizes Sacher-Masoch's dark obsession with a cruel, controlling goddess and the urges that drive the man held in her thrall. This special edition includes the letters exchanged between Sacher-Masoch and Emilie Mataja, an aspiring writer he sought to cast as the avatar of the forbidden desires expressed in his most famous work.

BADBOY

MIKE FORD, EDITOR
BUTCH BOYS
$6.50/523-9
A big volume of tales dedicated to the rough-and-tumble type who can make a man weak at the knees. From bikers to "gymbos," these no-nonsense studs know just what they want and how to go about getting it. Some of today's best erotic writers explore the many possible variations on the age-old fantasy of the dominant man.

WILLIAM J. MANN, EDITOR
GRAVE PASSIONS
$6.50/405-4
A collection of the most chilling tales of passion currently being penned by today's most provocative gay writers. Unnatural transformations, otherworldly encounters, and deathless desires make for a collection sure to keep readers up late at night—for a variety of reasons!

J. A. GUERRA, EDITOR
COME QUICKLY: FOR BOYS ON THE GO
$6.50/413-5
Here are over sixty of the hottest fantasies around—all designed to get you going in less time than it takes to dial 976. Julian Anthony Guerra, the editor behind the phenomenally popular *Men at Work* and *Badboy Fantasies*, has put together this volume especially for you—a busy man on a modern schedule, who still appreciates a little old-fashioned action.

JOHN PRESTON
HUSTLING: A GENTLEMAN'S GUIDE TO THE FINE ART OF HOMOSEXUAL PROSTITUTION
$6.50/517-4
The very first guide to the gay world's most infamous profession. John Preston solicited the advice and opinions of "working boys" from across the country in his effort to produce the ultimate guide to the hustler's world. *Hustling* covers every practical aspect of the business, from clientele and payment options to "specialties," sidelines and drawbacks. No stone is left unturned—and no wrong turn left unadmonished—in this guidebook to the ins and outs of this much-mythologized trade.

"...Unrivaled. For any man even vaguely contemplating going into business this tome has got to be the first port of call."
—*Divinity*

"Fun and highly literary. What more could you expect form such an accomplished activist, author and editor?"
—*Drummer*

Trade $12.95/137-3

BUY ANY 4 BOOKS & CHOOSE 1 ADDITIONAL BOOK, OF EQUAL OR LESSER VALUE, AS YOUR FREE GIFT

MASQUERADE BOOKS

MR. BENSON
$4.95/3041-5
Jamie is an aimless young man lucky enough to encounter Mr. Benson. He is soon led down the path of erotic enlightenment, learning to accept this man as his master. Jamie's incredible adventures never fail to excite—especially when the going gets rough! One of the first runaway best-sellers in gay erotic literature.

TALES FROM THE DARK LORD
$5.95/323-6
A new collection of twelve stunning works from the man Lambda Book Report called "the Dark Lord of gay erotica." The relentless ritual of lust and surrender is explored in all its manifestations in this heart-stopping triumph of authority and vision from the Dark Lord!

TALES FROM THE DARK LORD II
$4.95/176-4
The second volume of John Preston's masterful short stories. Includes an interview with the author, and a sexy screenplay written for pornstar Scott O'Hara.

THE ARENA
$4.95/3083-0
There is a place on the edge of fantasy where every desire is indulged with abandon. Men go there to unleash beasts, to let demons roam free, to abolish all limits. At the center of each tale are the men who serve there, who offer themselves for the consummation of any passion, whose own bottomless urges compel their endless subservience.

THE HEIR•THE KING
$4.95/3048-2
The ground-breaking novel The Heir, written in the lyric voice of the ancient myths, tells the story of a world where slaves and masters create a new sexual society. This edition also includes a completely original work, The King, the story of a soldier who discovers his monarch's most secret desires. A special double volume.

THE MISSION OF ALEX KANE

SWEET DREAMS
$4.95/3062-8
It's the triumphant return of gay action hero Alex Kane! In Sweet Dreams, Alex travels to Boston where he takes on a street gang that stalks gay teenagers. Mighty Alex Kane wreaks a fierce and terrible vengeance on those who prey on gay people everywhere!

GOLDEN YEARS
$4.95/3069-5
When evil threatens the plans of a group of older gay men, Kane's got the muscle to take it head on. Along the way, he wins the support—and very specialized attentions—of a cowboy plucked right out of the Old West. But Kane and the Cowboy have a surprise waiting for them....

DEADLY LIES
$4.95/3076-8
Politics is a dirty business and the dirt becomes deadly when a political smear campaign targets gay men. Who better to clean things up than Alex Kane! Alex comes to protect the dreams, and lives, of gay men imperiled by lies and deceit.

STOLEN MOMENTS
$4.95/3098-9
Houston's evolving gay community is victimized by a malicious newspaper editor who is more than willing to sacrifice gays on the altar of circulation. He never counted on Alex Kane, fearless defender of gay dreams and desires.

SECRET DANGER
$4.95/111-X
Homophobia: a pernicious social ill not confined by America's borders. Alex Kane and the faithful Danny are called to a small European country, where a group of gay tourists is being held hostage by ruthless terrorists. Luckily, the Mission of Alex Kane stands as firm foreign policy.

LETHAL SILENCE
$4.95/125-X
The Mission of Alex Kane thunders to a conclusion. Chicago becomes the scene of the right-wing's most noxious plan—facilitated by unholy political alliances. Alex and Danny head to the Windy City to take up battle with the mercenaries who would squash gay men underfoot.

MATT TOWNSEND

SOLIDLY BUILT
$6.50/416-X
The tale of the tumultuous relationship between Jeff, a young photographer, and Mark, the butch electrician hired to wire Jeff's new home. For Jeff, it's love at first sight; Mark, however, has more than a few hang-ups. Soon, both are forced to reevaluate their outlooks, and are assisted by a variety of hot men....

JAY SHAFFER

SHOOTERS
$5.95/284-1
No mere catalog of random acts, Shooters tells the stories of a variety of stunning men and the ways they connect in sexual and non-sexual ways. A virtuoso storyteller, Shaffer always gets his man.

ANIMAL HANDLERS
$4.95/264-7
In Shaffer's world, each and every man finally succumbs to the animal urges deep inside. And if there's any creature that promises a wild time, it's a beast who's been caged for far too long. Shaffer has one of the keenest eyes for the nuances of male passion.

FULL SERVICE
$4.95/150-0
Wild men build up steam until they finally let loose. No-nonsense guys bear down hard on each other as they work their way toward release in this finely detailed assortment of masculine fantasies. One of gay erotica's most insightful chroniclers of male passion.

D. V. SADERO

IN THE ALLEY
$4.95/144-6
Hardworking men—from cops to carpenters—bring their own special skills and impressive tools to the most satisfying job of all: capturing and breaking the male sexual beast. Hot, incisive and way over the top

MASQUERADE BOOKS

SCOTT O'HARA
DO-IT-YOURSELF PISTON POLISHING
$6.50/489-5
Longtime sex-pro Scott O'Hara draws upon his acute powers of seduction to lure you into a world of hard, horny men long overdue for a tune-up. Pretty soon, you'll pop your own hood for the servicing you know you need....

SUTTER POWELL
EXECUTIVE PRIVILEGES
$6.50/383-X
No matter how serious or sexy a predicament his characters find themselves in, Powell conveys the sheer exuberance of their encounters with a warm humor rarely seen in contemporary gay erotica.

GARY BOWEN
WESTERN TRAILS
$6.50/477-1
A wild roundup of tales devoted to life on the lone prairie. Gary Bowen—a writer well-versed in the Western genre—has collected the very best contemporary cowboy stories. Some of gay literature's brightest stars tell the sexy truth about the many ways a rugged stud found to satisfy himself—and his buddy—in the Very Wild West.

MAN HUNGRY
$5.95/374-0
By the author of *Diary of a Vampire*. A riveting collection of stories from one of gay erotica's new stars. Dipping into a variety of genres, Bowen crafts tales of lust unlike anything being published today.

KYLE STONE
HOT BAUDS 2
$6.50/479-8
Another collection of cyberfantasies—compiled by the inimitable Kyle Stone. After the success of the original *Hot Bauds*, Stone conducted another heated search through the world's randiest bulletin boards, resulting in one of the most scalding follow-ups ever published. Here's all the scandalous stuff you've heard so much about—sexy, shameless, and eminently user-friendly.

FIRE & ICE
$5.95/297-3
A collection of stories from the author of the infamous adventures of PB 500. Randy, powerful, and just plain bad, Stone's characters always promise one thing: enough hot action to burn away your desire for anyone else....

HOT BAUDS
$5.95/285-X
The author of *Fantasy Board* and *The Initiation of PB 500* combed cyberspace for the hottest fantasies of the world's horniest hackers. Stone has assembled the first collection of the raunchy erotica so many gay men cruise the Information Superhighway for.

FANTASY BOARD
$4.95/212-4
The author of the scalding sci-fi adventures of PB 500 explores the more foreseeable future—through the intertwined lives (and private parts) of a collection of randy computer hackers. On the Lambda Gate BBS, every hot and horny male is in search of a little virtual satisfaction—and is certain to find even more than he'd hoped for!

THE CITADEL
$4.95/198-5
The sequel to *The Initiation of PB 500*. Having proven himself worthy of his stunning master, Micah—now known only as '500'—will face new challenges and hardships after his entry into the forbidding Citadel. Only his master knows what awaits—and whether Micah will again distinguish himself as the perfect instrument of pleasure....

THE INITIATION OF PB 500
$4.95/141-1
He is a stranger on their planet, unschooled in their language, and ignorant of their customs. But this man, Micah—now known only by his number—will soon be trained in every last detail of erotic personal service. And, once nurtured and transformed into the perfect physical specimen, he must begin proving himself worthy of the master who has chosen him....

RITUALS
$4.95/168-3
Via a computer bulletin board, a young man finds himself drawn into a series of sexual rites that transform him into the willing slave of a mysterious stranger. Gradually, all vestiges of his former life are thrown off, and he learns to live for his Master's touch....

ROBERT BAHR
SEX SHOW
$4.95/225-6
Luscious dancing boys. Brazen, explicit acts. Unending stimulation. Take a seat, and get very comfortable, because the curtain's going up on a show no discriminating appetite can afford to miss.

JASON FURY
THE ROPE ABOVE, THE BED BELOW
$4.95/269-8
The irresistible Jason Fury returns—this time, telling the tale of a vicious murderer preying upon New York's go-go boy population. No one is who or what they seem, and in order to solve this mystery and save lives, each studly suspect must lay bare his soul—and more!

ERIC'S BODY
$4.95/151-9
Meet Jason Fury—blond, blue-eyed and up for anything. Fury's sexiest tales are collected in book form for the first time. Follow the irresistible Jason through sexual adventures unlike any you have ever read....

BUY ANY 4 BOOKS & CHOOSE 1 ADDITIONAL BOOK, OF EQUAL OR LESSER VALUE, AS YOUR FREE GIFT

MASQUERADE BOOKS

1 800 906-HUNK

THE connection for hot handfuls of eager guys! No credit card needed—so call now for access to the hottest party line available. Spill it all to bad boys from across the country! (Must be over 18.) Pick one up now.... $3.98 per min.

LARS EIGHNER

WHISPERED IN THE DARK
$5.95/286-8
A volume demonstrating Eighner's unique combination of strengths: poetic descriptive power, an unfailing ear for dialogue, and a finely tuned feeling for the nuances of male passion.

AMERICAN PRELUDE
$4.95/170-5
Eighner is widely recognized as one of our best, most exciting gay writers. He is also one of gay erotica's true masters—and American Prelude shows why. Wonderfully written, blisteringly hot tales of all-American lust.

B.M.O.C.
$4.95/3077-6
In a college town known as "the Athens of the Southwest," studs of every stripe are up all night—studying, naturally. Relive university life the way it was supposed to be, with a cast of handsome honor students majoring in Human Homosexuality.

DAVID LAURENTS, EDITOR

SOUTHERN COMFORT
$6.50/466-6
Editor David Laurents now unleashes a collection of tales focusing on the American South—reflecting not only Southern literary tradition, but the many contributions the region has made to the iconography of the American Male.

WANDERLUST: HOMOEROTIC TALES OF TRAVEL
$5.95/395-3
A volume dedicated to the special pleasures of faraway places. Gay men have always had a special interest in travel—and not only for the scenic vistas. Wanderlust celebrates the freedom of the open road, and the allure of men who stray from the beaten path....

THE BADBOY BOOK OF EROTIC POETRY
$5.95/382-1
Over fifty of today's best poets. Erotic poetry has long been the problem child of the literary world—highly creative and provocative, but somehow too frank to be "literature." Both learned and stimulating, The Badboy Book of Erotic Poetry restores eros to its rightful place of honor in contemporary gay writing.

AARON TRAVIS

BIG SHOTS
$5.95/448-8
Two fierce tales in one electrifying volume. In *Beirut*, Travis tells the story of ultimate military power and erotic subjugation; *Kip*, Travis' hypersexed and sinister take on film noir, appears in unexpurgated form for the first time.

EXPOSED
$4.95/126-8
A volume of shorter Travis tales, each providing a unique glimpse of the horny gay male in his natural environment! Cops, college jocks, ancient Romans—even Sherlock Holmes and his loyal Watson—cruise these pages, fresh from the throbbing pen of one of our hottest authors.

BEAST OF BURDEN
$4.95/105-5
Five ferocious tales. Innocents surrender to the brutal sexual mastery of their superiors, as taboos are shattered and replaced with the unwritten rules of masculine conquest. Intense, extreme—and totally Travis.

IN THE BLOOD
$5.95/283-3
Written when Travis had just begun to explore the true power of the erotic imagination, these stories laid the groundwork for later masterpieces. Among the many rewarding rarities included in this volume: "In the Blood"—a heart-pounding descent into sexual vampirism, written with the furious erotic power that is Travis' trademark.

THE FLESH FABLES
$4.95/243-4
One of Travis' best collections. *The Flesh Fables* includes "Blue Light," his most famous story, as well as other masterpieces that established him as the erotic writer to watch. And watch carefully, because Travis always buries a surprise somewhere beneath his scorching detail....

SLAVES OF THE EMPIRE
$4.95/3054-7
"A wonderful mythic tale. Set against the backdrop of the exotic and powerful Roman Empire, this wonderfully written novel explores the timeless questions of light and dark in male sexuality. The locale may be the ancient world, but these are the slaves and masters of our time...."   —John Preston

BOB VICKERY

SKIN DEEP
$4.95/265-5
So many varied beauties no one will go away unsatisfied. No tantalizing morsel of manflesh is overlooked—or left unexplored! Beauty may be only skin deep, but a handful of beautiful skin is a tempting proposition.

JR

FRENCH QUARTER NIGHTS
$5.95/337-6
Sensual snapshots of the many places where men get down and dirty—from the steamy French Quarter to the steam room at the old Everard baths. These are nights you'll wish would go on forever....

TOM BACCHUS

RAHM
$5.95/315-5
The imagination of Tom Bacchus brings to life an extraordinary assortment of characters, from the Father of Us All to the cowpoke next door, the early gay literati to rude, queercore mosh rats. No one is better than Bacchus at staking out sexual territory with a swagger and a sly grin.

MASQUERADE BOOKS

BONE
$4.95/177-2
Queer musings from the pen of one of today's hottest young talents. A fresh outlook on fleshly indulgence yields more than a few pleasant surprises. Horny Tom Bacchus maps out the tricking ground of a new generation.

KEY LINCOLN
SUBMISSION HOLDS
$4.95/266-3
A bright young talent unleashes his first collection of gay erotica. From tough to tender, the men between these covers stop at nothing to get what they want. These sweat-soaked tales show just how bad boys can really get.

CALDWELL/EIGHNER
QSFX2
$5.95/278-7
The wickedest, wildest, other-worldliest yarns from two master storytellers—Clay Caldwell and Lars Eighner. Both eroticists take a trip to the furthest reaches of the sexual imagination, sending back ten stories proving that as much as things change, one thing will always remain the same...

CLAY CALDWELL
JOCK STUDS
$6.50/472-0
A collection of Caldwell's scalding tales of pumped bodies and raging libidos. Swimmers, runners, football players... whatever your sport might be, there's a man waiting for you in these pages. Waiting to peel off that uniform and claim his reward for a game well-played....

ASK OL' BUDDY
$5.95/346-5
Set in the underground SM world, Caldwell takes you on a journey of discovery—where men initiate one another into the secrets of the rawest sexual realm of all. And when each stud's initiation is complete, he takes his places among the masters—eager to take part in the training of another hungry soul...

STUD SHORTS
$5.95/320-1
"If anything, Caldwell's charm is more powerful, his nostalgia more poignant, the horniness he captures more sweetly, achingly acute than ever."
—Aaron Travis
A new collection of this legend's latest sex-fiction. With his customary candor, Caldwell tells all about cops, cadets, truckers, farmboys (and many more) in these dirty jewels.

TAILPIPE TRUCKER
$5.95/296-5
Trucker porn! In prose as free and unvarnished as a cross-country highway, Caldwell tells the truth about Trag and Curly—two men hot for the feeling of sweaty manflesh. Together, they pick up—and turn out—a couple of thrill-seeking punks.

SERVICE, STUD
$5.95/336-8
Another look at the gay future. The setting is the Los Angeles of a distant future. Here the all-male populace is divided between the served and the servants—guaranteeing the erotic satisfaction of all involved.

QUEERS LIKE US
$4.95/262-0
"Caldwell at his most charming." —Aaron Travis
For years the name Clay Caldwell has been synonymous with the hottest, most finely crafted gay tales available. *Queers Like Us* is one of his best: the story of a randy mail-man's trek through a landscape of willing, available studs.

ALL-STUD
$4.95/104-7
This classic, sex-soaked tale takes place under the watchful eye of Number Ten: an omniscient figure who has decreed unabashed promiscuity as the law of his all-male land. One stud, however, takes it upon himself to challenge the social order, daring to fall in love. Finally, he is forced to fight for not only himself, but the man he loves.

CLAY CALDWELL AND AARON TRAVIS
TAG TEAM STUDS
$6.50/465-8
Thrilling tales from these two legendary eroticists. The wrestling world will never seem the same, once you've made your way through this assortment of sweaty, virile studs. But you'd better be wary—should one catch you off guard, you just might spend the rest of the night pinned to the mat....

LARRY TOWNSEND
LEATHER AD: S
$5.95/407-0
The second half of Townsend's acclaimed tale of lust through the personals—this time told from a Top's perspective. A simple ad generates many responses, and one man finds himself in the enviable position of putting these studly applicants through their paces....

LEATHER AD: M
$5.95/380-5
The first of this two-part classic. John's curious about what goes on between the leatherclad men he's fantasized about. He takes out a personal ad, and starts a journey of self-discovery that will leave no part of his life unchanged.

1 900 745-HUNG

Hardcore phone action for real men. A scorching assembly of studs is waiting for your call—and eager to give you the headtrip of your life! Totally live, guaranteed one-on-one encounters. (Must be over 18.) No credit card needed. $3.98 per minute.

BUY ANY 4 BOOKS & CHOOSE 1 ADDITIONAL BOOK, OF EQUAL OR LESSER VALUE, AS YOUR FREE GIFT

MASQUERADE BOOKS

BEWARE THE GOD WHO SMILES
$5.95/321-X
Two lusty young Americans are transported to ancient Egypt—where they are embroiled in regional warfare and taken as slaves by marauding barbarians. The key to escape from this brutal bondage lies in their own rampant libidos, and urges as old as time itself.

2069 TRILOGY
(This one-volume collection only $6.95)244-2
For the first time, Larry Townsend's early science-fiction trilogy appears in one massive volume! Set in a future world, the *2069 Trilogy* includes the tight plotting and shameless male sexual pleasure that established him as one of gay erotica's first masters.

MIND MASTER
$4.95/209-4
Who better to explore the territory of erotic dominance than an author who helped define the genre—and knows that ultimate mastery always transcends the physical.Another unrelenting Townsend tale.

THE LONG LEATHER CORD
$4.95/201-9
Chuck's stepfather never lacks money or clandestine male visitors with whom he enacts intense sexual rituals. As Chuck comes to terms with his own desires, he begins to unravel the mystery behind his stepfather's secret life.

MAN SWORD
$4.95/188-8
Très gai tale of France's King Henri III, who was unimaginably spoiled by his mother—the infamous Catherine de Medici—and groomed from a young age to assume the throne of France. Along the way, he encounters enough sexual schemers and politicos to alter one's picture of history forever!

THE FAUSTUS CONTRACT
$4.95/167-5
Two attractive young men desperately need $1000. Will do anything. Travel OK. Danger OK. Call anytime... Two cocky young hustlers get more than they bargained for in this story of lust and its discontents.

THE GAY ADVENTURES OF CAPTAIN GOOSE
$4.95/169-1
Hot young Jerome Gander is sentenced to serve aboard the *H.M.S. Faerigold*—a ship manned by the most hardened, unrepentant criminals. In no time, Gander becomes well-versed in the ways of horny men at sea, and the *Faerigold* becomes the most notorious vessel to ever set sail.

CHAINS
$4.95/158-6
Picking up street punks has always been risky, but in Larry Townsend's classic *Chains*, it sets off a string of events that must be read to be believed.

KISS OF LEATHER
$4.95/161-6
A look at the acts and attitudes of an earlier generation of gay leathermen, *Kiss of Leather* is full to bursting with the gritty, raw action that has distinguished Townsend's work for years. Sensual pain and pleasure mix in this tightly plotted tale.

RUN, LITTLE LEATHER BOY
$4.95/143-8
One young man's sexual awakening. A chronic underachiever, Wayne seems to be going nowhere fast. He finds himself bored with the everyday—and drawn to the masculine intensity of a dark and mysterious sexual underground, where he soon finds many goals worth pursuing....

RUN NO MORE
$4.95/152-7
The continuation of Larry Townsend's legendary *Run, Little Leather Boy*. This volume follows the further adventures of Townsend's leatherclad narrator as he travels every sexual byway available to the S/M male.

THE SCORPIUS EQUATION
$4.95/119-5
The story of a man caught between the demands of two galactic empires. Our randy hero must match wits—and more—with the incredible forces that rule his world.

THE SEXUAL ADVENTURES OF SHERLOCK HOLMES
$4.95/3097-0
A scandalously sexy take on this legendary sleuth. "A Study in Scarlet" is transformed to expose Mrs. Hudson as a man in drag, the Diogenes Club as an S/M arena, and clues only the redoubtable—and very horny—Sherlock Holmes could piece together. A baffling tale of sex and mystery.

DONALD VINING
CABIN FEVER AND OTHER STORIES
$5.95/338-4
Eighteen blistering stories in celebration of the most intimate of male bonding. Time after time, Donald Vining's men succumb to nature, and reaffirm both love and lust in modern gay life.

"Demonstrates the wisdom experience combined with insight and optimism can create."
—Bay Area Reporter

DEREK ADAMS
PRISONER OF DESIRE
$6.50/439-9
Scalding fiction from one of Badboy's most popular authors. The creator of horny P.I. Miles Diamond returns with this volume bursting with red-blooded, sweat-soaked excursions through the modern gay libido.

THE MARK OF THE WOLF
$5.95/361-9
I turned to look at the man who stared back at me from the mirror. The familiar outlines of my face seemed coarser, more sinister. An animal? The past comes back to haunt one well-off stud, whose unslakeable thirsts lead him into the arms of many men—and the midst of a perilous mystery.

MY DOUBLE LIFE
$5.95/314-7
Every man leads a double life, dividing his hours between the mundanities of the day and the outrageous pursuits of the night. The creator of sexy P.I. Miles Diamond shines a little light on the wicked things men do when no one's looking.

MASQUERADE BOOKS

HEAT WAVE
$4.95/159-4
"His body was draped in baggy clothes, but there was hardly any doubt that they covered anything less than perfection.... His slacks were cinched tight around a narrow waist, and the rise of flesh pushing against the thin fabric promised a firm, melon-shaped ass...."

MILES DIAMOND AND THE DEMON OF DEATH
$4.95/251-5
Derek Adams' gay gumshoe returns for further adventures. Miles always find himself in the stickiest situations—with any stud whose path he crosses! His adventures with "The Demon of Death" promise another carnal carnival.

THE ADVENTURES OF MILES DIAMOND
$4.95/118-7
The debut of Miles Diamond—Derek Adams' take on the classic American archetype of the hardboiled private eye. "The Case of the Missing Twin" promises to be a most rewarding case, packed as it is with randy studs. Miles sets about uncovering all as he tracks down the elusive and delectable Daniel Travis.

KELVIN BELIELE

IF THE SHOE FITS
$4.95/223-X
An essential and winning volume of tales exploring a world where randy boys can't help but do what comes naturally—as often as possible! Sweaty male bodies grapple in pleasure, proving the old adage: if the shoe fits, one might as well slip right in....

JAMES MEDLEY

THE REVOLUTIONARY & OTHER STORIES
$6.50/417-8
Billy, the son of the station chief of the American Embassy in Guatemala, is kidnapped and held for ransom. Frightened at first, Billy gradually develops an unimaginably close relationship with Juan, the revolutionary assigned to guard him.

HUCK AND BILLY
$4.95/245-0
Young love is always the sweetest, always the most sorrowful. Young lust, on the other hand, knows no bounds—and is often the hottest of one's life! Huck and Billy explore the desires that course through their young male bodies, determined to plumb the lusty depths of passion.

FLEDERMAUS

FLEDERFICTION: STORIES OF MEN AND TORTURE
$5.95/355-4
Fifteen blistering paeans to men and their suffering. Fledermaus unleashes his most thrilling tales of punishment in this special volume designed with Badboy readers in mind.

VICTOR TERRY

MASTERS
$6.50/418-6
A powerhouse volume of boot-wearing, whip-wielding, bone-crunching bruisers who've got what it takes to make a grown man grovel. Between these covers lurk the most demanding of men—the imperious few to whom so many humbly offer themselves....

SM/SD
$6.50/406-2
Set around a South Dakota town called Prairie, these tales offer compelling evidence that the real rough stuff can still be found where men roam free of the restraints of "polite" society—and take what they want despite all rules.

WHiPs
$4.95/254-X
Connoisseurs of gay writing have known Victor Terry's work for some time. Cruising for a hot man? You'd better be, because one way or another, these WHiPs—officers of the Wyoming Highway Patrol—are gonna pull you over for a little impromptu interrogation....

MAX EXANDER

DEEDS OF THE NIGHT: TALES OF EROS AND PASSION
$5.95/348-1
MAXimum porn! Exander's a writer who's seen it all—and is more than happy to describe every inch of it in pulsating detail. A whirlwind tour of the hypermasculine libido.

LEATHERSEX
$4.95/210-8
Hard-hitting tales from merciless Max Exander. This time he focuses on the leatherclad lust that draws together only the most willing and talented of tops and bottoms—for an all-out orgy of limitless surrender and control....

MANSEX
$4.95/160-8
"Mark was the classic leatherman: a huge, dark stud in chaps, with a big black moustache, hairy chest and enormous muscles. Exactly the kind of men Todd liked—strong, hunky, masculine, ready to take control...."

TOM CAFFREY

TALES FROM THE MEN'S ROOM
$5.95/364-3
From shameless cops on the beat to shy studs on stage, Caffrey explores male lust at its most elemental and arousing. And if there's a lesson to be learned, it's that the Men's Room is less a place than a state of mind—one that every man finds himself in, day after day....

HITTING HOME
$4.95/222-1
Titillating and compelling, the stories in *Hitting Home* make a strong case for there being only one thing on a man's mind.

BUY ANY 4 BOOKS & CHOOSE 1 ADDITIONAL BOOK, OF EQUAL OR LESSER VALUE, AS YOUR FREE GIFT

MASQUERADE BOOKS

TORSTEN BARRING

GUY TRAYNOR
$6.50/414-3
Some call Guy Traynor a theatrical genius; others say he was a madman. All anyone knows for certain is that his productions were the result of blood, sweat and tears. Never have artists suffered so much for their craft!

PRISONERS OF TORQUEMADA
$5.95/252-3
Another volume sure to push you over the edge. How cruel is the "therapy" practiced at Casa Torquemada? Barring is just the writer to evoke such steamy sexual malevolence.

SHADOWMAN
$4.95/178-0
From spoiled Southern aristocrats to randy youths sowing wild oats at the local picture show, Barring's imagination works overtime in these vignettes of homolust—past, present and future.

PETER THORNWELL
$4.95/149-7
Follow the exploits of Peter Thornwell as he goes from misspent youth to scandalous stardom, all thanks to an insatiable libido and love for the lash.

THE SWITCH
$4.95/3061-X
Sometimes a man needs a good whipping, and The Switch certainly makes a case! Packed with hot studs and unrelenting passions.

BERT McKENZIE

FRINGE BENEFITS
$5.95/354-6
From the pen of a widely published short story writer comes a volume of highly immodest tales. Not afraid of getting down and dirty, McKenzie produces some of today's most visceral sextales.

SONNY FORD

REUNION IN FLORENCE
$4.95/3070-9
Captured by Turks, Adrian and Tristan will do anything to save their heads. When Tristan is threatened by a Sultan's jealousy, Adrian begins his quest for the only man alive who can replace Tristan as the object of the Sultan's lust.

ROGER HARMAN

FIRST PERSON
$4.95/179-9
A highly personal collection. Each story takes the form of a confessional—told by men who've got plenty to confess! From the "first time ever" to firsts of different kinds, First Person tells truths too hot to be purely fiction.

J. A. GUERRA, ED.

SLOW BURN
$4.95/3042-3
Welcome to the Body Shoppe! Torsos get lean and hard, pecs widen, and stomachs ripple in these sexy stories of the power and perils of physical perfection.

DAVE KINNICK

SORRY I ASKED
$4.95/3090-3
Unexpurgated interviews with gay porn's rank and file. Get personal with the men behind (and under) the "stars," and discover the hot truth about the porn business.

SEAN MARTIN

SCRAPBOOK
$4.95/224-8
Imagine a book filled with only the best, most vivid remembrances...a book brimming with every hot, sexy encounter its pages can hold... Now you need only open up Scrapbook to know that such a volume really exists....

CARO SOLES & STAN TAL, EDITORS

BIZARRE DREAMS
$4.95/187-X
An anthology of stirring voices dedicated to exploring the dark side of human fantasy. Bizarre Dreams brings together the most talented practitioners of "dark fantasy," the most forbidden sexual realm of all.

CHRISTOPHER MORGAN

STEAM GAUGE
$6.50/473-9
This volume abounds in manly men doing what they do best—to, with, or for any hot stud who crosses their paths. Frequently published to acclaim in the gay press, Christopher Morgan puts a fresh, contemporary spin on the very oldest of urges.

THE SPORTSMEN
$5.95/385-6
A collection of super-hot stories dedicated to that most popular of boys next door—the all-American athlete. Here are enough tales of carnal grand slams, sexy interceptions and highly personal bests to satisfy the hungers of the most ardent sports fan. Editor Christopher Morgan has gathered those writers who know just the type of guys that make up every red-blooded male's starting line-up....

MUSCLE BOUND
$4.95/3028-8
In the New York City bodybuilding scene, country boy Tommy joins forces with sexy Will Rodriguez in a battle of wits and biceps at the hottest gym in town, where the weak are bound and crushed by iron-pumping gods.

MICHAEL LOWENTHAL, ED.

THE BADBOY EROTIC LIBRARY VOLUME I
$4.95/190-X
Excerpts from A Secret Life, Imre, Sins of the Cities of the Plain, Teleny and others demonstrate the uncanny gift for portraying sex between men that led to many of these titles being banned upon publication.

THE BADBOY EROTIC LIBRARY VOLUME II
$4.95/211-6
This time, selections are taken from Mike and Me and Muscle Bound, Men at Work, Badboy Fantasies, and Slowburn.

MASQUERADE BOOKS

ERIC BOYD

MIKE AND ME
$5.95/419-4
Mike joined the gym squad to bulk up on muscle. Little did he know he'd be turning on every sexy muscle jock in Minnesota! Hard bodies collide in a series of workouts designed to generate a whole lot more than rips and cuts.

MIKE AND THE MARINES
$6.50/497-6
Mike takes on America's most elite corps of studs—running into more than a few good men! Join in on the never-ending sexual escapades of this singularly lustful platoon!

ANONYMOUS

A SECRET LIFE
$4.95/3017-2
Meet Master Charles: only eighteen, and quite innocent, until his arrival at the Sir Percival's Royal Academy, where the daily lessons are supplemented with a crash course in pure, sweet sexual heat!

SINS OF THE CITIES OF THE PLAIN
$5.95/322-8
Indulge yourself in the scorching memoirs of young man-about-town Jack Saul. With his shocking dalliances with the lords and "ladies" of British high society, Jack's positively sinful escapades grow wilder with every chapter!

IMRE
$4.95/3019-9
What dark secrets, what fiery passions lay hidden behind strikingly beautiful Lieutenant Imre's emerald eyes? An extraordinary lost classic of fantasy, obsession, gay erotic desire, and romance in a small European town on the eve of WWI.

TELENY
$4.95/3020-2
Often attributed to Oscar Wilde, *Teleny* tells the story of one young man of independent means. He dedicates himself to a succession of forbidden pleasures, but instead finds love and tragedy when he becomes embroiled in a cult devoted to fulfilling only the very darkest of fantasies.

HARD CANDY

KEVIN KILLIAN

ARCTIC SUMMER
$6.95/514-X
Highly acclaimed author Kevin Killian's latest novel examines the many secrets lying beneath the placid exterior of America in the '50s. With his story of Liam Reilly—a young gay man of considerable means and numerous secrets—Killian exposes the contradictions of the American Dream, and the ramifications of the choices one is forced to make when hiding the truth.

STAN LEVENTHAL

BARBIE IN BONDAGE
$6.95/415-1
Widely regarded as one of the most refreshing, clear-eyed interpreters of big city gay male life, Leventhal here provides a series of explorations of love and desire between men. Uncompromising, but gentle and generous, *Barbie in Bondage* is a fitting tribute to the late author's unique talents.

SKYDIVING ON CHRISTOPHER STREET
$6.95/287-6
"Positively addictive." —Dennis Cooper
Aside from a hateful job, a hateful apartment, a hateful world and an increasingly hateful lover, life seems, well, all right for the protagonist of Stan Leventhal's latest novel. Having already lost most of his friends to AIDS, how could things get any worse? But things soon do, and he's forced to endure much more....

PATRICK MOORE

IOWA
$6.95/423-2
"Moore is the Tennessee Williams of the nineties—profound intimacy freed in a compelling narrative."
—Karen Finley
"Fresh and shiny and relevant to our time. *Iowa* is full of terrific characters etched in acid-sharp prose, soaked through with just enough ambivalence to make it thoroughly romantic." —Felice Picano
A stunning novel about one gay man's journey into adulthood, and the roads that bring him home again.

PAUL T. ROGERS

SAUL'S BOOK
$7.95/462-3
Winner of the Editors' Book Award
"Exudes an almost narcotic power.... A masterpiece." —*Village Voice Literary Supplement*
"A first novel of considerable power... Sinbad the Sailor, thanks to the sympathetic imagination of Paul T. Rogers, speaks to us all." —*New York Times Book Review*
The story of a Times Square hustler called Sinbad the Sailor and Saul, a brilliant, self-destructive, alcoholic, thoroughly dominating character who may be the only love Sinbad will ever know.

WALTER R. HOLLAND

THE MARCH
$6.95/429-1
A moving testament to the power of friendship during even the worst of times. Beginning on a hot summer night in 1980, *The March* revolves around a circle of young gay men, and the many others their lives touch. Over time, each character changes in unexpected ways; lives and loves come together and fall apart, as society itself is horribly altered by the onslaught of AIDS.

BUY ANY 4 BOOKS & CHOOSE 1 ADDITIONAL BOOK, OF EQUAL OR LESSER VALUE, AS YOUR FREE GIFT

MASQUERADE BOOKS

RED JORDAN AROBATEAU
LUCY AND MICKEY
$6.95/311-2
The story of Mickey—an uncompromising butch—and her long affair with Lucy, the femme she loves. A raw tale of pre-Stonewall lesbian life.
"A necessary reminder to all who blissfully—some may say ignorantly—ride the wave of lesbian chic into the mainstream." —Heather Findlay

DIRTY PICTURES
$5.95/345-7
"Red Jordan Arobateau is the Thomas Wolfe of lesbian literature... She's a natural—raw talent that is seething, passionate, hard, remarkable."
—Lillian Faderman, editor of *Chloe Plus Olivia*
Dirty Pictures is the story of a lonely butch tending bar—and the femme she finally calls her own.

DONALD VINING
A GAY DIARY
$8.95/451-8
Donald Vining's *Diary* portrays a long-vanished age and the lifestyle of a gay generation all too frequently forgotten.
"*A Gay Diary* is, unquestionably, the richest historical document of gay male life in the United States that I have ever encountered.... It illuminates a critical period in gay male American history."
—Body Politic

LARS EIGHNER
GAY COSMOS
$6.95/236-5
A title sure to appeal not only to Eighner's gay fans, but the many converts who first encountered his moving nonfiction work. Praised by the press, *Gay Cosmos* is an important contribution to the area of Gay and Lesbian Studies.

FELICE PICANO
THE LURE
$6.95/398-8
"The subject matter, plus the authenticity of Picano's research are, combined, explosive. Felice Picano is one hell of a writer." —Stephen King
After witnessing a brutal murder, Noel is recruited by the police, to assist as a lure for the killer. Undercover, he moves deep into the freneticism of Manhattan's gay highlife—where he gradually becomes aware of the darker forces at work in his life. In addition to the mystery behind his mission, he begins to recognize changes: in his relationships with the men around him, in himself...

AMBIDEXTROUS
$6.95/275-2
"Makes us remember what it feels like to be a child..."
—The Advocate
Picano's first "memoir in the form of a novel" tells all: home life, school face-offs, the ingenuous sophistications of his first sexual steps. In three years' time, he's had his first gay fling—and is on his way to becoming the widely praised writer he is today.

MEN WHO LOVED ME
$6.95/274-4
"Zesty...spiked with adventure and romance...a distinguished and humorous portrait of a vanished age." —Publishers Weekly
In 1966, Picano abandoned New York, determined to find true love in Europe. Upon returning, he plunges into the city's thriving gay community of the 1970s.

WILLIAM TALSMAN
THE GAUDY IMAGE
$6.95/263-9
"To read *The Gaudy Image* now...it is to see firsthand the very issues of identity and positionality with which gay men were struggling in the decades before Stonewall. For what Talsman is dealing with...is the very question of how we conceive ourselves gay."
—from the introduction by Michael Bronski

ROSEBUD

THE ROSEBUD READER
$5.95/319-8
Rosebud has contributed greatly to the burgeoning genre of lesbian erotica—to the point that our authors are among the hottest and most closely watched names in lesbian and gay publishing. Here are the finest moments from Rosebud's contemporary classics.

LESLIE CAMERON
WHISPER OF FANS
$6.50/542-5
"Just looking into her eyes, she felt that she knew a lot about this woman. She could see strength, boldness, a fresh sense of aliveness that rocked her to the core. In turn she felt open, revealed under the woman's gaze—all her secrets already told. No need of shame or artifice...." A fresh tale of passion between women, from one of lesbian erotica's up-and-coming authors.

RACHEL PEREZ
ODD WOMEN
$6.50/526-3
These women are sexy, smart, tough—some even say odd. But who cares, when their combined ass-ets are so sweet! An assortment of Sapphic sirens proves once and for all that comely ladies come best in pairs.

RANDY TUROFF
LUST NEVER SLEEPS
$6.50/475-5
A rich volume of highly erotic, powerfully real fiction from the editor of *Lesbian Words*. Randy Turoff depicts a circle of modern women connected through the bonds of love, friendship, ambition, and lust with accuracy and compassion. Moving, tough, yet undeniably true, Turoff's stories create a stirring portrait of contemporary lesbian life and community.

MASQUERADE BOOKS

RED JORDAN AROBATEAU
ROUGH TRADE
$6.50/470-4
Famous for her unflinching portrayal of lower-class dyke life and love, Arobateau outdoes herself with these tales of butch/femme affairs and unrelenting passions. Unapologetic and distinctly non-homogenized, *Rough Trade* is a must for all fans of challenging lesbian literature.

BOYS NIGHT OUT
$6.50/463-1
A *Red*-hot volume of short fiction from this lesbian literary sensation. As always, Arobateau takes a good hard look at the lives of everyday women, noting well the struggles and triumphs each woman experiences.

ALISON TYLER
VENUS ONLINE
$6.50/521-2
What's my idea of paradise? Lovely Alexa spends her days in a boring bank job, not quite living up to her full potential—interested instead in saving her energies for her nocturnal pursuits. At night, Alexa goes online, living out virtual adventures that become more real with each session. Soon Alexa—aka Venus—feels her erotic imagination growing beyond anything she could have imagined.

DARK ROOM: AN ONLINE ADVENTURE
$6.50/455-0
Dani, a successful photographer, can't bring herself to face the death of her lover, Kate. An ambitious journalist, Kate was found mysteriously murdered, leaving her lover with only fond memories of a too-brief relationship. Determined to keep the memory of her lover alive, Dani goes online under Kate's screen alias—and begins to uncover the truth behind the crime that has torn her world apart.

BLUE SKY SIDEWAYS & OTHER STORIES
$6.50/394-5
A variety of women, and their many breathtaking experiences with lovers, friends—and even the occasional sexy stranger. From blossoming young beauties to fearless vixens, Tyler finds the sexy pleasures of everyday life.

DIAL "L" FOR LOVELESS
$5.95/386-4
Meet Katrina Loveless—a private eye talented enough to give Sam Spade a run for his money. In her first case, Katrina investigates a murder implicating a host of society's darlings. Loveless untangles the mess—while working herself into a variety of highly compromising knots with the many lovelies who cross her path!

THE VIRGIN
$5.95/379-1
Veronica answers a personal ad in the "Women Seeking Women" category—and discovers a whole sensual world she never knew existed! And she never dreamed she'd be prized as a virgin all over again, by someone who would deflower her with a passion no man could ever show....

K. T. BUTLER
TOOLS OF THE TRADE
$5.95/420-8
A sparkling mix of lesbian erotica and humor. An encounter with ice cream, cappuccino and chocolate cake; an affair with a complete stranger, a pair of faulty handcuffs; and love on a drafting table. Seventeen tales.

LOVECHILD
GAG
$5.95/369-4
From New York's poetry scene comes this explosive volume of work from one of the bravest, most cutting young writers you'll ever encounter. The poems in *Gag* take on American hypocrisy with uncommon energy, and announce Lovechild as a writer of unforgettable rage.

ELIZABETH OLIVER
PAGAN DREAMS
$5.95/295-7
Cassidy and Samantha plan a vacation at a secluded bed-and-breakfast, hoping for a little personal time alone. Their hostess, however, has different plans. The lovers are plunged into a world of dungeons and pagan rites, as Anastasia steals Samantha for her own.

SUSAN ANDERS
CITY OF WOMEN
$5.95/375-9
Stories dedicated to women and the passions that draw them together. Designed strictly for the sensual pleasure of women, these tales are set to ignite flames of passion from coast to coast.

PINK CHAMPAGNE
$5.95/282-5
Tasty, torrid tales of butch/femme couplings. Tough as nails or soft as silk, these women seek out their antitheses, intent on working out the details of their own personal theory of difference.

ANONYMOUS
LAVENDER ROSE
$4.95/208-6
From the writings of Sappho, Queen of the island Lesbos, to the turn-of-the-century *Black Book of Lesbianism*; from *Tips to Maidens* to *Crimson Hairs*, a recent lesbian saga—here are the great but little-known lesbian writings and revelations.

LAURA ANTONIOU, EDITOR
LEATHERWOMEN
$4.95/3095-0
These fantasies, from the pens of new or emerging authors, break every rule imposed on women's fantasies. The hottest stories from some of today's newest and most outrageous writers make this an unforgettable exploration of the female libido.

BUY ANY 4 BOOKS & CHOOSE 1 ADDITIONAL BOOK, OF EQUAL OR LESSER VALUE, AS YOUR FREE GIFT

MASQUERADE BOOKS

LEATHERWOMEN II
$4.95/229-9
Another groundbreaking volume of writing from women on the edge, sure to ignite libidinal flames in any reader. Leave taboos behind, because these Leatherwomen know no limits....

AARONA GRIFFIN
PASSAGE AND OTHER STORIES
$4.95/3057-1
An S/M romance. Lovely Nina is frightened by her lesbian passions, until she finds herself infatuated with a woman she spots at a local café. One night Nina follows her, and finds herself enmeshed in an endless maze leading to a world where women test the edges of sexuality and power.

VALENTINA CILESCU
MY LADY'S PLEASURE: MISTRESS WITH A MAID, VOLUME I
$5.95/412-7
Claudia Dungarrow, a lovely, powerful, but mysterious professor, attempts to seduce virginal Elizabeth Stanbridge, setting off a chain of events that eventually ruins her career. Claudia vows revenge—and makes her foes pay deliciously....

DARK VENUS: MISTRESS WITH A MAID, VOLUME 2
$6.50/481-X
This thrilling saga of cruel lust continues! *Mistress with a Maid* breathes new life into the conventions of dominance and submission. What emerges is a picture of unremitting desire—whether it be for supreme erotic power or ultimate sexual surrender.

BODY AND SOUL: MISTRESS WITH A MAID 3
$6.50/515-8
The blistering conclusion to lesbian erotica's most unsparing trilogy! Dr. Claudia Dungarrow returns for yet another tour of depravity, subjugating every maiden in sight to her ruthless sexual whims. But, as stunning as Claudia is, she has yet to hold Elizabeth Stanbridge in complete submission. Will she ever?

THE ROSEBUD SUTRA
$4.95/242-6
"Women are hardly ever known in their true light, though they may love others, or become indifferent towards them, may give them delight, or abandon them, or may extract from them all the wealth that they possess." So says *The Rosebud Sutra*—a volume promising women's inner secrets.

MISTRESS MINE
$6.50/502-6
Sophia Cranleigh sits in prison, accused of authoring the "obscene" *Mistress Mine*. What she has done, however, is merely chronicle the events of her life. For Sophia has led no ordinary life, but has slaved and suffered—deliciously—under the hand of the notorious Mistress Malin. The uncensored tale of a life of sensuous suffering, by one of today's hottest lesbian writers.

LINDSAY WELSH
SECOND SIGHT
$6.50/507-7
The debut of Dana Steele—lesbian superhero! During an attack by a gang of homophobic youths, Dana is thrown onto subway tracks—touching the deadly third rail. Miraculously, she survives, and finds herself endowed with superhuman powers. Dana decides to devote her powers to the protection of her lesbian sisters, no matter how daunting the danger they face.

NASTY PERSUASIONS
$6.50/436-4
A hot peek into the behind-the-scenes operations of Rough Trade—one of the world's most famous lesbian clubs. Join Slash, Ramone, Cherry and many others as they bring one another to the height of torturous ecstasy—all in the name of keeping Rough Trade the premier name in sexy entertainment for women.

MILITARY SECRETS
$5.95/397-X
Colonel Candice Sproule heads a highly specialized boot camp. Assisted by three dominatrix sergeants, Col. Sproule takes on the talented submissives sent to her by secret military contacts. Then along comes Jesse—whose pleasure in being served matches the Colonel's own. This horny new recruit sets off fireworks in the barracks—and beyond....

ROMANTIC ENCOUNTERS
$5.95/359-7
Beautiful Julie, the most powerful editor of romance novels in the industry, spends her days igniting women's passions through books—and her nights fulfilling those needs with a variety of licentious lovers. Finally, through a sizzling series of coincidences, Julie's two worlds come together explosively!

THE BEST OF LINDSAY WELSH
$5.95/368-6
A collection of this popular writer's best work. Lindsay Welsh was one of Rosebud's early bestsellers, and remains one of our most popular writers. This sampler is set to introduce some of the hottest lesbian erotica to a wider audience.

NECESSARY EVIL
$5.95/277-9
What's a girl to do? When her Mistress proves too systematic, too by-the-book, one lovely submissive takes the ultimate chance—choosing and creating a Mistress who'll fulfill her heart's desire. Little did she know how difficult it would be—and, in the end, rewarding....

A VICTORIAN ROMANCE
$5.95/365-1
Lust-letters from the road. A young Englishwoman realizes her dream—a trip abroad under the guidance of her eccentric maiden aunt. Soon, the young but blossoming Elaine comes to discover her own sexual talents, as a hot-blooded Parisian named Madelaine takes her Sapphic education in hand.

MASQUERADE BOOKS

A CIRCLE OF FRIENDS
$4.95/250-7
The story of a remarkable group of women. The women pair off to explore all the possibilities of lesbian passion, until finally it seems that there is nothing—and no one—they have not dabbled in.

BAD HABITS
$5.95/446-1
What does one do with a poorly trained slave? Break her of her bad habits, of course! The story of the ultimate finishing school, *Bad Habits* was an immediate favorite with women nationwide.

"Talk about passing the wet test!... If you like hot, lesbian erotica, run—don't walk—and pick up a copy of Bad Habits." —*Lambda Book Report*

ANNABELLE BARKER
MOROCCO
$6.50/541-7
A luscious young woman stands to inherit a fortune—if she can only withstand the ministrations of her cruel guardian until her twentieth birthday. With two months left, Lila makes a bold bid for freedom, only to find that liberty has its own excruciating and delicious price....

A.L. REINE
DISTANT LOVE & OTHER STORIES
$4.95/3056-3
In the title story, Leah Michaels and her lover, Ranelle, have had four years of blissful, smoldering passion together. When Ranelle is out of town, Leah records an audio "Valentine:" a cassette filled with erotic reminiscences....

A RICHARD KASAK BOOK

SIMON LEVAY
ALBRICK'S GOLD
$12.95/518-2
From the man behind the controversial "gay brain" studies comes a chilling tale of medical experimentation run amok. Roger Cavendish, a diligent researcher into the mysteries of the human mind, and Guy Albrick, a researcher who claims to know the secret to human sexual orientation, find themselves on opposite sides of the battle over experimental surgery. Simon LeVay fashions a classic medical thriller from today's cutting-edge science.

SHAR REDNOUR, EDITOR
VIRGIN TERRITORY 2
$12.95/506-0
The follow-up volume to the groundbreaking *Virgin Territory*, including the work of many women inspired by the success of *VT*. Focusing on the many "firsts" of a woman's erotic life, *Virgin Territory 2* provides one of the sole outlets for serious discussion of the myriad possibilities available to and chosen by many contemporary lesbians.

VIRGIN TERRITORY
$12.95/457-7
An anthology of writing by women about their first-time erotic experiences with other women. From the ecstasies of awakening dykes to the sometimes awkward pleasures of sexual experimentation on the edge, each of these true stories reveals a different, radical perspective on one of the most traditional subjects around: virginity.

MICHAEL FORD, EDITOR
ONCE UPON A TIME:
EROTIC FAIRY TALES FOR WOMEN
$12.95/449-6
How relevant to contemporary lesbians are the lessons of these age-old tales? The contributors to *Once Upon a Time*—some of the biggest names in contemporary lesbian literature—retell their favorite fairy tales, adding their own surprising—and sexy—twists. *Once Upon a Time* is sure to be one of contemporary lesbian literature's classic collections.

HAPPILY EVER AFTER:
EROTIC FAIRY TALES FOR MEN
$12.95/450-X
A hefty volume of bedtime stories Mother Goose never thought to write down. Adapting some of childhood's most beloved tales for the adult gay reader, the contributors to *Happily Ever After* dig up the subtext of these hitherto "innocent" diversions—adding some surprises of their own along the way. Some of contemporary gay literature's biggest names are included in this special volume.

MICHAEL BRONSKI, EDITOR
TAKING LIBERTIES: GAY MEN'S ESSAYS ON POLITICS, CULTURE AND SEX
$12.95/456-9
"Offers undeniable proof of a heady, sophisticated, diverse new culture of gay intellectual debate. I cannot recommend it too highly."—Christopher Bram
A collection of some of the most divergent views on the state of contemporary gay male culture published in recent years. Michael Bronski here presents some of the community's foremost essayists weighing in on such slippery topics as outing, masculine identity, pornography, the pedophile movement, political strategy—and much more.

FLASHPOINT: GAY MALE SEXUAL WRITING
$12.95/424-0
A collection of the most provocative testaments to gay eros. Michael Bronski presents over twenty of the genre's best writers, exploring areas such as Enlightenment, True Life Adventures and more. Accompanied by Bronski's insightful analysis, each story illustrates the many approaches to sexuality used by today's gay writers. *Flashpoint* is sure to be one of the most talked about and influential volumes ever dedicated to the exploration of gay sexuality.

BUY ANY 4 BOOKS & CHOOSE 1 ADDITIONAL BOOK, OF EQUAL OR LESSER VALUE, AS YOUR FREE GIFT

MASQUERADE BOOKS

HEATHER FINDLAY, EDITOR
**A MOVEMENT OF EROS:
25 YEARS OF LESBIAN EROTICA**
$12.95/421-6
One of the most scintillating overviews of lesbian erotic writing ever published. Heather Findlay has assembled a roster of stellar talents, each represented by their best work. Tracing the course of the genre from its pre-Stonewall roots to its current renaissance, Findlay examines each piece, placing it within the context of lesbian community and politics.

CHARLES HENRI FORD & PARKER TYLER
THE YOUNG AND EVIL
$12.95/431-0
"*The Young and Evil* creates [its] generation as *This Side of Paradise* by Fitzgerald created his generation." —Gertrude Stein
Originally published in 1933, *The Young and Evil* was an immediate sensation due to its unprecedented portrayal of young gay artists living in New York's notorious Greenwich Village. From drag balls to bohemian flats, these characters followed love and art wherever it led them—with a frankness that had the novel banned for many years.

BARRY HOFFMAN, EDITOR
THE BEST OF GAUNTLET
$12.95/202-7
Gauntlet has, with its semi-annual issues, always publishing the widest possible range of opinions, in the interest of challenging public opinion. The most provocative articles have been gathered by editor-in-chief Barry Hoffman, to make *The Best of Gauntlet* a riveting exploration of American society's limits.

MICHAEL ROWE
**WRITING BELOW THE BELT:
CONVERSATIONS WITH EROTIC AUTHORS**
$19.95/363-5
"An in-depth and enlightening tour of society's love/hate relationship with sex, morality, and censorship." —James White Review
Journalist Michael Rowe interviewed the best erotic writers and presents the collected wisdom in *Writing Below the Belt*. Rowe speaks frankly with cult favorites such as Pat Califia, crossover success stories like John Preston, and up-and-comers Michael Lowenthal and Will Leber. A chronicle of the insights of this genre's most renowned practitioners.

LARRY TOWNSEND
ASK LARRY
$12.95/289-2
One of the leather community's most respected scribes here presents the best of his advice to leathermen. Starting just before the onslaught of AIDS, Townsend wrote the "Leather Notebook" column for *Drummer* magazine. Now, readers can avail themselves of Townsend's collected wisdom, as well as the author's contemporary commentary—a careful consideration of the way life has changed in the AIDS era. No man worth his leathers can afford to miss this volume of sage advice.

MICHAEL LASSELL
THE HARD WAY
$12.95/231-0
"Lassell is a master of the necessary word. In an age of tepid and whining verse, his bawdy and bittersweet songs are like a plunge in cold champagne."
—Paul Monette
The first collection of renowned gay writer Michael Lassell's poetry, fiction and essays. As much a chronicle of post-Stonewall gay life as a compendium of a remarkable writer's work.

AMARANTHA KNIGHT, EDITOR
LOVE BITES
$12.95/234-5
A volume of tales dedicated to legend's sexiest demon—the Vampire. Not only the finest collection of erotic horror available—but a virtual who's who of promising new talent. A must-read for fans of both the horror and erotic genres.

RANDY TUROFF, EDITOR
LESBIAN WORDS: STATE OF THE ART
$10.95/340-6
"This is a terrific book that should be on every thinking lesbian's bookshelf." —Nisa Donnelly
One of the widest assortments of lesbian nonfiction writing in one revealing volume. Dorothy Allison, Jewelle Gomez, Judy Grahn, Eileen Myles, Robin Podolsky and many others are represented by some of their best work, looking at not only the current fashionability the media has brought to the lesbian "image," but considerations of the lesbian past via historical inquiry and personal recollections.

ASSOTTO SAINT
SPELLS OF A VOODOO DOLL
$12.95/393-7
"Angelic and brazen."—Jewelle Gomez
A fierce, spellbinding collection of the poetry, lyrics, essays and performance texts of Assotto Saint—one of the most important voices in the renaissance of black gay writing. Saint, aka Yves François Lubin, was the editor of two seminal anthologies: 1991 Lambda Literary Book Award winner, *The Road Before Us: 100 Gay Black Poets* and *Here to Dare: 10 Gay Black Poets*. He was also the author of two books of poetry, *Stations* and *Wishing for Wings*.

WILLIAM CARNEY
THE REAL THING
$10.95/280-9
"Carney gives us a good look at the mores and lifestyle of the first generation of gay leathermen. A chilling mystery/romance novel as well."—Pat Califia
With a new introduction by Michael Bronski. First published in 1968, this uncompromising story of American leathermen received instant acclaim. Out of print even while its legend grew, *The Real Thing* returns from exile more than twenty-five years after its initial release. A guaranteed thriller and piece of gay and SM publishing history.

MASQUERADE BOOKS

EURYDICE
F/32
$10.95/350-3

"It's wonderful to see a woman...celebrating her body and her sexuality by creating a fabulous and funny tale."
—Kathy Acker

With the story of Ela, Eurydice won the National Fiction competition sponsored by Fiction Collective Two and Illinois State University. A funny, disturbing quest for unity, f/32 prompted Frederic Tuten to proclaim "almost any page... redeems us from the anemic writing and banalities we have endured in the past decade..."

CHEA VILLANUEVA
JESSIE'S SONG
$9.95/235-3

"It conjures up the strobe-light confusion and excitement of urban dyke life.... Read about these dykes and you'll love them."
—Rebecca Ripley

Based largely upon her own experience, Villanueva's work is remarkable for its frankness, and delightful in its iconoclasm. Unconcerned with political correctness, this writer has helped expand the boundaries of "serious" lesbian writing.

SAMUEL R. DELANY
THE MOTION OF LIGHT IN WATER
$12.95/133-0

"A very moving, intensely fascinating literary biography from an extraordinary writer....The artist as a young man and a memorable picture of an age."
—William Gibson

Award-winning author Samuel R. Delany's autobiography covers the early years of one of science fiction's most important voices. The Motion of Light in Water follows Delany from his early marriage to the poet Marilyn Hacker, through the publication of his first, groundbreaking work.

THE MAD MAN
$23.95/193-4/hardcover

Delany's fascinating examination of human desire. For his thesis, graduate student John Marr researches the life and work of the brilliant Timothy Hasler: a philosopher whose career was cut tragically short over a decade earlier. Marr soon begins to believe that Hasler's death might hold some key to his own life as a gay man in the age of AIDS.

"What Delany has done here is take the ideas of the Marquis de Sade one step further, by filtering extreme and obsessive sexual behavior through the sieve of post-modern experience...."
—Lambda Book Report

"Delany develops an insightful dichotomy between [his protagonist]'s two worlds: the one of cerebral philosophy and dry academia, the other of heedless, 'impersonal' obsessive sexual extremism. When these worlds finally collide ... the novel achieves a surprisingly satisfying resolution..."
—Publishers Weekly

FELICE PICANO
DRYLAND'S END
$12.95/279-5

The science fiction debut of the highly acclaimed author of Men Who Loved Me and Like People in History. Set five thousand years in the future, Dryland's End takes place in a fabulous techno-empire ruled by intelligent, powerful women. While the Matriarchy has ruled for over two thousand years and altered human society—But is now unraveling. Military rivalries, religious fanaticism and economic competition threaten to destroy the mighty empire.

ROBERT PATRICK
TEMPLE SLAVE
$12.95/191-8

"You must read this book."
—Quentin Crisp

"This is nothing less than the secret history of the most theatrical of theaters, the most bohemian of Americans and the most knowing of queens.... Temple Slave is also one of the best ways to learn what it was like to be fabulous, gay, theatrical and loved in a time at once more and less dangerous to gay life than our own."
—Genre

The story of Greenwich Village and the beginnings of gay theater—told with the dazzling wit and stylistic derring-do for which Robert Patrick is justly famous.

GUILLERMO BOSCH
RAIN
$12.95/232-9

"Rain is a trip..."
—Timothy Leary

An adult fairy tale, Rain takes place in a time when the mysteries of Eros are played out against a background of uncommon deprivation. The tale begins on the 1,537th day of drought—when one man comes to know the true depths of thirst. In a quest to sate his hunger for some knowledge of the wide world, he is taken through a series of extraordinary, unearthly encounters that promise to change not only his life, but the course of civilization around him. An acclaimed tale of passion, and a moving fable for our time.

LAURA ANTONIOU, EDITOR
LOOKING FOR MR. PRESTON
$23.95/288-4

Edited by Laura Antoniou, Looking for Mr. Preston includes work by Lars Eighner, Pat Califia, Michael Bronski, Joan Nestle, and others who contributed interviews, essays and personal reminiscences of John Preston—a man whose career spanned the gay publishing industry. Preston was the author of over twenty books, and edited many more. Ten percent of the proceeds from sale of this book will go to the AIDS Project of Southern Maine, for which Preston served as President of the Board.

BUY ANY 4 BOOKS & CHOOSE 1 ADDITIONAL BOOK, OF EQUAL OR LESSER VALUE, AS YOUR FREE GIFT

MASQUERADE BOOKS

CECILIA TAN, EDITOR
SM VISIONS: THE BEST OF CIRCLET PRESS
$10.95/339-2
"Fabulous books! There's nothing else like them."
—Susie Bright,
Best American Erotica and Herotica 3
Circlet Press, devoted exclusively to the erotic science fiction and fantasy genre, is now represented by the best of its very best: *SM Visions*—sure to be one of the most thrilling and eye-opening rides through the erotic imagination ever published.

RUSS KICK
OUTPOSTS:
A CATALOG OF RARE AND DISTURBING ALTERNATIVE INFORMATION
$18.95/0202-8
A huge, authoritative guide to some of the most bizarre publications available today! Rather than simply summarize the plethora of opinions crowding the American scene, Kick has tracked down and compiled reviews of work penned by political extremists, conspiracy theorists, hallucinogenic pathfinders, sexual explorers, and others. Each review is followed by ordering information for the many readers sure to want these publications for themselves. An essential reference in this age of rapidly proliferating information systems and increasingly extremes political and cultural perspectives. An indispensible guide to every book and magazine you're afraid you might have missed.

LUCY TAYLOR
UNNATURAL ACTS
$12.95/181-0
"A topnotch collection..." —*Science Fiction Chronicle*
Unnatural Acts plunges deep into the dark side of the psyche and brings to life a disturbing vision of erotic horror. Unrelenting angels and hungry gods play with souls and bodies in Taylor's murky cosmos: where heaven and hell are merely differences of perspective; where redemption and damnation lie behind the same shocking acts.

TIM WOODWARD, EDITOR
THE BEST OF SKIN TWO
$12.95/130-6
A groundbreaking journal from the crossroads of sexuality, fashion, and art, *Skin Two* specializes in provocative essays by the finest writers working in the "radical sex" scene. Collected here are the articles and interviews that established the magazine's reputation. Including interviews with cult figures Tim Burton, Clive Barker and Jean Paul Gaultier.

MICHAEL LOWENTHAL, EDITOR
THE BEST OF THE BADBOYS
$12.95/233-7
The very best of the leading Badboys is collected here, in this testament to the artistry that has catapulted these "outlaw" authors to bestselling status. John Preston, Aaron Travis, Larry Townsend, and others are here represented by their most provocative writing.

PAT CALIFIA
SENSUOUS MAGIC
$12.95/458-5
A new classic, destined to grace the shelves of anyone interested in contemporary sexuality.
"*Sensuous Magic* is clear, succinct and engaging even for the reader for whom S/M isn't the sexual behavior of choice.... When she is writing about the dynamics of sex and the technical aspects of it, Califia is the Dr. Ruth of the alternative sexuality set...." —*Lambda Book Report*
"Pat Califia's *Sensuous Magic* is a friendly, non-threatening, helpful guide and resource... She captures the power of what it means to enter forbidden terrain, and to do so safely with someone else, and to explore the healing potential, spiritual aspects and the depth of S/M." —*Bay Area Reporter*
"Don't take a dangerous trip into the unknown—buy this book and know where you're going!" —*SKIN TWO*

MICHAEL PERKINS
THE GOOD PARTS: AN UNCENSORED GUIDE TO LITERARY SEXUALITY
$12.95/186-1
Michael Perkins, one of America's only critics to regularly scrutinize sexual literature, presents this unprecedented survey of sex as seen/written about in the pages of over 100 major fiction and nonfiction volumes from the past twenty years.

COMING UP:
THE WORLD'S BEST EROTIC WRITING
$12.95/370-8
Author and critic Michael Perkins has scoured the field of erotic writing to produce this anthology sure to challenge the limits of even the most seasoned reader. Using the same sharp eye and transgressive instinct that have established him as America's leading commentator on sexually explicit fiction, Perkins here presents the cream of the current crop. One of the few available collections drawing on both American and European talent.

DAVID MELTZER
THE AGENCY TRILOGY
$12.95/216-7
"...The Agency' is clearly Meltzer's paradigm of society; a mindless machine of which we are all 'agents,' including those whom the machine supposedly serves...." —Norman Spinrad

When first published, *The Agency* explored issues of erotic dominance and submission with an immediacy and frankness previously unheard of in American literature, as well as presented a vision of an America consumed and dehumanized by a lust for power. All three volumes—*The Agency, The Agent, How Many Blocks in the Pile?*—are included in this one special volume, available only from Richard Kasak Books.

MASQUERADE BOOKS

JOHN PRESTON
MY LIFE AS A PORNOGRAPHER AND OTHER INDECENT ACTS
$12.95/135-7

A collection of renowned author and social critic John Preston's essays, focusing on his work as an erotic writer and proponent of gay rights.

"...essential and enlightening... [My Life as a Pornographer] is a bridge from the sexually liberated 1970s to the more cautious 1990s, and Preston has walked much of that way as a standard-bearer to the cause for equal rights...." —Library Journal

"My Life as a Pornographer...is not pornography, but rather reflections upon the writing and production of it. In a deeply sex-phobic world, Preston has never shied away from a vision of the redemptive potential of the erotic drive. Better than perhaps anyone in our community, Preston knows how physical joy can bridge differences and make us well."
—Lambda Book Report

CARO SOLES, EDITOR
MELTDOWN! AN ANTHOLOGY OF EROTIC SCIENCE FICTION AND DARK FANTASY FOR GAY MEN
$12.95/203-5

Editor Caro Soles has put together one of the most explosive collections of gay erotic writing ever published. Meltdown! contains the very best examples of the increasingly popular sub-genre of erotic sci-fi/dark fantasy: stories meant to shock and delight, to send a shiver down the spine and start a fire down below.

LARS EIGHNER
ELEMENTS OF AROUSAL
$12.95/230-2

A guideline for success with one of publishing's best kept secrets: the novice-friendly field of gay erotic writing. Eighner details his craft, providing the reader with sure advice. Because that's what Elements of Arousal is all about: the application and honing of the writer's craft, which brought Eighner fame with not only the steamy Bayou Boy, but the illuminating Travels with Lizbeth.

STAN TAL, EDITOR
BIZARRE SEX AND OTHER CRIMES OF PASSION
$12.95/213-2

From the pages of Bizarre Sex. Over twenty small masterpieces of erotic shock make this one of the year's most unexpectedly alluring anthologies. This incredible volume, edited by Stan Tal, includes such masters of erotic horror and fantasy as Edward Lee, Lucy Taylor and Nancy Kilpatrick.

MARCO VASSI
A DRIVING PASSION
$12.95/134-9

Marco Vassi was famous not only for his groundbreaking writing, but for the many lectures he gave regarding sexuality and the complex erotic philosophy he had spent much of his life working out. A Driving Passion collects the wit and insight Vassi brought to these lectures, and distills the philosophy that made him an underground sensation.

"The most striking figure in present-day American erotic literature. Alone among modern erotic writers, Vassi is working out a philosophy of sexuality."
—Michael Perkins, The Secret Record

THE EROTIC COMEDIES
$12.95/136-5

Short stories designed to shock and transform attitudes about sex and sexuality, The Erotic Comedies is both entertaining and challenging—and garnered Vassi some of the most lavish praise of his career. Also includes his groundbreaking writings on the Erotic Experience.

"The comparison to [Henry] Miller is high praise indeed.... But reading Vassi's work, the analogy holds—for he shares with Miller an unabashed joy in sensuality, and a questing after experience that is the root of all great literature, erotic or otherwise.... Vassi was, by all accounts, a fearless explorer, someone who jumped headfirst into the world of sex, and wrote about what he found...."
—David L. Ulin, The Los Angeles Reader

THE SALINE SOLUTION
$12.95/180-2

"I've always read Marco's work with interest and I have the highest opinion not only of his talent but his intellectual boldness." —Norman Mailer

The story of one couple's spiritual crises during an age of extraordinary freedom. While renowned for his sexual philosophy, Vassi also experienced success in with fiction; The Saline Solution was one of the high points of his career, while still addressing the issue of sexuality.

THE STONED APOCALYPSE
$12.95/132-2

"...Marco Vassi is our champion sexual energist."
—VLS

During his lifetime, Marco Vassi was hailed as America's premier erotic writer. The Stoned Apocalypse is Vassi's autobiography, financed by his other groundbreaking erotic writing and rife with Vassi's insight into the American character and libido. One of the most vital portraits of "the 60s," this volume is a fitting testament to the writer's talents, and the sexual imagination of his generation.

BUY ANY 4 BOOKS & CHOOSE 1 ADDITIONAL BOOK, OF EQUAL OR LESSER VALUE, AS YOUR FREE GIFT

ORDERING IS EASY

MC/VISA orders can be placed by calling our toll-free number
PHONE 800-375-2356/FAX 212-986-7355/E-MAIL masqbks@aol.com
or mail this coupon to:
MASQUERADE DIRECT
DEPT. BMRB17 801 2ND AVE., NY, NY 10017

BUY ANY FOUR BOOKS AND CHOOSE ONE ADDITIONAL BOOK, OF EQUAL OR LESSER VALUE, AS YOUR FREE GIFT.

QTY.	TITLE	NO.	PRICE
			FREE
			FREE

We Never Sell, Give or Trade Any Customer's Name.

SUBTOTAL

POSTAGE and HANDLING

TOTAL

In the U.S., please add $1.50 for the first book and 75¢ for each additional book; in Canada, add $2.00 for the first book and $1.25 for each additional book. Foreign countries: add $4.00 for the first book and $2.00 for each additional book. No C.O.D. orders. Please make all checks payable to Masquerade Books. Payable in U.S. currency only. New York state residents add 8.25% sales tax. Please allow 4-6 weeks for delivery.

NAME _____

ADDRESS _____

CITY _____ STATE _____ ZIP _____

TEL( ) _____

E-MAIL _____

PAYMENT: ☐ CHECK   ☐ MONEY ORDER   ☐ VISA   ☐ MC

CARD NO _____ EXP. DATE _____

The Rosebud Sutra

VALENTINA CILESCU